2 States

Chetan Bhagat is the author of four bestselling novels – *Five Point Someone* (2004), *One Night @ the Call Center* (2005), *The 3 Mistakes of My Life* (2008) and *2 States: The Story of My Marriage* (2009). Chetan's books have remained bestsellers since their release, and have been adapted into major Bollywood films. *The New York Times* called him the 'the biggest selling English language novelist in India's history.' *Time* magazine named him as one amongst the '100 Most Influential People in the world' and Fast Company, USA, listed him as one of the world's '100 most creative people in business.'

Chetan writes for leading English and Hindi newspapers, focusing on youth and national development issues. He is also a motivational speaker.

Chetan quit his international investment banking career in 2009, to devote his entire time to writing and make change happen in the country. He lives in Mumbai with his wife Anusha, an ex-classmate from IIM-A, and his twin sons Shyam and Ishaan.

To know more about Chetan visit www.chetanbhagat.com or email him at info@chetanbhagat.com.

Praise for previous work

Many writers are successful at expressing what's in their hearts or articulating a particular point of view. Chetan Bhagat's books do both and more.

– A R Rahman, in TIME magazine, on Chetan's inclusion in the Time 100 Most Influential People in the world

The voice of India's rising entrepreneurial class.

– Fast Company Magazine, on Chetan's inclusion in the 100 Most Creative People in business globally

India's paperback king.

– The Guardian

The biggest-selling English-language novelist in India's history.

– The New York Times

A rockstar of Indian publishing.

– The Times of India

Bhagat has touched a nerve with young Indian readers and acquired almost cult status.

– International Herald Tribune

2 States

THE STORY OF MY MARRIAGE

A novel by

Chetan Bhagat

RUPA

Published by
Rupa Publications India Pvt. Ltd 2013
7/16, Ansari Road, Daryaganj
New Delhi 110002

Sales centres:
Allahabad Bengaluru Chennai
Hyderabad Jaipur Kathmandu
Kolkata Mumbai

Copyright © Chetan Bhagat 2009, 2013

ISBN: 978-81-291-1530-0

105th impression 2014

110 109 108 107 106 105

The moral right of the author has been asserted.

Printed at Replika Press Pvt. Ltd, India

This may be the first time in the history of books, but here goes:

*Dedicated to my in-laws**

which does not mean I am henpecked, under her thumb or not man enough

Acknowledgements

No creation in this world is a solo effort. Neither is this book. From the person who makes Xerox copies of the draft to the delivery boy who makes the book reach shops, everyone has a role. In particular, I'd like to thank:

- My readers, you that is, have made me what I am. Last time I mentioned that I wanted to be India's most loved writer—and you gave me that. Thank you. Please continue with your support, and if possible, give me a tiny but permanent place in your heart.
- God, for his love and blessings.
- Shinie Antony, the first reader and editor of all my books so far, who tells me what works and what doesn't, not only in the book, but also in life.
- Abhishek Kapoor, for his wonderful suggestions. Prateek Dhawan, Shambhavi Kirawant, Ratika Kaul-Haksar, and Anusha Bhagat for great comments on the manuscript.
- My publishers Rupa & Co. for taking my stories across the nation.
- My family for their constant support.
- My friends from college, ex-colleagues at Deutsche Bank and Goldman Sachs, my current friends in Mumbai.
- The newspapers that publish my columns and give me a chance to share my views about new, progressive India that I dream of constantly.
- The filmmakers who were inspired by my stories and spent years bringing them to life.

I also want to make a couple of disclaimers. One, this story is inspired by my own family and experiences. However, this book should be seen as a work of fiction. Also, for authenticity, I have used names of some real places, people and institutions as they represent cultural icons of today and aid in storytelling. There is no intention to imply anything else. I'd also like to tell all South Indians I love them. My better half will vouch for that. I have taken the liberty to have some fun with you just like I have with Punjabis—only because I see you as my own. You only make digs at people you care for.

With that, I'd like to welcome you to *2 States*.

Prologue

'Why am I referred here? I don't have a problem,' I said.

She didn't react. Just gestured I remove my shoes and take the couch. She had an office like any other doctor's, minus the smells and cold, dangerous instruments.

She waited for me to talk more. I hesitated and spoke again.

'I'm sure people come here with big, insurmountable problems. Girlfriends dump their boyfriends everyday. Hardly the reason to see a shrink, right? What am I, a psycho?'

'No, I am the psycho. Psychotherapist to be precise. If you don't mind, I prefer that to shrink,' she said.

'Sorry,' I said.

'It's OK,' she said and reclined on her chair. No more than thirty, she seemed young for a shrink, sorry, psychotherapist. Certificates from top US universities adorned the walls like tiger heads in a hunter's home. Yes, another South Indian had conquered the world of academics. Dr Neeta Iyer, Valedictorian, Vassar College.

'I charge five hundred rupees per hour,' she said. 'Stare at the walls or talk. I'm cool either way.'

I had spent twelve minutes, or a hundred bucks, without getting anywhere. I wondered if she would accept a partial payment and let me leave.

'Dr Iyer. . . .'

'Neeta is fine,' she said.

'OK, Neeta, I don't think my problem warrants this. I don't know why Dr Ramachandran sent me here.'

She picked my file from her desk. 'Let's see. This is Dr Ram's brief to me – patient has sleep deprivation, has cut off human contact for a week, refuses to eat, has Google-searched on best ways to commit suicide.' She paused and looked at me with raised eyebrows.

'I Google for all sorts of stuff,' I mumbled, 'don't you?'

'The report says the mere mention of her name, her neighbourhood or any association, like her favourite dish, brings out unpredictable emotions ranging from tears to rage to frustration.'

'I had a break-up. What do you expect?' I was irritated.

'Sure, with Ananya who stays in Mylapore. What's her favourite dish? Curd rice?'

I sat up straight. 'Don't,' I said weakly and felt a lump in my throat. I fought back tears. 'Don't,' I said again.

'Don't what?' Neeta egged me on, 'Minor problem, isn't it?'

'Fuck minor. It's killing me.' I stood agitatedly. 'Do you South Indians even know what emotions are all about?'

'I'll ignore the racist comment. You can stand and talk, but if it is a long story, take the couch. I want it all,' she said.

I broke into tears. 'Why did this happen to me?' I sobbed.

She passed me a tissue.

'Where do I begin?' I said and sat gingerly on the couch.

'Where all love stories begin. From when you met her the first time,' she said.

She drew the curtains and switched on the air-conditioner. I began to talk and get my money's worth.

Act 1:
Ahmedabad

1

She stood two places ahead of me in the lunch line at the IIMA mess. I checked her out from the corner of my eye, wondering what the big fuss about this South Indian girl was.

Her waist-length hair rippled as she tapped the steel plate with her fingers like a famished refugee. I noticed three black threads on the back of her fair neck. Someone had decided to accessorise in the most academically-oriented B-school in the country.

'Ananya Swaminathan—best girl in the fresher batch,' seniors had already anointed her on the dorm board. We had only twenty girls in a batch of two hundred. Good-looking ones were rare; girls don't get selected to IIM for their looks. They get in because they can solve mathematical problems faster than 99.9% of India's population and crack the CAT. Most IIM girls are above shallow things like make-up, fitting clothes, contact lenses, removal of facial hair, body odour and feminine charm. Girls like Ananya, if and when they arrive by freak chance, become instant pin-ups in our testosterone-charged, estrogen-starved campus.

I imagined Ms Swaminathan had received more male attention in the last week than she had in her entire life. Thus, I assumed she'd be obnoxious and decided to ignore her.

The students inched forward on auto-pilot. The bored kitchen staff couldn't care if they were serving prisoners or future CEOs. They tossed one ladle of yellow stuff after another into plates. Of course, Ms Best Girl needed the spotlight.

'That's not rasam. Whatever it is, it's definitely not rasam. And what's that, the dark yellow stuff?'

'Sambhar,' the mess worker growled.

'Eew, looks disgusting! How did you make it?' she asked.

'You want or not?' the mess worker said, more interested in wrapping up lunch than discussing recipes.

While our lady decided, the two boys between us banged their plates on the counter. They took the food without editorials about it and left. I came up right behind her. I stole a sideways glance—*definitely above average. Actually, well above average. In fact, outlier by IIMA standards.* She had perfect features, with her eyes, nose, lips and ears the right size and in right places. That is all it takes to make people beautiful—normal body parts—yet why does nature mess it up so many times? Her tiny blue bindi matched her sky-blue and white salwar kameez. She looked like Sridevi's smarter cousin, if there is such a possibility.

The mess worker dumped a yellow lump on my plate.

'Excuse me, I'm before him,' she said to the mess worker, pinning him down with her large, confident eyes.

'What you want?' the mess worker said in a heavy South Indian accent. 'You calling rasam not rasam. You make face when you see my sambhar. I feed hundred people. They no complain.'

'And that is why you don't improve. Maybe they should complain,' she said.

The mess worker dropped the ladle in the sambhar vessel and threw up his hands. 'You want complain? Go to mess manager and complain . . . see what student coming to these days,' the mess worker turned to me, seeking sympathy.

I almost nodded.

She looked at me. 'Can you eat this stuff?' she wanted to know. 'Try it.'

I took a spoonful of sambhar. Warm and salty, not gourmet stuff, but edible in a no-choice kind of way. I could eat it for lunch; I had stayed in a hostel for four years.

However, I saw her face, now prettier with a hint of pink. I compared her to the fifty-year-old mess worker. He wore a lungi and had visible grey hair on his chest. When in doubt, the pretty girl is always right.

'It's disgusting,' I said.

'See,' she said with childlike glee.

The mess worker glared at me.

'But I can develop a taste for it,' I added in a lame attempt to soothe him.

The mess worker grunted and tossed a mound of rice on my plate. 'Pick something you like,' I said to her, avoiding eye contact. The whole campus had stared at her in the past few days. I had to appear different.

'Give me the rasgullas,' she pointed to the dessert.

'That is after you finish meal,' the mess worker said.

'Who are you? My mother? I am finished. Give me two rasgullas,' she insisted.

'Only one per student,' he said as he placed a katori with one sweet on her plate.

'Oh, come on, there are no limits on this disgusting sambhar but only one of what is edible,' she said. The line grew behind us. The boys in line didn't mind. They had a chance to legitimately stare at the best-looking girl of the batch.

'Give mine to her,' I said and regretted it immediately. *She'll never date you, it is a rasgulla down the drain*, I scolded myself.

'I give to you,' the mess worker said virtuously as he placed the dessert on my plate.

I passed my katori to her. She took the two rasgullas and moved out of the line.

OK buddy, pretty girl goes her way, rasgulla-less loser goes another. Find a corner to sit, I said to myself.

She turned to me. She didn't ask me to sit with her, but she looked like she wouldn't mind if I did. She pointed to a table with a little finger where we sat down opposite each other. The entire mess stared at us, wondering what I had done to merit sitting with her. I have made a huge sacrifice—my dessert—I wanted to tell them.

'I'm Krish,' I said, doodling in the sambhar with my spoon.

'I'm Ananya. Yuk, isn't it?' she said as I grimaced at the food's taste.

'I'm used to hostel food,' I shrugged. 'I've had worse.'

'Hard to imagine worse,' she said.

I coughed as I bit on a green chilli. She had a water jug next to her. She lifted the jug, leaned forward and poured water for me. A collective sigh ran through the mess. We had become everyone's matinee show.

She finished her two desserts in four bites. 'I'm still hungry. I didn't even have breakfast.'

'Hunger or tasteless food, hostel life is about whatever is easier to deal with,' I said.

'You want to go out? I'm sure this city has decent restaurants,' she said.

'Now?' We had a class in one hour. But Ms Best Girl had asked me out, even though for her own stomach. And as everyone knows, female classmates always come before class.

'Don't tell me you are dying to attend the lecture,' she said and stood up, daring me.

I spooned in some rice.

She stamped a foot. 'Leave that disgusting stuff.'

Four hundred eyes followed us as I walked out of the mess with Ms Ananya Swaminathan, rated the best girl by popular vote in IIMA.

'Do you like chicken?' The menu rested on her nose as she spoke. We had come to Topaz, a basic, soulless but air-conditioned restaurant half a kilometre from campus. Like all mid-range Indian restaurants, it played boring instrumental versions of old Hindi songs and served little marinated onions on the table.

'I thought Ahmedabad was vegetarian,' I said.

'Please, I'd die here then.' She turned to the waiter and ordered half a tandoori chicken with roomali rotis.

'Do you have beer?' she asked the waiter.

The waiter shook his head in horror and left.

'We are in Gujarat, there is prohibition here,' I said.

'Why?'

'Gandhiji's birthplace,' I said.

'But Gandhiji won us freedom,' she said, playing with the little onions. 'What's the point of getting people free only to put restrictions on them?'

'Point,' I said. 'So, you are an expert on rasam and sambhar. Are you South Indian?'

'Tamilian, please be precise. In fact, Tamil Brahmin, which is way different from Tamilians. Never forget that.' She leaned back as the waiter served our meal. She tore a chicken leg with her teeth.

'And how exactly are Tamil Brahmins different?'

'Well, for one thing, no meat and no drinking,' she said as she gestured a cross with the chicken leg.

'Absolutely,' I said.

She laughed. 'I didn't say I am a practising Tam Brahm. But you should know that I am born into the purest of pure upper caste communities ever created. What about you, commoner?'

'I am a Punjabi, though I never lived in Punjab. I grew up in Delhi. And I have no idea about my caste, but we do eat chicken. And I can digest bad sambhar better than Tamil Brahmins,' I said.

'You are funny,' she said, tapping my hand. I liked the tap.

'So where did you stay in hostel before?' she said. 'Please don't say IIT, you are doing pretty well so far.'

'What's wrong with IIT?'

'Nothing, are you from there?' She sipped water.

'Yes, from IIT Delhi. Is that a problem?'

'No,' she smiled, 'not yet.'

'Excuse me?' I said. Her smugness had reached irritating levels.

'Nothing,' she said.

We stayed quiet.

'What's the deal? Someone from IIT broke your heart?'

She laughed. 'No, on the contrary. I seem to have broken some, for no fault of my own.'

'Care to explain?'

'Don't tell anyone, but in the past one week that I've been here, I've had ten proposals. All from IITians.'

I mentally kicked myself. My guess was right; she was getting a lot of attention. I only wished it wasn't from my own people.

'Proposals for what?'

'The usual, to go out, be friends and stuff. Oh, and one guy from IIT Chennai proposed marriage!'

'Serious?'

'Yes, he said this past week has been momentous for him. He joined IIMA, and now he has found his wife in me. I may be wrong, but I think he had some jewellery on him.'

I smacked my forehead. No, my collegemates can't be doing this, whatever the deprivation.

'So, you understand my concern about you being from IIT,' she said, picking up a chicken breast next.

'Oh, so it is a natural reaction. If I am from IIT, I have to propose to you within ten minutes?'

'I didn't say that.'

'You implied that.'

'I'm sorry.'

'It's OK. I expected you to be like this. Let me guess—only child, rich parents?'

'Wrong, wrong. I have a younger brother. And my father works in Bank of Baroda in Chennai. Sorry, you expected me to be like what?'

'Some girls cannot handle attention. Two days of popularity and every guy in college should bow to you.'

'That's not true. Didn't I come out with you?' She neatly transferred the bare bones of the chicken on to another plate.

'Oh, that's huge. Coming out with a commoner like me. How much is the bill? I'll pay my share and leave.' I stood up.

'Hey,' she said.

'What?'

'I'm sorry. Please sit down.'

I had lost interest in the conversation anyway. If there is nothing as attractive as a pretty girl, there's nothing as repulsive as a cocky chick.

I sat back and focussed on the food and the irritating instrumental music for the next ten minutes. I ignored the Brahmin who stereotyped my collegemates.

'Are we OK now?' she smiled hesitantly.

'Why did you come out with me? To take your score to eleven?'

'You really want to know?'

'Yes.'

'I need some friends here. And you seemed like a safe-zone guy. Like the kind of guy who could just be friends with a girl, right?'

Absolutely not, I thought. *Why would any guy want to be only friends with a girl? It's like agreeing to be near a chocolate cake and never eat it. It's like sitting in a racing car but not driving it. Only wimps do that.*

'I'm not so sure,' I said.

'You can handle it. I told you about the proposals because you can see how stupid they are.'

'They are not stupid. They are IITians. They just don't know how to talk to women yet,' I said.

'Whatever. But you do. And I'd like to be friends with you. Just friends, OK?' She extended her hand. I gave her a limp handshake.

'Let's share, sixty each,' she said as the bill arrived.

That's right, 'just friends' share bills. I didn't want to be just friends with her. And I didn't want to be the eleventh martyr.

I paid my share and came back to campus. I had no interest in meeting my just friend anytime again soon.

2

'You OK?' I said, going up to my just friend. She remained in her seat as her tears re-emerged. The last lecture had ended and the classroom was empty.

I hadn't spoken much to Ananya after our lunch last week. Pretty girls behave best when you ignore them. (Of course, they have to know you are ignoring them, for otherwise they may not even know you exist.)

But today I had to talk to her. She had cried in class. We had auditorium-style classrooms with semi-circular rows, so everyone could see everyone. Students sat in alphabetical order. Ananya, like all kids doomed with names starting with the letter A, sat in the first row on the left side. She sat between Ankur and Aditya, both IITians who had already proposed to her without considering the embarrassment of being rejected and then sitting next to the rejector for the whole year.

I sat in the third row, between Kanyashree, who took notes like a diligent court transcripter, and five Mohits, who had come from different parts of India. But neither Ankur, nor Aditya, nor Kanyashree, nor the five Mohits had noticed Ananya's tears. Only I had caught her wiping her eye with a yellow dupatta that had little bells at its ends that tinkled whenever she moved.

In the past week, I had limited my communication with Ananya to cursory greetings every morning and a casual wave at the end of the day. During classes we had to pay attention to the teacher as we had marks for class participation – saying something that sounds intelligent. Most IITians never spoke while people from non-science backgrounds spoke non-stop.

Twenty-three minutes into the microeconomics class, the professor drew an L-shaped utility curve on the blackboard. He admired his curve for ten seconds and turned to the class.

'How many economics graduates here?' asked Prof Chatterjee, a two-decade IIMA veteran.

Fifteen students out of the seventy students in section A raised their hands, Ananya included.

Chatterjee turned to her. 'You recognise the curve, Ms Swaminathan?' He read her name from the nameplate in front.

'The basic marginal utility curve, sir,' Ananya said.

'So, Ms Swaminathan, how would you represent that curve mathematically?'

Ananya stood up, her eyes explaining clearly she had no clue. The remaining fourteen economics graduates lowered their hands.

'Yes, Ms Swaminathan?' Chatterjee said.

Ananya clutched the trinkets on her dupatta so they didn't make a noise as she spoke. 'Sir, that curve shows different bundles of goods between which a consumer is indifferent. That is, at each point on the curve, the consumer has equal preference for one bundle over another.'

'That's not my question. What is the mathematical formula?'

'I don't know that. In any case, this is only a concept.'

'But do you know it?'

'No. But I can't think of any real life situation where a mathematical formula like this would work,' Ananya said.

Prof raised his hand to interrupt her. 'Shsh. . . .' He gave a sinister smile. 'Notice, class, notice. This is the state of economics education in the country. Top graduates don't know the basics. And then they ask – why is India economically backward?'

Prof emphatically dropped the chalk on his table to conclude his point. He had solved what had dumbfounded policymakers for decades. Ananya Swaminathan was the reason for India's backwardness.

Ananya hung her head in shame. A few IITians brightened up. Microeconomics was an elective course in IIT and those who had done it knew the formula. They were itching to show off.

'Anyone knows?' Prof asked and Ankur raised his hand.

'Yes, tell us. Ms Swaminathan, you should talk to your neighbours more. And next time, don't raise your hand if I ask for economics graduates,' Prof said.

He went to the board to write lots of Greek symbols and calculus equations. The course had started with cute little things like how people choose between tea and biscuits. It had moved on to scary equations that would dominate exams. The class took mad notes. Kanyashree wrote so hard I could feel the seismic vibrations from her pen's nib.

I stole a glance at Ananya. As a smug Ankur saw his words inscribed on the board, Ananya's left hand's fingers scrunched up her yellow dupatta. She moved her left hand to her face even as she continued to write with her right. In subtle movements, she dabbed at her tears. Maybe Ms Best Girl had a heart, I thought. And maybe I should cut out my studied ignorance strategy and talk to her after class.

'You OK?' I said again.

She nodded while continuing to wipe her tears. She fixed her gaze down.

'I miss Topaz,' I said to change the topic.

'I've never been so humiliated,' she said.

'Nobody cares. All professors are assholes. That's the universal truth,' I offered. 'At least where I come from.'

'You want to see my economics degree? I'll show you my grades.'

'No,' I said.

'I came third in the entire Delhi University. These wannabe engineer profs have turned economics from a perfectly fine liberal arts subject to this Greek symbol junkyard,' she said as she pointed to the formulae on the board.

I kept silent.

'You are from IIT. You probably love these equations,' she said and looked up at me. Despite her tears, she still looked pretty.

I looked at the blackboard. Yes, I did have a fondness for algebra. It's nothing to be ashamed of. Yet, this wasn't the time. 'No, I am not a big fan. Greek symbols do take the fun out of any subject.'

'Exactly, but these profs don't think so. They will have these equations in the test next week. I am going to flunk. And he is going to turn me into this specimen of the educated but clueless Indian student. I bet I am the staff-room discussion right now.'

'They are all frustrated,' I said. 'We are half their age but will earn twice as them in two years. Wouldn't you hate an eleven-year-old if he earned double?'

She smiled.

'You need to hang that dupatta out to dry,' I said. She smiled some more.

We walked out of class. We decided to skip lunch and have tea and omelette at the roadside Rambhai outside campus.

'He is going to screw me in microeconomics. He's probably circled my name and put a D in front of it already,' she said, nestling the hot glass of tea in her dupatta folds for insulation.

'Don't freak out. Listen, you can study with me. I don't like these equations, but I am good at them. That's all we did at IIT for four years.'

She looked at me for a few seconds.

'Hey, I have no interest in being number eleven. This is purely for study reasons.'

She laughed. 'Actually, the score is thirteen now.'

'IITians?'

'No, this time from NIT. They are catching up.'

'I know, we are losing our edge. Whatever, I don't want to be number fourteen. I thought I could teach you . . .

She interrupted me, 'I can't learn economics from you. I am a university topper in economics. You are an engineer.'

'Then good luck,' I said and stood up to pay.

'I didn't say that. I said you can't teach me. But we can study together.'

I looked at her. She looked nice, and I couldn't blame the thirteen guys for trying.

'My room at eight? Ever been to the girl's dorm?'

'There is a first time for everything,' I said.

'Cool, carry lots of books to make it clear what you are there for,' Ananya advised.

3

I reached the girls' dorm at 8 p.m. I carried the week's case materials, the size of six telephone directories. I knocked at her door.

'One second, I am changing,' her muffled scream came from inside.

After three hundred seconds, she opened the door. She wore a red and white tracksuit. 'Sorry,' she said as she tied up her hair in a bun. 'Come in. We'd better start, there is so much to do.'

She gave me her study chair and sat on her bed. The rust-coloured bed-sheet matched the exposed brick walls. She had made a notice board out of chart paper and stuck family pictures all over.

'See, that's my family. That's my dad. He is so cute,' she said.

I looked carefully. A middle-aged man with neatly combed hair rationed his grin. He wore a half-sleeve shirt with a dhoti in most of the pictures. He looked like the neighbour who stops you from playing loud music. No, nothing cute about him. I scanned the remaining pictures taken on festivals, weddings and birthdays. In one, Ananya's whole family stood to attention at the beach. You could almost hear the national anthem.

'That's Marina Beach in Chennai. Do you know it is the second largest city beach in the world?'

I saw her brother, around fourteen years of age. The oiled hair, geeky face and spectacles made him look like an IITian embryo. His lack of interest in the world expression told me he would make it.

'And that's mom?' I quizzed. Ananya nodded.

Ananya's brother and father still seemed mild compared to her mother. Even in pictures she had a glum expression that made you wonder what did you do wrong. She reminded me of the strictest teachers I ever had in school. I immediately felt guilty about being in her daughter's room. My hands tingled as I almost expected her to jump out of the picture and slap me with a ruler.

'Mom and I,' Ananya said as she kneeled on the bed and sighed.

'What?' I looked at a wedding picture of her relatives. Given their dusky complexion, everyone's teeth shone extra white. All old women wore as much gold as their bodies could carry and silk saris shiny as road reflectors.

'Nothing, I wish I got along better with her,' Ananya said. 'Hey, you have pictures of your family?'

I shook my head. My family was too disorganised to ever pause and pose at the right moment. I don't think we even had a camera.

'Who is there in your family?' She sifted through the case materials to take out the economics notes.

'Mom, dad and me. That's it,' I said.

'Tell me more. What do they do? Who are you close to?'

'We met to study,' I pointed out and patted the microeconomics booklet.

'Of course, we will. I only asked to make conversation. Don't tell me if you don't want to,' she said and batted her eyelids. *How can such scary looking parents create something so cute?*

'OK, I'll answer. But after that, we study. No gossip for an hour,' I warned.

'Sure, I already have my book open,' she said and sat on the bed cross-legged.

'OK, my mother is a housewife. I am close to her, but not hugely close. That reminds me, I have to call her. I'll go to the STD booth later.'

'And dad? I am super close to mine.'

'Let's study,' I said and opened the books.

'You aren't close to your father?'

'You want to flunk?'

'Shsh,' she agreed and covered her lips with a finger. We studied for the next two hours in silence. She would look up sometimes and do pointless things like changing her pillow cover or re-adjusting her study lamp. I ignored all that. I had wasted enough of my initial years at IIT. Most likely due to a CAT computation error, I had another chance at IIMA. I wanted to make it count.

'Wow, you can really concentrate,' she said after an hour. 'It's ten. STD calls are cheap now.'

'Oh yes, I better go,' I said.

'I'll come with you. I'll call home, too,' she said and skipped off the bed to wear her slippers.

'Seri, seri, seri Amma . . . Seri!' she said, each seri increasing in pitch, volume and frustration. She had called home. Many students had lined up to make cheap calls at the STD booth, a five-minute walk from campus. Most carried their microeconomics notes. I helped Ananya with small change after her call.

'Is he dating her?' I overheard a student whisper to another.

'I don't think so, she treats him like a brother,' his friend guffawed.

I ignored the comment and went into the booth.

'Every girl wants an IIT brother, big help in quant subjects,' the first student said as several people around them laughed.

I controlled my urge to snap back at them and dialled home.

'Hello?' my father's voice came after four rings.

I kept silent. The meter started to click.

'Hello? Hello?' my father continued to speak.

I kept the phone down. The printer churned out the bill.

'Missed connection, you have to pay,' the shopkeeper said.

I nodded and dialled again. This time my mother picked up.

'Mom,' I screamed. 'I told you to be near the phone after ten.'

'I'm sorry. I was in the kitchen. He wanted to talk to you, so he picked up. Say hello to him first and then ask him for me.'

'I'm not interested.'

'OK, leave that. How are you doing? How is the place?'

'It's fine. But they make you cram even more than in the previous college.'

'How is the food?'

'Terrible. I am in a hostel. What do you expect?'

'I'm going to send some pickle.'

'The city has good restaurants.'

'They have chicken?' she asked, her voice worried as if she had asked about basic amenities like power and water.

'In a few places.'

'FMS was good enough. I don't know why you had to leave Delhi.'

'Mom, I am not going to make my career choices based on the availability of chicken,' I said and looked at the meter. I had spent eighteen bucks. 'I'll hang up now.'

'Tell me something more no. Did you make any friends?'

'Not really, sort of . . .' I looked at Ananya's face outside the booth. She looked at me and smiled.

'Who? What's their name?'

'An . . . Anant.'

'Punjabi?'

'Mom!'

'I'm sorry. I just thought you could have a friend who likes the same food. It's OK. We are very modern. Don't you know?'

'Yeah right. I'll catch you later. I have a test tomorrow.'

'Oh, really? Pray before the exam, OK?'

'Sure, let me finish studying first.'

I hung up and paid twenty-five bucks.

'Why did you hang up the first time? Your dad picked, right?' Ananya asked as we walked back.

I stopped in my tracks. 'How do you know?'

'I guessed. I do it with mom when I'm angry with her. We don't hang up; we just stay on the line and keep silent.'

'And pay?'

'Yes. Pretty expensive way to let each other know we are upset. Only sometimes though.'

'I never speak to my father,' I said.

'Why?' Ananya looked at me.

'Long story. Not for tonight. Or any night. I'd like to keep it to myself.'

'Sure,' she said.

We walked for a moment in silence before she spoke again. 'So your parents have big expectations from you? Which job are you going to take? Finance? Marketing? IT?'

'Neither of those,' I said. 'Though I will take up a job for the money first.'

'So what do you want to be? Like really?' She looked right into my eyes.

I couldn't lie. 'I want to be a writer,' I said.

I expected her to flip out and laugh. But she didn't. She nodded and continued to walk. 'What kind of writer?' she said.

'Someone who tells stories that are fun but bring about change too. The pen's mightier than the sword, one of the first proverbs we learnt, isn't it?'

She nodded.

'Sounds ridiculous?'

'No, not really,' she said.

'How about you? What do you want to be?'

She laughed. 'Well, I don't know. My mother already feels I'm too ambitious and independent. So I am trying not to think too far. As of now, I just want to do OK in my quiz and make my mother happy. Both are incredibly difficult though,' she said.

We reached her room and practised numericals for the next two hours.

'I am so glad you are here. I'd never be able to crack these,' she said after I solved a tricky one for her.

'You are not using me, are you?'

'Excuse me?'

'Like you are friends with me because I am from IIT? So I can help you with the quant subjects.'

'Are you kidding me?' she looked shocked.

'I don't want to be the IIT brother,' I said.

'What? Whatever that is, you are not. We are friends, right?'

She extended her hand. I looked into her eyes. No, those eyes couldn't use anyone.

'Good night,' I said and shook her hand.

'Hey Krish,' she said as I turned to leave.

'What?'

'The stuff you said, about being a writer who brings about change. It is really cool. I mean it,' she said.

I smiled.

'Good night,' she said and shut her door. A few sleepless girls wandered in the dorm with their notes. They gave me suspicious looks.

'I only came to study,' I said and walked out of the dorm fast. I don't know why I felt the need to give an explanation.

4

She came out of the research assistant's room with her microeconomics quiz results. She walked past the queued up students towards me. By this time, everyone on campus knew of her friendship, or as some would say, siblingship, with me. She wore denim shorts and a pink T-shirt, drawing extra long glances from the boys from engineering colleges.

'B-plus, people say it is a good grade,' she said, holding up her answer sheet.

'Your shorts are too short,' I said.

'Show me your grade,' she said, snatching my paper. 'A minus, wow, you cracked an A-minus!'

I didn't react. We walked back towards our dorms.

'You cannot score more than me in economics, I don't believe this,' she said. 'You are a mechanical engineer. I am a university gold medallist in the subject.'

'Show the medal to Prof Chatterjee,' I said in a serious tone.

'Hey, you OK?'

I kept quiet.

'Anyway, I owe you a treat. Your numericals saved me. Are you hungry?'

I nodded. People who live in hostels are always hungry.

'Let's go to Rambhai,' she said.

'You are not coming to Rambhai like this,' I said.

'Like what?'

'Like in these shorts,' I said.

'Excuse me. Is it a Delhi thing or a Punjabi thing? Controlling what women wear?'

'It is a common sense thing. It is outside campus. People stare,' I said.

'Enough people stare within campus. I'm fine, let's go,' she said and walked towards the campus gates.

'I don't need a treat. It's fine,' I said, turning in the opposite direction towards my dorm.

'Are you serious? You are not coming?' she called from behind.

I shook my head.

'Up to you.'

I ignored her and continued to walk.

'Are you going to come for the study session tonight?'

I shrugged to signify 'whatever'.

'Any dress code for me?' she said.

'You are not my girlfriend. Wear whatever. What do I care?' I said.

We didn't talk about the afternoon episode when I came to her room in the evening. She had changed into black track pants and an oversized full-sleeve black T-shirt. She was covered up enough to go for a walk in Afghanistan. I kind of missed her shorts, but I had brought it upon myself. I opened the marketing case that we had to prepare for the next day.

'Nirdosh – nicotine-free cigarettes,' I read out the title.

'Who the fuck wants that? I feel like a real smoke,' she said. I gave her a dirty look.

'What? Am I not allowed to use F words? Or is it that I expressed a desire to smoke?'

'What are you trying to prove?'

'Nothing. I want you to consider the possibility that women are intelligent human beings. And intelligent people don't like to be told what to wear or do, especially when they are adults. Does that make sense to you?'

'Don't be over-smart,' I said.

'Don't patronise me,' she said.

'There are other ways to attract attention than by wearing less clothes,' I said.

'I didn't do it to attract attention. I wear shorts because I like to wear shorts.'

'Can we study?' I opened the case again.

We kept quiet for half an hour and immersed ourselves in our books.

'I wasn't trying to attract attention,' she said again, looking up from her books.

'It doesn't matter to me,' I said.

'Are you jealous?'

'Are you kidding me?' I slammed my book shut.

'No, just checking. Let's study,' she said. She turned back to her books, a smile on her face.

I threw the pillow at her. She laughed and slammed it on my head. I realised this was the first contact sport I had played with her apart from shaking hands.

5

We studied together every day for the next month. Even though I pretended to be fine with the 'just friends' thing, it was killing me. Every time I looked up from my books, I saw her face. Every time I saw her, I wanted to grab her face and kiss her. The only way I could focus was by imagining that Prof Chatterjee was in our room.

Even outside the study sessions, it wasn't easy. Every time I saw a guy talk to her or laugh with her, a hot flush started from my stomach and reached my face. Sometimes, she would tell me how funny some guy in section A was or how cute some guy in section B was and I wanted to go with a machine gun and shoot the respective guys in sections A and B.

'What? They should go full on with the advertising campaign, right?' she referred to the marketing case.

I had been staring at her lips, researching ways of kissing her. 'Huh? Yes, I agree with you,' I said.

'Your mind is elsewhere. What are you thinking of right now?' she snapped her fingers.

'Nothing, sorry, I was thinking how . . . how insightful you are in marketing.'

'Thank you,' she smiled, believing me. 'Yes, I like this subject. I think I will be good at a marketing job. So I will go with this recommendation tomorrow.'

We finished the case at midnight. I stood up to leave.

'Tea?' she said, suggesting we go to Rambhai.

'No. I can't fall asleep then,' I said.

'Maggi? I will make it in the pantry upstairs.'

'No, I'd better go.'

She came to the door with me. 'You are so serious these days. What do you keep thinking about? Grades?'

'I can't study with you any longer,' I blurted out.

'What?' she said, surprised.

'We've figured out a rhythm for ourselves. We don't need to study together anymore.'

'Yeah, but we like to study together, at least I do. . . . What's up? Did I do anything wrong?'

'It's not you. It's me,' I said.

'Don't do an "it's not you, it's me" on me,' Ananya screamed.

Her loud voice woke up a girl in the next room who switched on her light.

'We are not dating, OK? Stop behaving like we are having a break-up,' I whispered. 'And go to sleep. There's a quiz tomorrow.'

I didn't speak to her in class the next day. She came up to me twice, once to return my pen that I had left in her room and another time during the mid-morning break to ask me if I wanted to go for tea. Once you start liking someone, their mere presence evokes a warm feeling in you. I fought the feeling before it took control of me.

'I'd rather read up for the next class. You go have tea,' I said.

She didn't insist as she left the room. She had worn a long maroon skirt and a light brown top. I wish she'd turn back and look at me. But she didn't. She joined her dorm-mates and went out for tea.

I dodged her for the next five days. I came late to class and left first, so there was no time for greetings.

'You are not talking to her?' the Mohit right next to me asked while the other four craned their necks to listen. Even Kanyashree paused from her frantic note-taking and turned her profile ten degrees towards me.

'You seem quite concerned?' I said and everyone promptly backed off.

6

Ananya knocked on my door at nine in the night. I had just sat down to study after dinner. Girls rarely visited boys' dorms. She had come to my room only once before. It had excited my dorm-mates into an impromptu Frisbee match set to loud music in the dorm corridor.

'She reminds me of Bhagyashree,' one of the boys had screamed outside our room. Even I couldn't resist a smile. He went on to play a song from *Maine Pyar Kiya* that urged a pigeon to play postman.

'That's it. We are never studying at your dorm again,' she had fumed as she packed her books. She opened the door to eight boys playing Frisbee in the corridor.

'For the record, I hate Bhagyashree,' she had said and stormed off.

But here she was again. And the firmness in her step meant my dorm-mates didn't act like Neanderthals and had disappeared into their rooms.

I opened the door. She stood there, wearing the blue and white salwar kameez that she wore the first time I saw her. When you are in campus, you can figure out a pattern in people's clothes. Her blue salwar kameez repeated itself every three weeks.

She had brought two Frootis with her. 'Can I come in? Can I distract the scholar for ten minutes from his studies?'

Unlike her room, there was no aesthetic appeal to mine. I had left the red bricks bare, and they looked like prison walls. My originally white bed-sheet had turned grey after being washed in acid in the IIT hostels. My desk only had books, unlike Ananya's who always had cut flowers from campus lawns or arty incense holders or other objects that men never put on their shopping lists.

'Wait,' I said. I turned around to do a quick scan. No, there was no underwear or smelly socks or porn magazines or old razor blades in sight. I held the door open.

'Mugging away?' she asked as she sat on the bed.

'No choice.' I pulled back my study chair.

'Your grades will improve as you don't study with me anymore.'

'It's nothing like that,' I said.

'Then, what is the matter? What is this childish behaviour? Like you don't even acknowledge me in class.'

I looked away from her.

'Eye contact please.'

I looked at her. I had missed her so much I wanted to lock my room and never let her go.

'I can't,' I said.

'Can't what?'

'I can't be just friends. I'm sure some guys can be friends with girls. I can't. Not with you.'

'What?' She sat up straight.

'I know you are out of my league and I don't deserve you and whatever so spare me all that and. . . .'

'What are you talking about?' she sounded confused.

'Forget it. Thanks for the Frooti,' I said. I took a long, gurgling sip to finish the drink. I slammed the tetrapack on the table like a retro Hindi film hero who takes the last sip of his VAT69. Yes, leave me alone as I drown my suffering in mango juice, I thought.

'Hey.' She touched my shoulder.

'Don't put your hand on my shoulder,' I said as her touch sent tingles down the back of my neck.

'OK, peace.' She moved her hand away. 'But this is sort of not fair. We had a deal.'

'Screw the deal,' I said as I crumpled the Frooti carton and threw it in my dustbin.

We exchanged glances, silent for a minute.

'What do you want?' she asked.

'I want us to be a couple,' I said. 'And this is not a proposal. I am not Mr Fourteen.'

She stared at me. I stared back, to show I was unfazed. 'If this isn't a proposal, what is it?'

'*You* have come to my room. *You* asked me what I want. It's different.'

'But *you* want us to be a couple.' Her voice was still defiant.

I nodded.

'We used to practically be a couple, studying together, going to the STD booth together, having meals in the mess together.'

'All that stuff you can do with anyone,' I said.

'You aren't making any sense,' she said.

'OK, I will explain it,' I said and stood up. 'I will explain it so it makes sense. To sit and study with you is an exercise in double self-control. First, I have to force myself to pay attention to these boring cases. Second, I have to avoid looking at your face as much as possible because when I look at your face, all I want to do is kiss you. But we have this stupid just-friends deal and you are all cool about it and so that leaves me whipping my mind to study nicotine-free cigarettes and not think about your lips and the little mole that is there below the lower one.'

'You noticed that mole? It's tiny.' She touched it.

'It may be tiny, but it at least has a fifty percent market share in terms of my mind-space. But hey, I am just a friend. I don't get the mole. I only get the full stops.'

She laughed.

'I am not being funny. You girls don't know what it is like to be a guy.'

'Those lips talk a lot. Yours I mean,' she said.

I froze. Ms Swaminathan didn't as she came close to me. In a second, her Frooti-laced lips were on mine. We kissed for three seconds.

'And now, before I realise the stupidity of what I have done, I am out of here,' she said and opened the door. I was too dumbstruck to move.

Four boys from my dorm removed their ears from the door as Ananya pushed the door open.

'We were just locating our Frisbee,' one of the four boys said.

'It won't be in this room. This boy only likes to study,' she said and walked out of my dorm.

I didn't move an inch for five minutes. The sensation of her lips stayed with me for two minutes. The remaining three minutes were spent realising that the hottest girl in the campus had kissed me. I didn't know what I'd done right. But I didn't care. Maybe she had missed me too. Maybe it wasn't such a big deal for her. Maybe I was just imagining this and this hadn't really happened. Maybe I should stop dreaming like an idiot and run to her room. Maybe I shouldn't, as I had no idea what to do when I meet her. Maybe I should let a night pass and talk to her in class tomorrow.

'Don't keep mentioning it,' she said as the same lips that were on mine thirteen hours and twenty-two minutes ago sipped tea during class break.

'Yes, sure, OK . . .' I had already thanked her seven times. I changed the topic. 'The normal distribution is totally overrated,' I said, referring to the statistics class we had attended.

'And don't expect more,' Ananya said.

'More what?' I said. She had brought the topic back now.

'More meaning not anymore. Now, just back to what you said about the normal curve,' she said.

'Sorry, only one clarification. By more you mean no more kisses or no more than kissing?'

'Can you stop it? We are in the middle of a class.'

'But I am in the middle of a life crisis. Please tell me.'

'Is that all you guys think about? We have to study all these normal curve problems tonight.'

I looked at her and smiled.

'Any jokes about curves and I will kill you,' she promised as the bell rang for class.

7

Needless to say, one thing led to another and within two weeks we had sex. You put a boy and a girl in a room for a week and add lots of boring books, and sparks are sure to fly.

'This is my first time,' she said after we did it and pointed to her mother's picture on the wall. 'And if she finds out, she will flip.'

'We should cover these pictures when we do it. They freak me out,' I said, scanning her family members.

She laughed. 'Was this your first time?'

'I'd rather not talk about it,' I said.

'Did you have a girlfriend in IIT?' She sat up to wear her top.

I kept quiet.

'Did you have sex with a guy?' Ananya asked, eyebrows up.

'No,' I screamed and sat up. 'Are you stupid? You, of all people, are asking me if I am gay.'

'I heard they make you do all sorts of stuff in ragging.'

'No, it wasn't that bad. I had a girlfriend.'

'Really?' She blinked. 'How come you never told me!'

'I don't want to talk about it. It's over. It ended when I left college, two years ago.'

'Why? Who was she? A student?'

'Prof's daughter.'

'My, my, my! We have a stud here.' Then, 'Pretty? Prettier than me?'

I looked at Ananya. Why do women size each other up in looks so much?

'Similar, though you are smarter,' I said.

'Similar?'

'OK, you are better looking,' I said. The girl who asks the question is the better looking one, always.

'Thank you,' she said as she stepped off the bed to wear her track pants. 'Why did it end?'

'I sort of had a deal with her father.'

'Father? What, he bought you out? Gave you a blank cheque like in films?' she laughed.

'No, he let me have my degree on time. Because of which I am here. But the implicit deal was, don't push it. Don't dream of being family. There was no future, so it died.'

My throat closed up as I thought about my previous girlfriend. Somehow, it never really gets over with an ex. You merely learn to push their thoughts aside. Unless someone prods your brain again to think of them. 'Can we leave it now?'

'Where is she now? Campus?'

'No, father went to the US to a senior faculty post in MIT. She found a geeky guy of the same community. Engaged in six months, married in a year. Rest I don't know. Now, even though we were naked a few moments ago, I do think I can make a case for invasion of privacy.'

'Well, it affects me. In case you are still involved with her.'

'I'm not. It took me a long time to get over her, but I am not involved anymore.'

'Did you love her?'

'Yes. And I feel sick I didn't have the courage to fight her father. And no more talk about her please,' I said. My ex-girlfriend and my father were off-limit topics.

'One last question. Is she South Indian?'

'How did you know?'

'You mentioned IIT, MIT, geeky software programmer, it wasn't that hard.'

I laughed.

'My parents are pretty conservative too,' she said, switching on her electric kettle.

'We haven't planned to get married yet.'

She stared at me. I wondered if I had said the wrong thing. I was being factual.

'You are right. We are just friends with benefits, right? Or what is it? Fuck buddies?'

She looked upset. It is amazing how the vulnerability in a relationship shifts from the guy to the girl after you've had sex.

'Hey, we. . . .'

But she interrupted me, 'Sorry, I am freaking out. Have tea.' She passed me a cup. I twiddled with the handle for two minutes. Despite the sexual possibilities, we still had to study.

'Should we open the HR case? It is about a strike in a hotel,' I said as I opened my folder.

She nodded without eye contact. I racked my brains hard on what I could say that could make her feel better. 'I love you,' I said.

She carefully closed her case materials and looked up at me. 'Mean it?' she said, her eyes wet.

'Yes,' I said.

'You are not just saying it so you can have sex with me again?'

'No. But are you saying that. . . .'

'I am not saying anything. Is that all you think about?'

'We study together, eat together, go out together, sit in class looking at each other all day, the only time we are apart is when I have to go to sleep or when I have to use the toilet. So,' I paused.

'So what?'

'I love you, damn it! Don't you get it?' I yelled.

'That's better. Now you sound convincing,' she smiled.

'And you?' I asked.

'I'm going to think about it.'

'Excuse me?'

'Well, I could be only using you for sex,' she said.

'Excuse me?' I said, this time louder.

She laughed. I threw a pillow at her.

'I told you, I have to think about it.'

Even though she never said 'I love you', Ms Swaminathan moved in with me. I had freaked out about the idea when she arrived at my room one day with a backpack for overnight clothes. I'd have much preferred her place, as I didn't want her to be the only woman in the dorm with twenty testosterone-charged men.

Still, it was kind of nice. She brought her electric kettle, sweet smile and Maggi-making abilities with her. While we used to study together earlier, now there was even more discipline. When a woman comes into your life, things organise themselves.

We woke up in the morning, she half an hour earlier than me. She would rush to her dorm a hundred metres away and bathe there. I'd get ready and meet her at the mess for breakfast.

'This is your assignment and this is my quant worksheet.' She'd take out the stack of work from last night and divide it in the mess. We'd go to class together, and if Kanyashree was in a good mood, she'd switch places with Ananya for a day. Otherwise, we'd take our original seats and stare at each other through class. The five Mohits were quite amused at first, but later adjusted quite well and turned to check us out only when the lecture got boring. In fact, her moving in with me created a mini scandal. Like it always happens, I earned the tag of a stud. And she earned tags ranging from stupidly-in-love to slut. But it didn't matter to her as maybe she was stupidly in love. Every day in class, she would pass me a note.

'I miss you. Can't wait to cuddle with you after class,' it said, and it came to me via Ankur, Anoop, Bipin, Bhupin, Bhanu, ten other students and Kanyashree. We lived with each other, yet she missed me in class from six rows away.

'Stop sending such notes in class. People will open them,' I warned.

'You are no fun,' she replied with several sad smilies. Bipin smiled as he passed that note. OK, so someone had entertainment in class.

'You are a whisker away from being in the top ten. One more A in the statistics final exam and you are there,' she said one night three months after she had moved in with me.

'I can't believe I'm studying so much. In IIT, all we'd do is chat all night.' I switched off the lights.

'We could chat all night,' she said as we tucked under the quilt together.

'About what? And why? We are with each other all the time. Why sacrifice sleep?'

'Still, we could talk. Future plans and stuff.'

The word 'future' and females is a dangerous combination. Still, in a business school future could merely mean placement. 'We've good grades. You'll easily get HLL. It is the best marketing job, right? And I'll go for WPM.'

'WPM?'

'Whoever pays more, so I can save as much money as fast as possible,' I grinned.

'You still serious about becoming a writer, right?' She ran her fingers through my hair.

'Yes, but I'm still wondering what I'd write about,' I yawned.

'About anything. Like that girlfriend of yours.'

'Ananya, we had a pact. We will not talk about my ex-girlfriend again.'

'Sorry, sorry. You said you had a deal with the Prof for grades, so I thought maybe it will make an interesting story.'

'Good night, my strategist.' I kissed her and lay down.

'I love you,' she said.

'Mean it?'

'Yes.'

'How come you said it now?'

'I think about it a lot. I only articulated it now. Good night,' she said.

One-and-a-half years later

'Tell me your thoughts. Don't you like to talk after making love?'

Actually, I prefer to look at the fan above. Or drift into a nap. Why do women want to talk all the time? We were in my room. We were snugly wrapped up on a cloudy, winter afternoon.

'I love to talk,' I said carefully. 'Do you have something in mind?'

'It's one week to placement and I'm nervous,' she said.

'Don't worry, every company has short-listed you. You will hit the jackpot.'

'I'm not nervous about receiving a job offer. What after that?'

'After that? Finally, we will have money in the bank. No more scrimping while ordering in restaurants, no more front row seats in theatres, no more second-class train travel. College is fun, but sorry, I've had my share of slumming it. Imagine, you can shop every month!'

'I don't like shopping.'

'Fine, you can save the money. Or travel to exotic places.'

Her face turned more thoughtful.

'You OK?' I asked.

'Do you realise we leave campus in four weeks?'

'Good riddance. No more mugging and grades, hopefully for life,' I said.

Her voice dropped an octave. 'What about us?'

'About us what?' I asked with an idiotic, confused expression exclusive to men when they have to get all meaningful with women.

She sat up and wore her top. She stepped off the bed to wear the rest of her clothes. Despite the serious mood, I couldn't help but notice how wonderful women look when they change. 'I'm going to my room. Enjoy your nap,' she said.

'Hey,' I extended my arm and stopped her. 'What's up? I am talking, no?'

'But like a dork. We could be in different cities in four weeks. It will never be like this again.'

'What do you mean never?' I said, my mouth open.

'Wear your clothes first. I want to have a serious discussion.'

She kept quiet until I finished dressing. We sat across, cross-legged on the bed.

'Here is the deal,' I said, collecting my thoughts. 'You are the career-focussed one, I am doing it for the money. So, I will try to get a job in the same city as you. But the issue is, we don't know which city you will be in. So how can I do anything about it now?'

'And what will you do next week? We are all going to get placed around the same time. You can't wait for me to get a job.'

'So let fate play out,' I said.

'And what about our future? Or sorry, I should ask, is there a future?'

'I can't talk about that right now,' I said.

'Oh really, can you give me a time in the future when we can talk about the future?'

I kept quiet.

'Forget it, I'm leaving,' she said and made for the door.

'I need time to think,' I said.

'Two years are not enough?'

I kept quiet.

'You know it baffles me,' Ananya said, 'how you men need so much time to think about commitment, but how you need no time at all to decide when you have to sleep with the girl.'

'Ananya,' I began only to hear the door slam shut.

'You'll be fine,' she told me for the fifth time. We took a four-kilometre walk outside campus to reach Navrangpura. I wanted to be as far from the madness as possible. Day Zero, or the first day of placement, had ended and I hadn't got a job.

'I thought with my grades I will crack Day Zero,' I said.

'Who cares? There're six more days left for placements,' she said.

We stopped at a roadside vendor for pao-bhaji. She ordered two plates with less butter. 'You will be fine. See, marketing companies don't even start until tomorrow. I have my big HLL interview. I'm not stressed.'

'You'll get in. I can't think of a single company who can say no to you,' I said.

She looked at me and smiled. 'You do realise that not everyone is in love with me.'

'You have good grades and a passion for marketing. You are so HLL, I can see it on your face.'

'You have two more banks tomorrow.'

'I want Citibank,' I said. 'I should have better answers than "I like the money". I need to lie better in interviews.'

The waiter served us. She broke a piece of the pao and fed me. 'But that's the only reason why anyone would work in a bank, right?'

'Yes, but the interviewers like to believe they are doing something meaningful. Like they work for the Mother Teresa Foundation or something.'

'Well, you should say this – I want Citibank as I want Indians to have access to world-class financial services. And use words like "enormous growth" and "strategic potential",' she said.

'I have to say all that without throwing up?'

'And remember, the Citi never sleeps. So say you will work hard,' she said.

'I can't lie that much,' I said.

She laughed as she wiped a bit of bhaji off the corner of my mouth. I thought how lucky I was to have her. She could be running HLL in a few years, but today her priority was to wipe bhaji off my stupid face. Guilt knotted within me. She deserved an answer about the future. Do it, loser, I told myself. Do it now. Even if it is a makeshift pao bhaji stall in Navrangpura. I gathered the courage to speak.

'What? You want to say something?'

'Do you want more pao?' I said.

'You are third,' a first-year student volunteer who assisted in placements told me. I sat on a stool with seven other candidates outside the interview room. We resembled patients at a dentist's clinic, only more stressed.

The HLL interviews were on in the room across me. Ananya had moved up all the rounds and now waited to be called one last time. I reflected on what had gone wrong on Day Zero. OK, I only wanted a job for the money, but I had hidden that when they spoke to me. *Then why did I screw up with five banks yesterday? What if Citi also screws me?* I thought. Sweat beads popped on my forehead. *Was it destiny leading me to doom after all these degrees and grades? Is God not on my side?* I wondered if I had given any reason to God not to be on my side. I saw the HLL room from a distance. Ananya stood outside, looking beautiful in a peacock blue sari. *Maybe God will not let me decide my future unless I give her clarity on her future.*

'Krish Malhotra,' the student volunteer called my name.

I offered mental prayers and stood up. I checked my tie knot and shirt collars. *Remember, you need this job,* I told myself. Banks pay double, I could quit a corporate career twice as fast to do whatever I wanted to. I breathed in deeply and exhaled.

'Welcome, take your seat,' a man in an impeccable black suit spoke from his chair. He was rich enough to wear a Rolex watch and obnoxious enough not to look at me while he addressed me. He rifled through a pile of resumes to find mine.

'Good afternoon.' I extended my hand. I flexed my forearm muscles as people say a tight handshake is a sign of confidence and world domination.

'Rahul Ahuja, managing director, corporate finance,' he said and shook hands with me. He pointed to his colleague on the right. 'And this is Devesh Sharma, vice-president in HR.'

I looked at Devesh, a thirty-year-old executive with the timidity of a three-year-old. He came across as someone who could be kicked around despite being called vice-president. Anyway, I'd heard Citibank had four hundred vice-presidents to accommodate careers and egos of hundreds of new MBAs that joined every year. Of course, it took away the relevance of the title but at least it gave you a good introduction. Rahul signalled Devesh to start.

'So Krish, I notice you have poor grades in your undergrad,' Devesh spoke in a voice so effeminate, he'd be the obvious choice for female leads in college plays.

'You are pretty observant,' I said.

'Excuse me?' Devesh said, surprised.

Cut the wisecracks, I told myself. 'Nothing,' I cleared my throat.

'So, what happened?'

A girlfriend, fun-loving friends, alcohol, grass and crap profs happened, I wanted to say. But Ananya had told me the right answer.

'Actually, Mr Sharma,' I said, emphasising his name so he felt good, 'when I entered IIT, I didn't realise the rigours demanded by the system. And once you have a bad start, due to relative grading, it is quite hard to come back. I did get good grades in the last semester and my IIMA grades are good. So, as you can see, I've made up.'

There were twenty minutes of stupid questions like 'will credit cards grow in India?' or 'can India improve its banking services?' where you easily answer what they want to hear (yes, they will grow and, yes, India can improve heaps). Finally, they asked the big question, 'Why Citibank?'

I want Citibank because none of the other five banks worked out. I sucked in my breath along with my stupid thoughts. *BS time, buddy,* I thought, *the ten seconds that will determine your career start now.*

'Mr Ahuja, the question is not why Citi. The real question is why would any ambitious young person want to go anywhere else? It is the biggest private bank in the world, it has a great reputation, it is committed to India, and there are opportunities in almost every area of the bank. It is not a bank, it is a growth machine.'

I paused to see if I had gone over the top. But Rahul listened with rapt attention and Devesh nodded. Yes, they were falling for it.

'And, ultimately the biggest reason is, Rahul,' I said, switching to the first name to show my closeness to him, 'I really want to work with people I look up to. When I see you, I want to be you. And Citi gives me a shot at it.'

Rahul flushed with pride. 'How . . . I mean, how do you know you want to be me?'

No matter how accomplished people get, they don't stop fishing for compliments. 'I saw you at the pre-placement talk. I've attended dozens of talks, but the way you presented showed more thought clarity than anyone else. I think it is a Citibank thing. Your people have a different confidence. Right, Devesh?'

Devesh looked at me, perplexed. 'Actually, we at human resources pick the best talent,' he parroted, probably from a manual.

'HR does nothing. I personally pick everyone for the job,' Rahul said as the two jostled for my attention.

'It shows,' I said.

Rahul pushed back his chair and stood up. 'Listen Krish, I like you. So between us, let me be honest. We are mostly done with the recruiting and have only one place left. But we have internal criteria; we need a seven-point grade in undergrad to take new recruits.'

Fuck. My past sins would not let go of me. Maybe that is why the five banks had rejected me.

'And this missed semester . . .' he tapped my undergrad grade sheet.

'Research semester, sir,' I corrected.

'I don't know about that. Devesh?'

Devesh, like anyone who works in HR, had never taken a real decision in his life. 'It's a business call, sir,' he said.

'I head my business,' Rahul said.

'Yes, but you may want to talk to the country manager,' Devesh said, scared to make a suggestion.

'I'm senior to him. I came from New York. He's just connected so he became country manager. You know that, right?'

'Sir, but grade-wise . . .' Devesh paused and both of them looked at me.

'Can you give us five minutes?' Rahul asked.

'Sure, I'll wait outside,' I obliged with an ingratiating grin.

'Thanks, we'll call you in again. So, don't send the next candidate.'

8

I stepped out of the Citi interview room. I scanned the list of remaining companies on the notice board. Everyone else paid half of Citibank. I found an empty stool to sit on and closed my eyes to pray. God appeared in front of me.

'Hello God,' I said, 'I've not said one true thing in that interview today. But I want the job, please.'

'They don't want to hear the truth. So, that's OK,' God said. 'But that's not what you should be worried about.'

'Then what?'

'You have lived with a girl for two years.'

'I love her, God,' I said.

'Love is not enough. You know what you have to do.'

'I will, I just need time.'

'You are well past your time. In four minutes, I could let your last bank job slip away,' God said.

'No God, I want Citibank.'

'I want you to do the right thing first.'

'How?' I opened my eyes. I looked at the HLL room. Ananya had gone inside the room. I closed my eyes again. 'How?' I repeated. 'She is in an interview. I promise to do it after I get my Citibank job.'

'I don't trust you. Anyway, upto you. You don't listen to me, I don't listen to you,' God said.

I opened my eyes. I had three minutes. Ananya would kill me if I went inside that room. But a voice inside told me that if I didn't go to her, the Citi country manager or Rahul or Devesh could decide against me. Of course, my rational mind knew I was being completely moronic. Both the events were not connected. But there is only so much our rational mind knows. Maybe, events and karma are connected. I ran to the HLL room.

'Excuse me,' the volunteer on the door said, blocking me.

'I need to go inside,' I said, 'urgent.'

'There's an inter . . .'

I forced my way inside. HLL was conducting its final interviews in one of the classrooms. The company staff sat in the front row of the class while the candidate sat in the prof's chair.

Ananya faced a panel of five elderly people in the room. She was moving her hands in an animated manner as she spoke. 'The rural market doesn't need different products. They need affordability. . . .' She stopped mid-sentence upon noticing me. Her eyebrows elevated in shock and stayed there.

'Yes?' a sixtyish-year-old gentleman turned to me.

Ananya's face turned pink, then red. The colour coordination came from embarrassment and anger, respectively.

'I need to talk to her,' I said slowly, scanning everyone in the room.

'Can't it wait?' the old gentleman asked. 'She is having her final interview. All our senior management is here.'

'Actually, it can't,' I said.

'Everything OK?' another panellist said.

'Yes, I only need a minute,' I said and signalled to Ananya to come out.

'What? Just tell me here,' she said, throwing me a dirty look.

I saw the panel's confused expression. I went up to Ananya.

'What?' she whispered, 'Are you mad?'

I knelt down next to her, my mouth close to her ear. 'Sorry, how is it going?' I whispered.

'Krish Malhotra, this better be important. What's up?' she whispered, loud enough for the panel to hear.

'Ananya Swaminathan, I, Krish Malhotra, am deeply in love with you and want to be with you always. Apart from when we go to office, of course. Will you marry me?'

Ananya's mouth fell open. She alternated her glance between the panel and me. 'Krish,' she said. She tried hard but a tear slipped out of her carefully eye-lined eyes.

'Everything OK?' one panel member asked as he noticed Ananya's restlessness. 'It's not bad news, I hope.'

Ananya shook her head as she took a sip from the glass of water in front of her. 'No, it's not bad news at all. It's good.'

'Ananya,' I whispered again. My knees hurt as they rubbed against the rough classroom floor.

'What now?'

'Is that a yes? Will you be with me, always?' I asked.

She tigthened her lips to hide a laugh. 'Yes, you idiot. I will be with you. Just not right now. So, go!'

9

'Wow, this feels special,' Ananya said.

She opened her HLL offer letter for the third time at Rambhai's. I had collected mine from Citibank the day before and, after confirming the salary, had dumped it in my cupboard.

'It's an invitation to be a slave, don't get so excited,' I said as I ordered a samosa sandwich.

'Aw, don't be morbid. They are thrilled about hiring me. HLL has a serious South India strategy.'

Rambhai's minions served us tea. During placement time, tips peaked for them.

'Do you go to school?' Ananya asked the thirteen-year-old boy who served us.

'Yes, Rambhai sends me,' the boy said.

'Good, because if he doesn't, report him to the police,' Ananya said and gave the boy a fifty rupee note.

'They will post you in South India,' I said, 'in one of those unpronounceable places without an STD code.'

'No, they won't. And if they do, my husband will come and rescue me,' she winked.

'Ananya, you don't get it. *We* have decided to get married. Our parents haven't approved – yet,' I reminded her.

'C'mon, mine are a bit conservative. But we are their overachieving children, the ultimate middle-class fantasy kids. Why would they have an issue?'

'Because they are parents. From biscuits to brides, if there is anything their children really want, parents have a problem,' I said.

'Your parents will have a problem with me?' Ananya pulled her hair back to tie it in a loose bun. She clenched a pin in the middle of her teeth.

'They'd have a problem with anyone I choose. And you are South Indian, which doesn't help at all. OK, it's not as bad as marrying someone from another religion. But pretty close.'

'But I also aced my college. I have an MBA from IIMA and work for HLL. And sorry to brag, but I am kind of pretty.'

'Irrelevant. You are Tamilian. I am Punjabi.'

Ananya folded her offer letter and rearranged things in her bag.

'What? Say something?'

'Can't be part of this backward conversation,' she said. 'Please, discuss your woes with the Punjabi brethren.'

She stood up to leave. I tugged her down by her hand. 'C'mon Ananya, aren't your parents going to flip out when they find out you have a Punjabi boyfriend?'

'No. I don't think so.'

'Have you told them?'

'No.'

'Why?'

'Waiting for the appropriate time. The convocation is in two weeks. They'll be here, I will introduce you. Tell them what you have done in life, not where your ancestors were born. They can meet your parents. They are coming, right?'

'My mother, yes. Father, I don't know.'

'What's the deal?'

'Let's not talk about it.'

'You won't tell your future wife? Have you invited him?'

'No.'

She stood up, I followed suit. 'Let's go to the STD booth,' she said.

'Now?'

'This strong and silent warfare between you and your dad is becoming too much.'

'It's peak hour rates.'

'I don't care.'

We walked to the STD booth near Vijay Char Rasta. I called home.

'Hi, mom, it is me.'

'Krish, we should book tickets. I am coming, Shipra masi wants to come. Rajji mama and Kamla aunty, too.'

'Mom, is dad coming?'

'No,' she said and fell silent.

'It's my convocation,' I said.

'He said he has work.'

'He's retired. What work?' The meter rode up twenty rupees.

'You talk to him, he expects a personal invitation,' my mother said.

'I won't. Doesn't he want to come by himself?'

'No, why don't you ask him to?' She prepared to put me on hold.

'Mom, no. I don't want to call him if he doesn't want to come.'

'Fine. Can masi and mama come?'

'Don't get any relatives,' I pleaded.

'Why? They love you so much. They want to see you. . . .'

'I want you to meet someone, mom.'

'Who?'

'You'll find out,' I said.

I came out of the booth. Ananya and I walked back. *Which father needs an invitation from his son to attend his convocation? Screw him,* I said to myself.

'You invited him?' Ananya asked.

'Dad's not coming,' I said.

'Why?'

'We have no relationship, Ananya. Don't try and fix it ever. OK?'

'What happened though?'

'I don't want to talk about it.'

'Standard answer.'

'Yours was a standard question.'

'You do care for him. You are upset.'

'I'm upset about paying peak hour rates. Now listen, I've fended off my aunts with great difficulty. It's only my mom. You have a plan, right?'

She skipped ahead of me. 'Let's make it a great first meeting of the families. We should do something fun together.'

'Like shoot each other?'

'Shut up. It'll be fine. They'd love it that my boyfriend is from IIT.'

'They won't ask my grades, right?'

'They might. But who cares, you will be in Citibank. Listen, should we organise an outing for them?'

'I am not so sure if our families would like to spend so much time together.'

'Of course, they would. You leave it to me. Your mom will love me more than you after this,' she said as we reached the campus gates.

I received my mother at the Ahmedabad railway station a day before the convocation. Ananya's parents flew down, her father using his LTC that allowed him to fly once every four years. My mother arrived with two suitcases. One had her clothes and the other contained mithai boxes sourced from various shops in Delhi.

'I'm in college for five more days. Why so many sweets?' I asked in the auto back to campus.

'We will eat them, no? And we might meet people. They will say her son is graduating and she has nothing to offer us. I almost brought packed meals. I don't want to eat the Gujarati daal with sugar. Is it really sweet?'

'It's not that sweet. Anyway, I want you to meet someone, mom,' I said as the auto struggled to penetrate the narrow lanes near the railway station.

'Who?'

'There's this girl,' I said.

'You have a Girlfriend? *Girlfriend*?' she said as if I had contracted AIDS.

'A good friend,' I said to calm her down.

'Good friend? What, you have bad friends also?'

'No, mom. We used to study together. We did a lot of projects together.'

'OK. Did she get a job?'

'Yes, in HLL. It's a good job.'

'HLL?'

'The company that makes Surf. And Rin and Lifebuoy and Kissan Sauce.' I named products, hoping that one of them would impress her.

'Kissan Jams also?' she asked after thinking for thirty seconds.

'Yes. She is in marketing. It's the most prestigious marketing job.'

'She will get free jams then?'

'I guess,' I said, wondering how to bring the conversation back on track. 'But that's not the point.'

'Yes, it's not. So, should we stop for lunch before we go to your college or do we eat in college? Bhaiya, any good restaurants here?' she addressed the auto driver.

'Mom, stop. I am talking about something important.'

But my mother said, 'These auto drivers always know good places.'

'Stopping is extra, madam,' the auto driver said, ignoring me along with every speed-breaker on the road.

'What?' my mother said as I continued to stare at her to get her attention.

'Her name is Ananya. Her parents are also there. I want you to meet them and be nice to them.'

'I will meet whoever you want me to meet. And when am I not nice? We are nice people only.'

'Mom. . . .' I said before she interrupted me.

'Let's take some Nice biscuits on the way. They are good with tea.'

'Mom,' I screamed. 'This is what I don't want. I want you to meet them properly and not obsess about meals or snacks or tea or whatever. They should have a good impression.'

My mother gave me a dirty look. I didn't respond.

'Bhaiya, turn the auto. I am going back,' my mother said. 'One, I come all the way from Delhi to attend your convocation, get mithai from four different shops, and now I can't make a good impression. It's OK, if we can't make a good impression then we won't come.'

My mother kept mumbling to herself. She had officially entered her drama mode. The driver stopped the auto.

'What? Why have you stopped?' I asked, exasperated.

'Madam is telling me to turn back.'

'Mom,' I said as she continued to sulk.

'So, you remember I am your mother? I thought you only cared about your friend's parents?'

Anger filled my mother's voice. I had to take emergency measures. 'There is an excellent pao-bhaji place round the corner. Bhaiya, just take us to Law Garden.'

'I'm not hungry,' my mother said.

'Only for tasting,' I said. I tapped the auto driver on his shoulder. The driver turned towards Law Garden.

I ordered paneer pao-bhaji with extra butter and a lassi on the side. Nothing soothes an upset Punjabi like dairy products.

'Who is this girl?' she asked after finishing her lassi.

'Nobody important. She wanted to meet you after I told her how much trouble you took to bring me up because of dad,' I lied.

Maybe it was the extra butter or my words. My mother calmed down. 'You told her everything?' she asked.

'No, only a little. Also, her parents may be a bit formal. That's why I spoke about making a good impression. Otherwise, who wouldn't love to meet you?'

'What do Gujaratis eat for dessert? Or do they put all the sugar in their food?' My mother picked up the menu again.

10

The next morning, two hundred fresh MBA graduates and their insanely proud parents sat in the Louis Kahn Plaza lawns for the convocation. The chief guest, a third generation silver-spoon-at-birth industrialist, told students to work hard and come to the top. He also had the tough job of handing out degrees and posing for pictures with two hundred students.

Today, we had to collect our post-graduate diploma in management, a ticket to a lifetime of overpaid jobs. Ananya wanted everything to be perfect. She had reached the venue half an hour earlier to secure six seats for her family and mine.

My mother wore her best sari. I wore graduation robes rented for thirty bucks.

'Mom, this is Ananya. Ananya, my mother,' I said when we reached the premises.

Ananya extended her arm to shake my mother's hand. My mother looked shocked. While Ananya touching her feet would be too much, I felt Ananya should have stuck to a namaste. Anything modern doesn't go down well with parents.

'Hello, aunty. I have heard so much about you,' Ananya said.

'Actually, since I have arrived I am only hearing about you.' My mother smiled, making it difficult to spot the sarcasm.

'Let's sit down. Ananya, where is your family?' I asked as we sat down.

'My mother takes forever to put on her sari. I came first to get good seats.'

Ananya wore the same peacock blue sari that she wore to her HLL interview. She caught me staring and blew a kiss. Fortunately, my mother didn't notice. I shook my head, beseeching Ananya to maintain decorum.

Ananya's parents arrived ten minutes later. Her father wore a crisp white shirt, like the ones in detergent ads. Ananya's mother walked behind in a glittery haze. Her magenta and gold Kanjeevaram sari could be noticed from any corner of the lawn. She looked as if she had fallen into a drum of golden paint. Behind her walked a fourteen-year-old boy with spectacles; a miniature version of the MBA men who would get a degree this evening.

'Hello mom,' Ananya said and stood up, her voice her cheerful best.

'Safety pin illa something something,' her mother replied. Mother and daughter lapsed into Tamil. Ananya's father took out his camera and started taking random pictures of everything around us – the lawns, the stage, the chairs, the mikes. Little brother didn't have much to do but looked uncomfortable in his new button-down collar shirt. My mother heard them talk and her mouth fell open.

I whispered, 'Get up. Let us introduce ourselves.'

'They are Madrasi?' my mother asked, shocked.

'Shsh, Tamilian,' I said.

'Tamilian?' my mother echoed even as Ananya continued the introductions.

'Mom, this is Krish, and this is Krish's mother.'

'Hello,' Ananya's mother said, looking just as stunned as my mother.

'Isn't this cool? Our families meeting for the first time,' Ananya cooed even as everyone ignored her.

'Krish's father has not come?' Ananya's father asked.

'He is not well,' my mother said, her voice butter-soft. 'He is a heart patient. Advised not to travel.'

My mother faked it so well, even I felt like sympathising with her.

Ananya's parents gave understanding nods. They whispered to each other in Tamil as they took their places.

'I better go, I'm one of the first ones.' Ananya giggled and ran up to join the line of students.

I sat sandwiched between my mother on one side and Ananya's mother on the other.

'You want to sit next to Ananya's mother?' I asked my mother.

'Why? Who are these people?' she frowned.

'Don't panic, mom. I said it because I have to join that line soon.'

'Then go. I have come to see you, not sit next to Madrasis. Now let me watch,' she said.

The chief guest started the diploma distribution. The audience broke into continuous applause for the initial students. Then they got tired and went back to fanning themselves with the convocation brochures.

'Get to know them. We'll probably go for lunch together,' I said.

'You go for lunch with them. I can eat alone,' my mother said.

'Mom . . .' I said as the announcer read out Ananya's name. Ananya walked on to the stage, probably the only student whose picture was worth taking. I stood up and applauded.

My mother gave me a dirty look. 'Sit. Even her parents are not standing.'

Maybe they don't love her like I do, I wanted to say but didn't. I sat down. Ananya's parents clapped gently, craning their necks to get a better view. Ananya's mother looked at me with suspicion. I realised that I hadn't yet spoken to her. *Start a conversation, you idiot*, I thought.

'Your daughter is such a star. You must be so proud,' I said.

'We are used to it. She always did well in school,' Ananya's mother replied.

I tried her father. 'How long are you here for, uncle?'

Uncle looked up and down at me as if I had questioned him about his secret personal fantasies.

'We leave day after. Why?' he said.

Some whys have no answer, apart from the fact that I was trying to make small talk. 'Nothing, Ananya and I were wondering if you wanted to see the city. We can share a car,' I said.

Ananya's mother sat between us and listened to every word. She spoke to her husband in Tamil. 'Something something Gandhi Ashram something recommend something.'

'Gandhi Ashram is nice. My mother also wants to see it.' I said.

'What?' my mother said from her seat. 'Don't you have to go on stage, Krish? Your turn is coming.'

'Yes,' I said and stood up. Gandhi Ashram would be a good start for the families. He stood for peace and national integration, maybe that could inspire us all.

'Then go,' my mother said.

'Wait,' I said and bent to touch her feet.

'Thank god, you remembered. I thought you were going to touch Ananya's mother's feet,' she said.

My mother said it loud enough for Ananya's mother to hear. They exchanged cold glances that could be set to the backdrop of AK-47 bullets being fired. Surely, it would take a Mohandas Karamchand Gandhi to make them get along.

'Mom, control,' I whispered to her as I turned to leave.

'I am under control. These South Indians don't know how to control their daughters. From Hema Malini to Sridevi, all of them trying to catch Punjabi men.'

My mother had spoken so loud that the entire row heard her. For a few moments, people's attention shifted from the convocation ceremony to us.

Ananya's mother elbowed her husband. They stood up, pulled up Ananya's scrawny brother between them and found some empty seats five rows away.

'Mom, what are you doing?' I struggled to balance the graduation cap on my head.

'Kanyashree Banerjee,' the announcer said over the mike and I realised I was horribly late. I had missed my last convocation as I had overslept. I didn't want to miss it this time.

'What have I said? It's a fact,' my mom said, talking to me but addressing everyone who had tuned into our conversation that beat the boring degree distribution hollow any day.

'Krish . . .' I heard my name and ran up. The five Mohits were waiting near the stage. I smiled at them as I climbed the steps to the stage. The chief guest gave me my diploma.

My mother was standing and clapping. 'I love you,' she screamed. I smiled back at her. For the last ten years my father had told her that her son would get nowhere in life. I held up my diploma high and looked up to thank God.

'Move, the next student has to come,' the announcer said as I emotionally thanked the chief guest again and again. As I walked down the steps, I saw Ananya's parents. They had not applauded or even reacted to my being on stage. I came back towards my seat. Ananya stood at our row's entrance, looking lost. 'I stayed back to get some pictures with friends. Where are my parents?'

'Five rows behind,' I said.

'Why? What happened?'

'Nothing. They wanted a better view,' I said.

'I've booked the car. We are all going afterwards, right?'

'Go to your parents, Ananya,' I said firmly as I saw my mother staring at me.

11

'We've already paid for the taxi,' I said. 'So, you can pretend to get along. See it as a budget exercise.'

My mother and I walked towards the taxi stand outside campus. She had no inclination to see where Mr Gandhi lived. The Sabarmati Ashram, on the outskirts of the city, was a key tourist attraction. Ananya had got lunch packed in little packets from Topaz. According to her, it would be a Kodak moment to picnic somewhere by the Sabarmati river. Of course, she had no idea about her missed Kodak moment when my mother had made insightful comments about certain South Indian actresses.

'We had booked a Qualis,' I told the driver who stood next to an Indica. Ananya and her family were already at the taxi stand. Her mother looked like she had just finished a grumble session, maybe her natural expression.

'The Qualis is on election duty. We only have this.' The driver crushed tobacco in his palm.

'How can we all fit in?' I wondered.

'We take double the passengers, squeeze in,' the driver said.

'Let's take an auto,' I said.

'I'm not taking an auto,' my mother said as she slid into the backseat.

'You can sit in front and make madam sit in your lap,' the driver pointed Ananya to me. Ananya's mother gave the driver a glare strong enough to silence him for the rest of the day.

'Mom, can you take an auto?' Ananya requested her mother.

'Why, we have also paid for this,' she said. 'Something something illa illa!'

'Seri, seri, Amma,' Ananya said.

We finally arrived at an arrangement. Ananya's dad sat in front with Ananya in his lap. Ananya's mother sat behind with her son in her lap. My mother had already taken a window seat behind the driver. I squished myself between the two ladies in the middle.

The Sabarmati Ashram is eight kilometres away from campus. The twenty-minute drive felt like an hour due to the silence. Ananya tried to make conversation with her parents. They pretended not to hear her as they kept their heads out of the window. My mother took out a packet of Nice biscuits and started eating them without offering them to anyone. She took one biscuit and put it in my mouth, to assert maternal rights on me. Of course, I couldn't refuse.

'Why is everyone so silent,' Ananya said to me as we went to the ticket counter at the ashram.

'My mother made a silly comment at the convocation,' I said, hoping Ananya won't seek details.

'What did she say?' Ananya said as she fished for the required amount of money for six tickets.

'It's not important. But your parents left after that.'

'What exactly did she say?' Ananya persisted.

'Nothing, something about South Indian women being loose or something. No big deal.'

'What?' Ananya looked at me, shocked.

'I didn't say it. She did. Silly comment, ignore it.'

'I don't know what to say,' Ananya said.

'Nothing. Let's get everyone talking again,' I said as we walked to the main entrance.

We came inside the ashram. Gandhi lived here from 1915 to 1930. The famous Salt March started from this ashram. Ananya appointed a guide, for no other reason than to keep everyone walking together. We passed the exhibits – various pictures, paintings, letters and articles of Gandhi.

'And when Mr Gandhi left in 1930 for the Dandi March, he vowed never to return to the ashram until India won its independence,' the guide said in a practised dramatic voice. 'And he didn't after that day.'

'Did he come back after India became free?' Ananya's mother wanted to know.

'Alas,' the guide sighed, 'he couldn't. He was shot dead within six months of independence.'

My mother, not to be left behind in asking of questions, turned to the guide. 'Why is it called Dandi March? Because he carried a stick?'

The guide laughed. Like all his mannerisms, his laugh was dramatic, too. 'How little we know about the greatest man in India. No madam, Dandi is the name of a place, five hundred kilometres away from here.' The guide took us to an exhibit of the map and pointed to the coastal town.

Ananya's mother turned to her father and spoke in Tamil. 'Something something illa knowledge Punjabi people something.'

'Seri, seri,' Ananya's father said in a cursory manner, engrossed in the map. Ananya's mother continued. 'Intellectually, culturally zero. Something something crass uneducated something.'

I don't know if Ananya's mother realised her use of the few English words, or maybe she planted them intentionally. She had made her comeback. My mother heard her and looked at me. The guide looked worried as his tip was in danger.

'So you see, Gandhiji strongly believed that all Indians are one. Anyway, let us now see Gandhiji's personal belongings. This way, please,' the guide said, breaking the Antarctic glances between the two mothers.

We sat down for lunch under a tree in the ashram complex, looking like we were on death row. Everyone ate in silence as Ananya dropped the news. 'We like each other.'

Everyone looked at each other in confusion. Most people did not like each other in this group.

'Krish and I, we like each other,' Ananya smiled.

'I told you. I smelt something fishy. . . .' My mother tore her chapatti.

'There's nothing fishy. There's nothing to be worried about. We just wanted to share our happiness. We are just two people in love,' Ananya said as her mother interrupted her.

'Shut up, Ananya!' Ananya's mother glared at her. I wondered if she would slap her. And I wondered if Ananya would offer her second cheek, considering we were in Gandhi's ashram.

'This is what I meant when I said about South Indian girls. There are so many cases in Delhi only,' my mother said, itching to slam Ananya's mom again.

'Mom, chill,' I said.

'What have I said? Did I say anything?' my mother asked.

'Get up,' Ananya's mother said to her husband. Like a TV responding to a remote, he stood. Ananya's brother followed. 'We will take an auto back,' Ananya's mother said.

Ananya sat under the tree, perplexed.

'Now you will stay with them?' Ananya's mother asked.

'Mom, please!' Ananya sounded close to tears.

Ananya's mother tugged at Ananya and pulled her away. The guide noticed them leave and looked puzzled. I paid him off and came back to my mother. She finished the last few spoons of Topaz's paneer tikka masala under the tree.

'They are gone,' I said.

'Good. There'll be more space in the car,' she said.

Act 2:
Delhi

12

'What are you reading with such concentration?' my mother asked as she chopped bhindi on the dining table.

'It's the Citibank new employee form. I have to fill fifty pages. They want to know everything, like where was your mother born.'

'On the way from Lahore to Delhi. Your grandmother delivered me in a makeshift tent near Punjabi Bagh.'

'I'll write Delhi,' I said.

I had come home for the two-month break before joining Citibank. Even in April, Delhi temperature had already crossed forty degrees centigrade. There wasn't much to do, apart from calling Ananya once a day or waiting for her call. I sat with my mother as she prepared lunch. My father wasn't home, nobody really sure or caring about where he was.

'Is this the form where you fill your location preference?' my mother asked.

I looked at her hands, a little more wrinkled than before I left home to join college. She cut the top and tail of a bhindi and slit it in the middle.

'Yes,' I said.

'You chose Delhi, right?'

I kept quiet.

'What?'

'Yes I will,' I said.

The phone rang. I rushed to pick it up. It was Sunday and cheaper STD rates meant Ananya would call at noon.

'Hi, my honey bunch,' Ananya said.

'Obviously, your mother is not around,' I said. I spoke in a low volume as my own mother kept her eyes on the bhindi but her ears on me.

'Of course not. She's gone to buy stuff for *Varsha Porupu* puja tomorrow.'

2 States • 55

'*Varsha* what?'

'*Varsha Porupu*, Tamil new year. Don't you guys know?'

'Uh, yes of course. Happy New Year,' I said.

'And have you sent in your Citibank form yet?'

'No, have to fill a few final items,' I said.

'You've given Chennai as your top location choice?'

'I will . . . wait.'

I picked up the phone and went as far from my mother as the curly landline wire allowed me. 'My mother expects me to put in Delhi,' I whispered.

'And what do you want? HLL has placed me in Chennai. I told you weeks ago. How are we going to make this work?'

'We will. But if I come to Chennai, she'll know it is for you.'

'Fine, then tell her that.'

'How?'

'I don't know. They didn't give me a choice, else I would have come to Delhi. I miss you sweets, a lot. Please, baby, come soon.'

'I'm someone else's baby too, quite literally. And she is watching me, so I better hang up.'

'Please say "I love you".'

'I do.'

'No, say it nicely.'

'Ananya!'

'Just once. The three words together.'

I looked at my mother. She picked up the last bunch of bhindis and wiped them with a wet cloth. Her shiny knife, symbolic of her current position in my love story, gleamed in the afternoon light.

'Movies I love. You should see them, too.'

'Aww, that's not fair,' Ananya mock-cried at the other end.

'Bye,' I said.

'OK, love you. Bye,' she ended the call.

I came back to the dining table. Out of guilt, I picked up a few bhindis and started wiping them with a wet cloth.

'Madrasi girl?'

'Ananya,' I said.

'Stay away from her. They brainwash, these people.'

'Mom, I like her. In fact, I love her.'

'See, I told you. They trap you,' my mother declared.

'Nobody has trapped me, mom,' I said as I thwacked a bhindi on the table. 'She is a nice girl. She is smart, intelligent, good-looking. She has a good job. Why would she need to trap anyone?'

'They like North Indian men.'

'Why? What's so special about North Indian men?'

'North Indians are fairer. The Tamilians have a complex.'

'A complexion complex?' I chuckled.

'Yes, huge,' my mother said.

'Mom, she went to IIMA, she is one of the smartest girls in India. What are you talking about? And not that it matters, but you have seen her. She is fairer than me.'

'The fair ones are the most dangerous. Sridevi and Hema Malini.'

'Mom, stop comparing Ananya to Sridevi and Hema Malini,' I screamed and pushed the bhindi bowl on the table aside with my arm. The bowl pushed the knife, which in turn rammed against my mother's fingers. She winced in pain as drops of blood flooded her right index and middle fingers.

'Mom, I am so sorry,' I said. 'I am so sorry.'

'It's OK. Kill me. Kill me for this girl,' she wailed.

'Mom, I am not. . . .' A drop of blood fell on my Citibank form. *Now would be the time to betray your mother, you idiot*, I thought.

'I am going to write Delhi,' I said.

'What?'

'Nothing. Where are the band-aids? Don't worry, I will cook the bhindi. Give me the masala.'

I bandaged my mother and had her recline on the sofa. I switched on the TV. I tried to find a channel with a soap opera that didn't show children disrespecting their parents. I filled each bhindi with masala over the next hour.

'Do you know how to switch on the gas?' she screamed from the living room as I hunted for matches in the kitchen.

'I do. Don't worry.'

'I can show you Punjabi girls fair as milk,' she said, her volume louder than the TV. I ignored her as I checked the cupboard for a vessel. 'Should we give a matrimonial ad? Verma aunty downstairs gave it; she got fifty responses even though her son is from donation college. You will get five hundred,' my mother said.

'Let it be, mom,' I said.

I ignited the gas stove and kept the pan over it. I poured cooking oil and opened the drawers to find cumin seeds. It was kept in the same place as when I left home for college over seven years ago.

'Actually, I have a girl in mind. You have seen Pammi aunty's daughter?'

'No. And I don't want to,' I said.

'Wait,' my mother said as a new wave of energy was unleashed within her. I heard her open the Godrej cupboard in her bedroom. She brought a wedding album to the kitchen. 'Lower the flame, you'll burn it. And why haven't you switched on the exhaust?' She snatched the ladle from me and took control of the stove. She stirred the bhindi with vigour as she spoke again. 'Open this album. See the girl dancing in the baraat next to the horse. She is wearing a pink lehnga.'

'Mom,' I protested.

'Listen to me also sometimes. Didn't I meet Jayalalitha's family on your request?'

'What?'

'Nothing, see the picture.'

I opened the album. It was my second cousin Dinki's wedding to Deepu. The first five pages of the album were filled with face shots of the boy and girl in various kaleidoscopic combinations and enclosed by heart-filled frames. I flipped through the album and came to the pictures with the horse.

I saw a girl in pink lehnga, her face barely visible under a lot of hair. She was in the middle of a dance step with her hands held high and index fingers pointing up.

'Isn't she pretty?' My mother switched on the other gas stove and put a tava on it to make rotis. She took out a rolling pin and dough.

'I can't make out,' I said.

'You should meet her. And here, keep stirring the bhindi while I make the rotis,' She handed me the ladle.

'I don't want to meet anyone.'

'Only once.'

'What's so special about her?'

'They have six petrol pumps.'

'What?'

'Her father. He has six petrol pumps. And the best part is, they have only two daughters. So each son-in-law will get three, just imagine.'

'What?' I said as I imagined myself sitting in a gas station.

'Yes, they are very rich. Petrol pumps sell in cash. Lots of black money.'

'And what does the girl do? Is she educated?'

'She is doing something. These days you can do graduation by correspondence also.'

'Oh, so she is not even going to college?'

'College degrees you can get easily. They are quite rich.'

'Mom, that's not the point. I can't believe you are going to marry me to a twelfth pass . . . oh, forget it. Put this album away. And are the rotis done? I am hungry.'

'We can get an educated Punjabi girl. Do you like doctors?'

'No, I don't like any Punjabi girl.'

'Your mother is Punjabi,' my mother said in an upset tone.

'That's not the point, mom,' I said and opened the fridge to take out curd. 'I don't want any other girl. I have a girlfriend.'

'You'll marry that Madrasi girl?' my mother asked, seriously shocked for the first time since she found out about Ananya.

'I want to. In time, of course.'

My mother slapped a roti on the tawa and then slapped her forehead.

'Let's eat,' I said, ignoring her demonstrations of disappointment. We placed the food on the living-room coffee table and sat down to eat in front of the TV.

The doorbell rang twice.

'Oh no, it's your father,' my mother said. 'Switch off the TV.'

'It's OK,' I said.

My mother gave me a stern glance. I reluctantly shut the television. My mother opened the door. My father came inside and looked at me. I turned away and came back to the table.

'Lunch?' my mother asked.

My father did not answer. He came to the dining table and examined the food. 'You call this food?' he said.

I glared at him. 'It took mom three hours to make it,' I said.

My mother took out a plate for him.

'I don't want to eat this,' my father said.

'Why don't you say you've already eaten and come?' I butted in again.

My father stared at me and turned to my mother. 'This is the result of your upbringing. All degrees can go to the dustbin. You only have this at the end.'

This, and a job at Citibank that pays me three times at the start than what you ever earned in your life, I wanted to say but didn't. I pulled the Citibank form close to me.

My father went and touched the TV top. 'It's hot. Who watched TV?'

'I did. Any problem?' I said.

'I hope you leave home soon,' my father said.

I hope you leave this world soon, I responded mentally as I took my plate and left the room.

I lay down in bed at night, waiting to fall asleep. My mind oscillated between wonderful thoughts of Ananya's hair as they brushed against my face when we slept in campus and the argument with my father this afternoon. My mother came to my room and switched on the light.

'I've fixed the meeting. We'll go to Pammi aunty's place day after tomorrow.'

'Mom, I don't. . . .'

'Don't worry, I've only told them we are coming for tea. Let me show you off a little. You wait and see, they will ask me first.'

'I am not interested.' I sat up on my bed.

'Come for the snacks. They are very rich. Even for ordinary guests, they give dry fruits.'

'Mom, why should I come, really?'

'Because it will make me happy. Is that reason enough?' she said and I noticed her wrinkled hand with the bandage.

'OK,' I shrugged and slid back into bed. 'Now, let me sleep.'

'Excellent,' she said and switched off the lights as she left the room. I allowed my mind to be trapped again by thoughts of my South Indian girl.

13

Pammi aunty lived in Pitampura, a hardcore Punjabi neighbourhood. Each lane in this area has more marble than the Taj Mahal. Every street smells of tomatoes cooking with paneer. We took an auto as my father never allowed us to take the car. My mother told the auto driver to stop a few houses away. We couldn't tell Pammi aunty we hadn't come by car.

'He had a meeting, he dropped us outside and left,' my mother said as Pammi aunty came to greet us at the door.

'He should have come for a cold drink at least,' Pammi aunty said and escorted us in. Pammi aunty's weight roughly matched the decade she lived in, and that correlation had continued into the current nineties. Pammi aunty had been Miss Chandigarh thirty-seven years ago. A rich businessman snapped her soon after the title and gave her a life of extra luxury and extra calories. Now, she weighed more than the three finalists put together.

We walked up five steps to get to their living room. Pammi aunty had difficulty climbing them. 'My knees,' she mumbled as she took the last step.

'You are going for morning walk nowadays?' my mother asked.

'Where Kavita-ji, it is so hot. Plus, I have satsang in the morning. Sit,' Pammi aunty said as she told her maid to get khus sharbat.

We sank into a red velvet sofa with a two-feet deep sponge base.

'Actually, even if you walk to satsang, it can be good exercise,' my mother said.

'Six cars, Kavita-ji. Drivers sitting useless. How to walk?' Pammi aunty asked. She had demonstrated a fine Punjabi skill – of showing off her wealth as part of an innocent conversation.

My mother turned to me to repeat her comment. 'Six cars? Krish, you heard, they have six cars.'

I didn't know how to respond. Maybe I was supposed to applaud.

'Which ones?' I said, only because they kept staring at me.

'I don't know. My husband knows. Just last week he bought a Honda.'

'How much for?' my mother asked. It is almost courteous among Punjabis to encourage someone who is flaunting his wealth to brag some more.

'Seven lakh, plus stereo changed for thirty thousand,' Pammi aunty said.

'Wow!' my mother said. 'He has also got a job with Citibank, four lakh a year.'

To a non-Punjabi, my mother's comment would be considered a non-sequitur. To a Punjabi, it is perfect continuation. We are talking about lakh, after all.

'Good. Your son has turned out bright,' she said.

I guess to be rich is to be bright, as she didn't ask for my IQ.

'Your blessings, Pammi-ji,' my mother said.

'No, no,' Pammi aunty said as she gloated over her possible role in my bagging a job.

We had smiled at each other for another minute when Pammi aunty spoke again. 'Dry fruits?'

'No, no, Pammi-ji, what formalities you are getting into?' my mother demurred.

'Rani, get cashews and those Dubai dates,' Pammi-ji screamed.

My mother gave a mini nod in appreciation of the international nuts. 'Where's our Dolly?' my mother enquired, claiming the heiress of three gas station as hers without hesitation.

'Here only. Dolly!' Pammi aunty screamed hard to reach the upper floors of the hydrocarbon-funded mansion.

The servants were summoned to call Dolly downstairs.

'She takes forever to have a bath and get ready,' Pammi aunty said in mock anger, as she took a fistful of cashews and forced them in my hands.

'Don't stop our daughter from looking beautiful, Pammi-ji,' my mother said. Yes, Dolly was already ours.

'Who knows ji about whose daughter she will become? We only have two girls, everything is theirs,' Pammi said and spread her arms to show everything. Yes, the sofas, hideous marble coffee tables, curios, fans, air conditioners—everything belonged to the daughters and their future husbands. I have to say, for a second the thought of owning half this house made me wonder if my mother was right. But the next second the thought of losing Ananya came to me. No, I wouldn't give up Ananya for all the cashews and cash in the world. If only Pammi aunty allowed me to live in this house with Ananya.

Dolly came scurrying down the steps with her perfume reaching us three seconds before her. 'Hello Aunty-ji,' Dolly said and went on to give my mother a tight hug.

'How beautiful our daughter has become!' my mother exclaimed.

Dolly and I greeted each other with slight nods. She wore a wine-red salwar kameez with vertical gold stripes running down it. She was abnormally white, and my mother was right; she did remind me of milk. She sucked in her stomach a little, though she wasn't fat. Her ample bosom matched Pammi aunty's and it made me wonder how these women would ever wean their children off without suffocating them.

'What are you doing these days, Dolly?' my mother asked.

'BA pass, aunty, correspondence.'

'You are also doing computer course, tell that,' Pammi aunty said and turned to my mother, 'I'll get more snacks?'

Dolly tried to say something but was ignored as we had moved on to the more interesting topic of food.

'No, Pammi-ji. This is enough,' my mother said, obviously daring her to serve us more.

'What are you saying? You haven't come at meal time, so I just arranged some heavy snacks. Raju, get the snacks. And get both the red and green chutneys!' she shrieked to her servant.

Raju and another servant brought in a gigantic tray with samosas, jalebis, chole bhature, milk cake, kachoris and, of course, the red and green chutneys. Twenty thousand calories were plonked on the table.

'You shouldn't have!' my mother said as she signalled the servant to pass the jalebis.

'Nothing ji, just for tasting. You should have come for dinner.'

I felt I would come across as a retard if I didn't talk to Dolly now. 'What computer course are you doing?'

'Microsoft Word, Power Point, Email, I don't know, just started. Looks quite hi-fi.'

'Sure, it does sound like a challenging programme,' I said, and instantly felt guilty for my sarcasm.

'My friends are doing it, so I joined. If it is too difficult, I'll stop. You know all these things, no?'

'Sort of,' I said.

My mother and Pammi aunty had stopped talking the moment Dolly and I began a conversation. Dolly and I became quiet as we noticed them staring at us.

'It's OK. Keep talking,' my mother beamed and looked at Pammi-ji. Both of them gave each other a sly grin. They winked at each other and then folded their hands and looked up to thank God.

Dolly looked at my mother and smiled. 'Aunty-ji, tea?' she asked.

'No ji, we don't make our daughters work,' my mother said. The work in this case being screaming at the servant.

'Raju, get tea,' Dolly exerted herself and earned affectionate glances from my mother. *Why couldn't my mother give Ananya one, just one, glance like that?*

'Son, tea?' Pammi aunty offered me. I shook my head. 'You young people have coffee, I know. Should we get coffee? Or wait, what is that new place at the District Centre, Dolly? Where they sell that expensive coffee? Barsaat?'

'Barista, mom.' Dolly switched to a more anglicised accent when asked to describe something trendy.

'Yes, that. Take him there in the Honda. See ji, we are quite modern, actually,' she said to my mother.

'Modern is good ji. We are also not old-fashioned. Go Krish, enjoy,' my mother said. Of course, hating Tamilians is not old-fashioned at all.

I stood up to partly enjoy myself with Dolly, but mainly to get away from here and ride in the new Honda.

'Come here, Dolly,' Pammi-ji said and did the unthinkable. She slid a hand into her bosom ATM and pulled out a wad of notes. I wondered if Pammi aunty's cleavage also contained credit cards.

Dolly took the wad and put it in her golden handbag without counting it. She screamed at the servant to scream at the driver to scream at the security guard to open the gate so the Honda could be taken out.

We reached the District Centre, a ghetto of salwar-kameez shops, beauty parlours and STD booths. Dolly insisted on going to her favourite clothes boutique. I watched her choose clothes for half an hour. I wondered if it would be appropriate to call Ananya from one of the STD booths. I dropped the idea and hung around the shop, watching Punjabi mothers and daughters buy salwar kameezes by the dozen. The daughters were all thin and the mothers were all fat. The boutique specialised in these extreme sizes.

'Healthy figure range is there,' one salesman said as he pointed a mother to the right direction.

Dolly finished her shopping and paid for three new suits with her wad of notes.

'You like these?' she asked, opening her bag.

'Nice,' I said as we entered Barista. The air-conditioning and soothing music were a respite from the blazing forty-degree sun outside.

'One cold coffee with ice-cream,' Dolly said. 'What do you want?'

I ordered the same and we sat on a couch, sitting as far apart as possible. We mutely stared at the music channel on the television in front of us.

'I've never spoken to an IITian before,' she said after some time.

'You are not missing much,' I said.

She shifted in her seat. Her clothes bag fell down. She lifted it back up.

'Sorry, I get nervous in front of hi-fi people,' she said.

'Don't be,' I said. 'Enjoy your coffee.'

'You have a girlfriend, no? South Indian?'

'What?' I jumped off my seat. 'Who told you?'

'Kittu told me,' she said.

Kittu was my first cousin and Shipra masi's daughter. Kittu's father was Pammi aunty's cousin. In some sense, Dolly was my third or fourth cousin, though we weren't related by blood.

'Kittu? How did she know?'

'Shipra masi must have told her. And your mother must have told Shipra masi.'

'And now the whole clan knows,' I guessed.

'Sort of.'

'What else do you know about her?'

'Nothing,' Dolly said as her eyes shifted around.

'Tell me.'

'Oh, some stuff. That she is very aggressive and clever and has you totally under her control. But South Indian girls are like that, no?'

'Do you know any South Indian girls?'

'No,' Dolly said as she twirled her straw. 'Sorry, I didn't want to tell you. You guys serious or is it just time-pass?'

I tried to curb my anger. 'What about you? You have a boyfriend?'

'No, no. Never,' she swore.

'Not even time-pass?'

She looked at me. I smiled to show friendliness.

'Just one colony guy. Don't tell my mom, please. Or your mother, or even Kittu.'

'I won't.'

'He sent me a teddy bear on Valentine's day.'

'Cute,' I said.

'Have you kissed anyone?' she asked. 'Like this South Indian girl.'

I thought hard about how I should answer her question without saying the truth, that I lived with Ananya in one tiny hostel room for two years.

'No,' I said.

'OK, because this guy is insisting I kiss him. But I don't want to get pregnant.'

'How did you meet him?'

'It's a very sweet story. He called a wrong number at my home one day. And we started talking. I've only met him once.'

'You are seeing someone who called a wrong number?'

'He's not my boyfriend yet. But you know I have a didi in Ludhiana who married a guy who called her as a wrong number. They have two kids now.'

'Wow,' I said. I wondered if I should gulp my coffee down so we could leave sooner.

'Do you like me?' Dolly asked.

'What?'

'You know why we have been sent here, right? For match-making.'

'Dolly, I can't marry anyone but Ananya.'

'Oh, that's her name. Nice name.'

'Thanks, and she is nice, too. And I am involved. I am sorry my mother dragged me into this.'

'But you said you haven't even kissed her.'

'I lied. We lived together for two years. But please don't tell anyone this.'

'Lived together?' Her eyebrows peaked. 'Like *together*? You mean, you have done everything?'

'That's not important. I only told you so you don't feel bad about my lack of interest in you.'

'Two years? She didn't get pregnant?'

'Dolly, stop. Thanks for the coffee.'

'I can make you forget her,' Dolly said as she opened out her waist-length hair.

'What?'

'I know what guys want.'

'You don't. And try to stay away from wrong numbers.'

We left Barista and drove back in her spacious Honda. I realised this Honda could be mine if only I didn't believe in stupid things like love.

'What should I tell my mother?' Dolly asked.

'Say you didn't like me.'

'Why? She'll ask.'

'It's easy to slam an IITian down. Say I am a geek, boring, lecherous, whatever,' I said.

'She doesn't understand all that,' Dolly said.

'OK, tell her Krish has no plans to continue in the bank. He'll quit in a few years to be a writer.'

'Writer?'

'Yes.'

'You are too hi-fi for me,' she said as we reached her house.

14

'I can't believe you said no to Dolly,' my mother said. 'There has to be a reason, no?'

She had brought up the topic for the twentieth time three days later. My father didn't come home until late so my mother had taken the risk and invited her sister home for lunch. Some Indian men cannot stand any happiness in their wives' lives, which includes her meeting her siblings.

'Pammi is buying one more house in the next lane. She told me it is for her daughter,' Shipra masi said, rubbing salt into my mother's wounds. My mother hung her head low.

'You are making the same mistake again. You chose an army person for your own marriage. You said they are sacrificing people. We have seen how much. You have spent your whole life in misery and poverty.'

My mother nodded as she accepted her elder sister's observation. Shipra masi had married rich. Her husband, a sanitary-fittings businessman, had struck gold building toilets. My mother had valued stupid things like virtue, education and nature of profession, and suffered. And according to Shipra masi, I planned to do the same.

'How much will that Madrasin earn?' Shipra masi inquired. 'Dolly would have filled your house. When was the last time you bought anything new? Look, even your dining table shakes.'

Shipra masi banged on the dining table and its legs wobbled. I pressed the top with my palm to neutralise her jerks.

'I say, meet Pammi once again and close it,' Shipra masi suggested. 'What are you thinking?' she said after a minute. 'Do you know Pammi bought that phone, the one you can walk around with everywhere?'

'Cordless . . .' my mother said.

'Not cordless, that new one costing twenty thousand rupees. You can take it all over Delhi. Pass me the pickle,' Shipra masi said. She ate fast to catch up for the lost time she spent on her monologue.

Cell-phones had recently arrived in India. A minute's talktime cost more than a litre of petrol. Needless to say, it was the newest Punjabi flaunt toy in Delhi.

'And what is this writer thing? Dolly said you will leave the bank to be a writer one day.'

'What?' my mother gasped.

'In time, after I have saved some money,' I said and picked up my plate to go to the kitchen.

'This is what happens if you educate children too much,' my masi said.

'I have no idea about him becoming a writer. When did this start?' my mother turned to me as I returned from the kitchen.

'That South Indian girl must have told him. They love books,' Shipra masi said.

I banged my fist on the table. The legs wobbled. Maybe we did need to change it.

'Nobody asked me to be a writer. Anyway, it is none of your business, Shipra masi.'

'Look at him, these black people have done their black magic,' Shipra masi said. 'Don't be foolish, Kavita, tell Pammi he will remain in Citibank and make a lot of money. Get his price properly.'

I glared at everyone at the table, went to the living-room sofa and picked up the newspaper. The matrimonial page opened out. I threw it in disgust.

'Let's look at some educated girls. You want to see educated girls?' my mother threw a pacifier at me.

'I have an educated girl. I like her. She has a job, she is pretty, decent, hard-working and has a lot of integrity. What is your problem?'

'Son,' Shipra masi said, her voice soft for reconciliation, 'that is all fine. But how can we marry Madrasis? Tomorrow your cousins will want to marry a Gujarati.'

'Or Assamese?' my mother added.

'My god!' Shipra masi said.

'So what? Aren't they all Indian? Can't they be good human beings?' I said.

Shipra masi turned to my mother. 'Your son is gone. I am sorry, but this boy belongs to Jayalalitha now.'

The bell rang twice. Panic spread in the house as my father had arrived earlier than usual. I never welcome my father home. However, I was happy as it meant Shipra masi would leave now.

'Hello Jija-ji,' Shipra masi said as my father entered the house.

My father didn't answer. He picked up the newspaper thrown on the floor and folded it.

'I said hello Jija-ji,' Shipra masi said and smiled. She didn't give up easily.

'I like your goodbye more than hello,' my father replied. No one can beat him in the asshole stakes.

'My sister has invited me,' Shipra masi said.

'Useless people invite useless people,' my father said.

Shipra masi turned to my mother. 'I don't come here to get insulted. Only you can bear him. The worst decision of your life,' Shipra masi mumbled as she packed her handbag to leave.

'I would appreciate it if you don't interfere in our family matters,' my father said and gave her a brown bag. It was the mithai Shipra masi had brought for us. They exchanged glares.

'Take it or I will throw it in the dustbin,' my father said.

I stood up to argue. My mother signalled me to back off. Shipra masi reached the main door. I came with her to shut it. I touched her feet, more out of ritual than respect.

'Son, now don't make foolish decisions like your mother. Marry a good Punjabi girl before they find out about your father. Dolly is good.'

My father's ears are as sharp as his tongue. 'What is going on? Who is Dolly?' my father shouted.

Shipra masi shut the door and left. Nobody answered.

'Are you seeing girls?' my father demanded of my mother.

My mother kept quiet.

'Did you see a girl?'

'Yes,' I said. I was kind of glad I did, just to piss him off.

'I will . . .' he screamed at my mother, lifting his hand.

'Don't even fucking think about it!' I came close to him.

'In this house, I make the decisions,' my father said. He picked up a crystal glass and smashed it on the floor. The violence intended at my mother had to come out somehow.

'You sure seem mature enough to take them,' I said and moved towards the kitchen.

'Don't walk barefoot,' my mother called out. She bent to pick up the splintered shards. Anger seethed within me. Not only at my father, but also my mother; how could she let him get away with this and start cleaning up calmly?

'I don't know why I come to this house,' my father said.

'I was thinking the same thing,' I said.

'Bastard, mind it!' he shouted at me like he did at his army jawans ten years ago.

'Krish, go to the other room,' my mother said.

'Not until this nutcase leaves,' I said.

'He can't be my son. Nobody talks to their father like this.'

'And no father behaves like this,' I said.

My mother pushed me towards the bedroom. My father looked around for new things to shout at or break. He couldn't find much. He turned around and walked out. The loud sound of the door banging shut sent a sigh of relief through the whole house.

My mother came to my room after cleaning up the glass in the living area. She came and sat next to me on the bed. I didn't look at her. She held my chin and turned my face towards her.

'You let him do this, so he does it. Why did you have to start cleaning up?' I sulked.

'Because he'll break the other glasses, too. And then we will have no more glasses for guests,' my mother said. 'Don't worry. I can manage him.'

I looked at my mother, a tear rolled down her eye. I felt my eyes turn wet, too.

'You have to leave him,' I said after we composed ourselves.

'It's not that simple,' she said.

'I will earn now,' I said.

'I am fine. Ninety percent of the time he is not even here. He goes to his army mess, he visits his partners with whom he tries his harebrained business schemes.'

'What? Like that security agency?' I scoffed.

'Yes, but he picks up fights with customers at the first meeting. Doesn't exactly make them feel safe,' my mother said.

I laughed.

'I can handle him. It is you who gets angry and fights with him,' my mother said.

'He starts it. What was the need to insult Shipra masi?'

'He won't change. Shipra is used to him. I worry how you will stay with him when you work in Delhi. Maybe you should take the company accommodation.'

'Or maybe I should not be in Delhi.'

'What are you saying?'

'I can't stand him.'

'Where are you planning to go?'

'I don't know, mom. I can only give a preference to Citibank. It's no guarantee. Plus you get posted out after two years.'

'You chose Delhi, no?'

I didn't answer. Somehow the thought of being in Delhi and seeing ditzy Punjabi girls by day and dad by night didn't seem terribly exciting.

'You come with me wherever I go,' I said.

'Where? I can't leave Delhi. All my relatives are here. You will be in office all day. What will I do in a new city?'

'I want to go to Chennai,' I said.

'Oh God!' my mother's mellow mood shifted gears to overdrive. She got up from the bed. 'I find this harder to deal with than your father. Are you mad?'

'No, I like Ananya. I want to give our relationship a shot.'

'You'll become a Madrasi?'

'I am not becoming anything. I'm only going there to live. And Citibank transfers you in two years.'

'I should meet an astrologer. I don't know what phase you are going through.'

'There is no phase. I love someone.'

'Love is nothing, son,' my mother patted my cheek and left the room.

I didn't submit the Citibank form until the last date. I kept taking my pen to the 'location preference' question. It had asked for three choices in order. I couldn't fill it.

'You've sent your form?' Ananya asked on the phone.

'I will. Almost ready,' I said.

'Are you crazy? It is the last day. You put Chennai, right?'

'Yeah,' I said and hung up.

I gave one final glance at the form. I looked at God above and asked him to decide my love-life. I filled up the form:

Location Preference:
1. Chennai or Delhi (equal preference)
2. –
3. –

I sealed the form and dropped it off at the bank branch. In my bed I opened Ananya's letter from last week. I read it every night before going to bed.

Hello my Punjabi hunk,

Miss me? I do. I miss our cuddles, I miss our walks in campus, I miss studying together and then going for midnight chai, I miss running to my dorm every morning to brush my teeth, I miss eating pao-bhaji on the char rasta with you, I miss playing footsie in the library, I miss the glances we stole in class, I miss my bad grades and the tears afterwards that you wiped, I miss how you made me laugh, I miss how you played with my hair, I miss how you used to watch me put eye-liner, I miss . . . oh, you get the drift, I miss you like hell.

Meanwhile, I am fine in Chennai. My mother is at her neurotic best, my father is quiet as usual and my brother always has a book that says Physics, Chemistry or Maths on the cover. In other words, things are normal. I mentioned you again to my mother. She called a priest home who gave me a pendant to make me forget you. Wow, I never thought they'd react to you like this. Well, it is going to take more than a pendant to forget you, but for good measure I tossed it into the Bay of Bengal on Marina Beach. I haven't mentioned you since, because I know you will come to Chennai and charm them yourself – just as you charmed me.

Bye, my Love,
Ananya.
PS: Oh did I mention, I miss the sex too.

I read the letter ten times. I read the last sentence a hundred times. I wanted to be with her right that moment. I realised I could have written 'Chennai' in the form but I had played roulette with my love-life due to some vague sense of responsibility and guilt towards home. I wondered if Citi would need more people in Delhi as this is where all the money is. After all, a Punjabi is far more likely to want a foreign bank account than a Tamilian. And I am Punjabi, so they would give me Delhi. Something yelped inside me. I read the letter again and again until I fell asleep.

One week later, I received a call at home. Mother picked it up and said it was from a guy who sounded like a girl.

'Hello?' I said.

'Hi Krish, it's Devesh from Citi HR.'

'Oh, hi Devesh. How are you?'

'Good, I just wanted to give you your joining date and location.'

My heart started to beat fast. 'Yes,' I said, excited and nervous.

'So you start on June 1.'

'OK.'

'And we are placing you in Chennai.'

Imaginary fireworks exploded all over the Delhi sky. I felt real love for Devesh, the HR department and Citibank for the first time in my life.

Act 3:
Chennai

15

My flight landed in Chennai at 7 p.m. We had a six-hour delay in Delhi because a psycho called the airport and said the plane had a bomb. My bags took another hour to arrive on the conveyor belt. As I waited, I looked at the people around me. The first thing I noticed, excuse my shallowness, was that almost ninety percent of the people were dark complexioned. Of these ninety percent, eighty percent had dabbed talcum that gave them a grey skin tone. I understood why Fair & Lovely was invented. I couldn't understand why people wanted to be fair so bad.

Most women at the conveyor belt looked like Ananya's mother; I couldn't tell one from the other. They all wore tonnes of gold, but somehow it looked more understated than Pammi aunty's necklaces that had precious stones and pearls hanging from them like shapeless dry fruits.

I came out of the airport. I had to find an auto to go to my chummery. I fumbled through my pockets to find the slip of paper with my new address. I couldn't find them in my jeans and almost panicked. I didn't know any place in Chennai except T. Nagar. And I knew T. Nagar as I took Brilliant Tutorials once upon a time. Somehow, I didn't think they'd shelter one of their lakh of students from eight years ago.

I opened my wallet and found my address. I heaved a sigh of relief. I came to the auto stand. Four drivers argued with each other over the next passenger.

'Enga?' one driver pushed back three drivers and asked me. 'Enga hotel?'

'No hotel,' I said and took out my wallet. I opened it and the drivers saw the ten hundred-rupee notes my mother had given me before leaving Delhi. He smacked his lips. I pulled out the slip with the address.

'English illa,' he said.

I looked around. No one proficient in English seemed visible. I read the address.

'Nunga-ba-ka-ma-ma?' I said.

'Nungambakkam?' the driver laughed as if it was the easiest word to say in the world.

'Yeah,' I said and remembered a landmark Devesh had told me. 'Near Loyola College. You know Loyola College.'

'Seri, seri,' the driver said. My stay with Ananya had told me that 'seri' meant an amiable Tamilian.

I loaded the luggage. 'Meter?'

He laughed again as if I had made a bawdy joke.

'What?' I tapped the meter.

'Meter illa,' the driver said loudly, his personality taking on a more aggressive form as he left the airport.

'How much?' I asked.

'Edhuvum,' he said.

'I don't understand. Stop, how much?'

He didn't stop or answer. I tapped his shoulder. He looked back. I played dumb charades with him, acting out 'how much money, dude?'

He continued to drive. After ten seconds he raised his right palm and stretched out his five fingers wide.

'Five what?'

He flashed his fingers again.

'Fifty?'

He nodded.

'OK,' I said. He understood this word.

'Vokay,' he said and extended his hand for a handshake. I shook his hand. He laughed and zoomed off into the Chennai sunset.

I saw the city. It had the usual Indian elements like autos, packed public buses, hassled traffic cops and tiny shops that sold groceries, fruits, utensils, clothes or novelty items. However, it did feel different. First, the sign in every shop was in Tamil. The Tamil font resembles those optical illusion puzzles that give you a headache if you stare at them long enough. Tamil women, all of them, wear flowers in their hair. Tamil men don't believe in pants and wear lungis even in shopping districts. The city is filled with film posters. The heroes' pictures make you feel even your uncles can be movie stars. The heroes are fat, balding, have thick moustaches and the heroine next to them is a ravishing beauty. Maybe my mother has a point in saying that Tamil women have a thing for North Indian men.

'Hey, that's IIT?' I said out aloud as I noticed the board for IIT Chennai.

'Guindy, guindy,' the auto driver said a word which would have led to trouble if he had spoken it in Delhi.

I looked at the campus wall that lasted for over a kilometre. The driver recited the names of neighbourhoods as we passed them – Adyar, Saidapet, Mambalam and other unpronounceable names so long they wouldn't fit on an entire row of Scrabble. I felt bad for residents of these areas as they'd waste so much of their time filling the address columns in forms.

We passed a giant, fifty-feet-tall film poster as we entered Nungambakkam. The driver stopped the auto. He craned his neck out of the auto and folded his hands.

'What?' I gestured.

'Thalaivar,' he said, pointing to the poster.

I looked out. The poster was for a movie called *Padayappa*. I saw the actors and recognised only one. 'Rajnikant?'

The auto driver broke into a huge grin. I had recognised at least one landmark in this city.

He drove into the leafy lanes of Nungambakkam till we reached Loyola College. I asked a few local residents for Chinappa Towers and they pointed us to the right building.

I stepped out of the auto and gave the driver a hundred-rupee note. I wondered if I should give him a ten-rupee tip for his friendliness.

'Anju,' the driver said and opened his palm again.

I remained puzzled and realised it when he gestured three times.

'You want five hundred? Are you mad?'

'Illa mad,' the driver said, blocking the auto to prevent me from taking out the luggage.

I looked at the desolate street. It was only nine but felt like two in the morning in the quiet lane. Two autos passed us by. My driver stopped them. One of the autos had two drivers, both sitting in front. The four of them spoke to each other in Tamil, their voices turning louder.

'Five hundred,' one driver who spoke a bit of English turned to me.

'No five hundred. Fifty,' I said.

'Ai,' another driver screamed. The four of them surrounded me like baddies from a low-budget Kollywood film.

'What? Just give me my luggage and let me go,' I said.

'Illa luggage. Payment . . . make . . . you,' the Shakespeare among them spoke to me.

They started moving around me slowly. I wondered why on earth didn't I choose to work in an air-conditioned office in Delhi when I had the chance.

'Let's go to the police station,' I said, mustering up my Punjabi blood to be defiant.

'Illa police,' screamed my driver, who had shaken hands with me just twenty minutes ago.

'This Chennai . . . here police is my police . . . this no North India . . . illa police, ennoda poola oombuda,' the English-speaking driver said.

Their white teeth glistened in the night. Any impressions of Tamil men being timid (influenced by Ananya's father) evaporated as I felt a driver tap my back.

'Fuck,' I said as I noticed one of the drivers take out something from his pocket. Luckily, it wasn't a knife but a pack of matches and cigarettes. He lit one in style, influenced by too many Tamil movies. I looked down the street, for anybody, anyone who would get me out of this mess.

One man came out of the next building. I saw him and couldn't believe it. He had a turban – a Sardar-ji in Chennai was akin to spotting a polar bear in Delhi. He had come out to place a cover on his car. Tingles of relief ran down my spine. Krishna had come to save Draupadi.

'Uncle!' I shouted as loudly as I could.

Uncle looked at me. He saw me surrounded by the autos and understood the situation. He came towards us.

The drivers turned, ready to take him on as well.

'Enna?' the uncle said.

The drivers gave their version of the story to him. Uncle spoke to them in fluent Tamil. It is fascinating to see a Sardar-ji speak in Tamil. Like Sun TV's merger with Alpha TV.

'Where are you coming from?' he said.

'Airport.'

'Airport cannot be five hundred rupees. Hundred maximum,' he said.

The four drivers started speaking simultaneously with lots of 'illas'. However, they had softened a little due to uncle's Tamil. After five minutes, we settled for a hundred bucks and disgusted glances from the drivers. My driver took out my luggage and dumped it on the street as he sped off.

'Thanks, uncle,' I said. 'You've lived in Chennai long?'

'Too long. Please don't stay as long as me,' Uncle said as he helped me with my luggage to the lift. 'Punjabi?'

I nodded.

'Come home if you need a drink or chicken. Be careful, your building is vegetarian. No alcohol also.'

'Really?'

'Yes, people here are like that. For them, anything fun comes with guilt,' he said as the lift doors shut.

I rang the chummery doorbell. It was ten o'clock. A sleepy guy opened the door. The apartment was completely dark.

'Hi,' I said. 'Krish from Delhi. I am in consumer finance.'

'Huh?' the guy said. 'Oh, you are that guy. The only North Indian trainee in Citibank Chennai. Come in, you are so late.'

'Flight delay,' I said as I came into the room.

He switched on the drawing-room light. 'I am Ramanujan, from IIMB,' he said. I looked at him. Even just out of bed, his hair was oiled and combed. He looked like someone who would do well at a bank. With my harried look after the scuffle with the auto drivers, I looked like someone who couldn't even open a bank account.

'That's Sendil's room, and that's Appalingam's.'

He pointed me to my room.

'Anything to eat in the house?' I said.

'I don't know,' he said and opened the fridge. 'There is some curd rice.' He took out the bowl. It didn't look like a dish. It looked like rice had accidentally fallen into the curd.

'Anything else? Any restaurant open nearby?'

He shook his head as he picked up two envelopes and passed them to me. 'Here, some letters for you. The servant said a girl had come to see you.'

I looked at the letter. One was the welcome letter from Citibank. The second envelope had Ananya's handwriting on it. I looked at the curd rice again and tried to imagine it as something yummy but I couldn't gather the courage to eat it.

I came to my room and lay down on the bed. Ramanujan shut the lights in the rest of the house and went back to sleep.

'Should we wake you up?' he had asked before going to his room.

'What time is office?'

'Nine, but trainees are expected to be there by eight. We target seven-thirty. We wake up at five.'

I thought about my last two months in Delhi, when waking up at nine was an early start. 'Is there even daylight at five?'

'Almost. We'll wake you up. Good night.'

I closed my door and opened Ananya's letter.

Hey Chennai boy,

I came to see you, but you hadn't arrived in the afternoon as you told me. Anyway, I can't wait any longer as mom thinks I am with friends at the Radha Silks Shop. I have to be back. Anyway there is a bit of drama at home but I don't want to get into that now.

Don't worry, we shall meet soon. Your office is in Anna Salai, not far from mine. However, HLL is making me travel a lot all over the state. I have to sell tomato ketchup. Hard, considering it has no tamarind or coconut in it!

I'll leave now. Guess what, I am wearing jasmine flowers in my hair today! It helps to have a traditional look in the interiors. I broke a few petals and have included them in this letter. Hope they remind you of me.

Love and kisses,
Ananya.

I opened the folds of the letter. Jasmine petals fell into my lap. They felt soft and smelt wonderful. It was the only thing about this day that made me happy. It reminded me why I was here.

16

It is bad news when you hate your job in the first hour of the first day of office. It isn't like Citibank did anything to piss me off. In fact, they tried their best to make me feel at home. I already had an assigned cubicle and computer. My first stint involved working in a group that served 'priority banking' clients, a politically correct term to address 'stinking rich' customers. There is little a customer needed to do to become priority except wave bundles of cash at us. Priority customers received special service, which included sofas for waiting areas instead of chairs, free tea while the bank representative discussed new ways to nibble . . . oops sorry, invest clients' money. And the biggest touted perk was you would get direct access to your Customer Services Managers. These were supposed to be financial wizards from top MBA schools who would take your financial strategy to a whole new level. Yes, that would be me. Of course, we never mentioned that your customer service manager could hate his job, do it only for the money and would have come to the city only because his girlfriend was here.

I had to supervise eight bank representatives. The bank representatives were younger, typically graduates or MBAs from non-blue-blooded institutions. And I, being from an IIM and therefore injected with a sense of entitlement for life, would obviously be above them. I didn't speak Tamil or know anything about banking. But I had to pretend I knew what I was doing. At least to my boss Balakrishnan or Bala.

'Welcome to the family,' he said as we shook hands.

I wondered if he was related to Ananya. 'Family?'

'The Citibank family. And of course, the Priority Banking family. You are so lucky. New MBAs would die to get a chance to start straight in this group.'

I smiled.

'Are you excited, young man?' Bala asked in a high-pitched voice.

'Super-excited,' I said, wondering if they'd let me leave early as it was my first day.

He took me to the priority banking area. Eight reps, four guys and four girls read research reports and tips from various departments on what they could sell today. I met everyone though I forgot their similar sounding South Indian names the minute I heard them.

'Customers start coming in at ten, two hours from now,' Bala said. 'And that is when the battle begins. We believe trainees learn best by facing action. Ready for war?'

I looked at him. I could tell he was a Citibank lifer. At forty, he had probably spent twenty years already in the bank.

'Ready? Any questions, champ?' Bala asked again.

'Yeah, what exactly am I supposed to do?'

Bala threw me the first of his many disappointed looks at me. He asked a rep for the daily research reports. 'Two things you need to do, actually three,' Bala said as he took me to my desk. 'One, read these reports everyday and see if you can recommend any investments to the clients. Like look at this.' He pulled out a report from the equities group. It recommended shares of Internet companies as their values had dropped by half.

'But isn't the dot com bubble bursting?' I asked. 'These companies would never make money.'

Bala looked at me like I had spoken to him in pure Punjabi.

'See, our research has given a buy here. This is Citibank's official research,' Bala spoke like he was quoting from the Bible. Official research was probably written by a hung-over MBA three years out of business school.

'Fine, what else?'

'The second important job is to develop a relationship. Tamilians love educated people. You, being from IIT and IIM, must develop a relationship with them.'

I nodded. I was the endangered species in the priority-banking zoo that customers could come throw bananas at.

'Now, it is going to be hard for you as you are a. . . .' Bala paused as if he came to a swear word in the conversation.

'Punjabi?'

'Yes, but can you befriend Tamilians?'

'I am trying to. I have to,' I said, wondering where I could call Ananya apart from her home number. If only these damn cell-phone prices would drop fast.

'Good. And the last thing is,' Bala moved forward to whisper, 'these reps are quite lazy. Keep an eye on them. Anyone not doing their job, tell me.' He winked at me and stood up to leave. 'And come to office early.'

'I came at seven-thirty. Isn't the official time nine?'

'Yes, but when I was your level, I came at seven. If you want to be like me, wake up, soldier,' Bala said and laughed at his own joke. The Tamil sense of humour, if there is any, is really an acquired taste.

I didn't want to be like him. I didn't even want to be here. I took a deep breath after he left and meditated on my salary package. *You are doing it for the money,* I told myself. *Four lakh a year, that is thirty-three thousand a month,* I chanted the mantra in my head. My father had worked in the army for thirty years and still never earned half as much. I had to push bubble stocks and the cash would be mine. Life isn't so bad, I said to myself.

'Sir, can I go to the toilet?' one female rep came to me.

'What?'

She looked at me, waiting for permission.

'What's your name?'

'Sri.'

'Where are you from?'

'Coimbatore,' she said, adjusting her oversized spectacles with cockroach-coloured borders. Fashion is not a Chennai hallmark.

'You went to college?'

'Yes sir. Coimbatore University, distinction, sir.'

'Good. Then why are you asking me for permission?'

'Just like that, sir,' she said.

'No one needs to ask me permission for going to the toilet,' I said.

'Thank you, sir.'

I read reports for the next two hours. Each one had financial models done by overenthusiastic MBAs who were more keen to solve equations than to question what they were doing. One table compared value of Internet companies with the number of visitors to the site. The recommended company had the lowest value to eyeball ratio, a trendy term invented by the analyst. Hence, BUY! screamed the report. Of course, the analyst never questioned that none of the site visitors ever paid any money to the Internet company. 'It is trading cheap on every multiple conceivable!' the report said, complete with the exclamation mark.

'Sir, my customer is here. Can I bring them to you?' Sri requested well after her return from the toilet.

'Sure,' I said.

'Sir, this is Ms Sreenivas,' Sri said. A fifty-year-old lady with gold bangles thicker than handcuffs came to my cubicle. We moved to the sofa area, to give a more personal, living room feel as we robbed the customer.

'You are from IIT?' she peered at me.

'Yes,' I said even as I readied my pitch about which loss-making company to buy.

'Even my grandson is preparing for it,' she said. She had dark hair, with oil that made it shine more.

'You don't look old enough to have a grandson preparing for IIT,' I said.

Ms Sreenivas smiled. Sri smiled back at her. Yes, we had laid the mousetrap and the cheese. Walk in, baby.

'Oh no, I am an old lady. He is only in class six though.'

'How much is madam's balance?' I asked.

'One crore and twenty lakh, sir,' Sri supplied.

I imagined the number in my head; I'd need to work in this job for thirty years to get there. It almost felt right to part her from her money. 'Madam, have you invested in any stocks? Internet stocks are cheap these days,' I said.

Ms Sreenivas gave me a worried look. 'Stocks? Never. And my son works in an Internet company abroad. He said they might close down.'

'That's USA, madam. This is India, we have one billion population, or two billion eyeballs. Imagine the potential of the Internet. And we have a mutual fund, so you don't have to invest in any one company.'

We cajoled Ms Sreenivas for five minutes. I threw in a lot of MBA terms like strategic advantage, bottom-line vs. top line, top down vs. bottom up and it made me sound very intelligent. Ms Sreenivas and Sri nodded at whatever I said. Ultimately, Ms Sreenivas agreed to nibble at the toxic waste.

'Let's start with ten lakh,' I said to close the case.

'Five. Please, five,' Ms Sreenivas pleaded with us on how to use her own money.

I settled at five and Sri was ecstatic. I had become their favourite customer service manager.

Bala took me out for lunch at Sangeetha's, a dosa restaurant.

'What dosas do you have?' I asked the waiter.

'We have eighty-five kinds,' the waiter pointed to the board. Every stuffing imaginable to man was available in dosa form.

'Try the spinach dosa. And the sweet banana dosa,' Bala said as he smiled at me like the father I never had. 'So, how does it feel, to get your first investment? Heart pumping?'

My heart didn't pump. It only ached. I'd been in Chennai for fifteen hours and had not spoken to Ananya yet. I wanted to buy a cell-phone as soon as possible. Wait, I'd need two.

'I see myself in you. You are like me,' Bala said as he dunked his first piece of dosa in sambhar. I had no clue how he reached that conclusion.

I had Ananya's home landline number. But she didn't reach home until seven. She had a sales field job so no fixed office number as well. I remembered how we'd finish lunch in campus and snuggle up for our afternoon nap. It is official, life after college sucks.

'Isn't this fun?' Bala said. 'I get a rush every time I come to the bank. And it is twenty years. Wow, I still remember the day my boss first took me out for lunch. Hey, what are you thinking? Stop work thoughts now. It is lunch-time.'

'Of course,' I said and collected myself. 'How far is HLL office from here?'

'Why? You have a potential client?' Bala asked as if the only reason people existed was to become priority banking customers.

'Possibly,' I said. One good thing about banking is you don't feel bad about lying at all.

'It is in Nungambakkam. Apex Plaza,' he said.

The waiter reloaded our sambhar and delivered the banana dosa. The latter tasted like a pancake, and I have to say, wasn't bad at all. 'Oh, that's where I am staying, right?'

'Yes, the Citi chummery. My first home too,' he leaned forward and patted my back.

I suppose I had a good boss. I should have felt happy but didn't. I wondered if I should call HLL first or straight land up there.

I came back to my desk in the afternoon. I met some customers, but most of them didn't have time to stay long. Ms Sreenivas had given me a lucky break, but it wasn't that easy to woo conservative Tamilians, after all.

'Fixed deposit. I like fixed deposit,' one customer told me when I asked him for his investment preferences.

At three in the afternoon, I had a call.

'It is for you, sir,' Sri said as she transferred the line to my extension.

'Hi, I'd like to open a priority account, with my hot-shot sexy banker.'

'Ananya?' I said, my voice bursting with happiness, 'Where are you? When are we meeting? Should I come to HLL? I am sorry my flight. . . .'

'Easy, easy. I am in Kancheepuram.'

'Where's that?'

'Three hours from Chennai. I'll head back soon. Why don't you come home for dinner?'

'Home? Your home? With your mom and dad?'

'Yes, why not? You have to know them anyway. Mom's a little low these days, but that is OK.'

'Why is she low? Because of us?'

'No, she finds other reasons to be miserable. Luckily, this time it has nothing to do with me.'

'Ananya, let's go out, OK?'

'I can't today. My aunt is visiting from Canada. Come at eight.' She gave me her address. I noted it down after making her spell it thrice. 'See you in five hours,' she said and hung up.

I stared at the watch, hoping it would move faster. The reps left at six, and as Citi's great culture goes, MBAs never left until eight.

I killed time reading reports on the Indian economy. Smart people had written them, and they made GDP forecasts for the next ten years with confidence that hid the basic fact—*how can you really tell, dude?*

At seven-thirty I stood up to leave. Bala came towards me. 'Leaving?' he asked, puzzled as if I had planned to take a half day.

'Yeah,' I said. 'Not much to do.'

'One tip, never leave before your boss,' he said and winked at me. He laughed, and I didn't find it funny at all. I want to see what a Tamil joke book looks like.

'What time do you leave?' I said, tired.

'Soon, actually let me call it a day. Kusum will be waiting. You want to come home for dinner?'

'No, thanks,' I said.

He gave me the second disappointed look.

'I have to go somewhere, distant relatives,' I said.

'Oh,' he said, his voice still a little sad.

I am sorry, dude, I am not handing you the remote of my life because you are my boss, I thought.

17

'Swaminathan', the name plate of Ananya's small standalone house proclaimed in arched letters. I pressed the doorbell even as a buzzing grinder drowned the ring.

'Yes?' Ananya's father opened the door with a puzzled expression. I bet he recognised me but feigned ignorance to rattle me. He wore a half-sleeve white vest with a front pocket and a checked blue and white lungi.

'Krish, sir, Ananya's friend,' I said. For no particular reason, fear makes me address people as sir. I had brought a gift pack of biscuits, as my Punjabi sensibilities had taught me to never go to someone's house without at least as many calories as you would consume there.

'Oh, come in,' he said after I reintroduced myself.

2 STATES • 89

I stepped inside and handed him the gift pack.

'Shoes!' he said in a stern voice when I had expected 'thanks'.

'What?' I said.

He pointed at the shoe rack outside the house.

I removed my shoes and checked my socks for smells and holes. I decided to take them off, too. I went inside.

'Don't step on the rangoli,' he warned.

I looked down. My right foot rested on a rice flour flower pattern.

'Sorry, I am really sorry, sir,' I said and bent down to repair the pattern.

'It's OK. It can't be fixed now,' he said and ushered me into the living room. The long rectangular room looked like what would be left if a Punjabi drawing room was robbed. The sofas were simple, with cushions thinner than Indian Railways sleepers had and from the opposite of the decadent red velvet sofas of Pammi aunty. The walls had a pale green distemper finish. There were pictures of various South Indian gods all around the room. The dining area had floor seating. At one corner, there was a daybed with a tambura (which looks like a sitar) kept on it. An old man sat there. I wondered if Ananya's parents were cool enough to arrange live music for dinner.

'Sit,' Ananya's father said, pointing at the sofa.

We sat opposite each other as I faced Ananya's dad for the first time in my life. I strained my brain hard for a suitable topic. 'Nice place,' I said.

'What is nice? No water in this area,' uncle said as he picked up a newspaper.

I hung my head, as if to apologise for the water problem in Mylapore.

Uncle opened the newspaper, which blocked his face from mine. I didn't know if it was intentional. I kept quiet and turned to the man with the tambura. I smiled, but he didn't react. The house had an eerie silence. A Punjabi house is never this silent even when people sleep at night.

I bent forward to see if uncle was reading the paper or avoiding me. He had opened the editorial page of *The Hindu*. He read an opinion piece about AIADMK asking the government to do an inquiry on the defence minister who had sacked the naval chief. It was heavy-duty stuff. No one in my family, correction, no one in my extended clan ever read editorial pages of newspapers, let alone articles about AIADMK.

Uncle caught me peeking over him and grunted, 'What?'

'Nothing,' I said. I didn't know why I felt so guilty.

Uncle continued to read for five minutes. I had an opportunity to speak again when he turned the page. 'No one is at home, sir?'

'Where will they go?'

'I can't see anyone.'

'Cooking. Can't you hear the grinder?' he said.

I didn't know if Ananya's father was naturally like this or extra grumpy today. *Maybe he is pissed about me being here,* I thought.

'You want water?' he said.

'No sir,' I said.

'Why? Why you don't want water?'

I didn't have an answer except that I felt scared and weird in this house. 'OK, give me water,' I said.

'Radha,' uncle screamed. 'Tanni!'

'Is that Ananya's grandfather,' I said, pointing to the old man.

'No,' he said.

I realised Ananya's father answered exactly what was asked. 'Who is he?' I asked slowly.

'It's Radha's Carnatic music teacher who came to see her. But she is busy in the kitchen making dinner for you. Now what to do?'

I nodded.

Ananya's mother came in the living room. She held a tray with a glass of water and a plate of savouries. The spiral-shaped, brown-coloured snacks resembled fossilised snakes.

'Hello, aunty,' I stood up.

'Hello, Krish,' she said.

'I am sorry I came at the wrong time,' I said, looking at the teacher.

'It's OK. Ananya invited you. And she has a habit of not consulting me,' Ananya's mother said.

'Aunty, we can all go out,' I said.

'It's OK. Food is almost ready,' she said and turned to her husband. 'Give me half an hour with Guruji.' She went up to Guruji and touched his feet. The Guruji blessed her. Ananya's mother picked up the tambura and they left the room.

'So, Citibank placed you in Chennai?' uncle said, initiating conversation with me for the first time.

'Yes, sir,' I said. Ananya had told him the bank had transferred me.

'Why do they send North Indians here?'

'I don't know, sir.'

'Useless buggers,' he mumbled and buried himself in his newspaper again.

I cleared my throat and finally gathered the courage to ask. 'Where's Ananya?'

Uncle looked up in shock as if I had asked him where he kept his porn collection. 'She had gone for a bath. She will come after evening prayers.'

I nodded. Ananya never did any evening prayers in Ahmedabad. I heard noises from the other room. They sounded like long wails, as if someone was being slowly strangled. I looked puzzled and uncle looked at me.

'Carnatic music,' uncle said. 'You know?'

I shook my head.

'Then what do you know?' he asked and sank into *The Hindu* without waiting for me to respond.

I had an urge to run out of the house. *What the fuck am I doing here in this psycho home?* I heard footsteps outside.

'Sorry,' Ananya said, coming in.

I turned to look at her. I was seeing her after two months. She wore a cream-coloured cotton sari with a thin gold border. She seemed prettier than I last saw her. I wanted to grab her and plant the biggest kiss on her lips ever. Of course, things had to be different with Mr Hindu-addict Grumpyswami in front of me.

'Hi Ananya, good to see you,' I greeted her like a colleague at work. I kept my hands close to my body.

'What? Give me a hug,' she said and uncle finally lost interest in *The Hindu.*

'Sit here, Ananya,' he said and carefully folded the newspaper like he would read it again every day for the rest of his life.

'Hi dad,' Ananya said and kissed her father on the cheek. I felt jealous.

'Oh, mom is singing,' she said, upon hearing her mother shriek again.

'Yes, finally,' Ananya's father said. 'Can you tell the raga?'

Ananya closed her eyes to listen. She looked beautiful but I had to look away as uncle eyed every move of mine.

'It's malhar, definitely malhar,' she said.

Uncle nodded his head in appreciation.

'How many ragas are there?' I asked, trying to fit in.

'A thousand, yeah dad?' Ananya said.

'At least. You don't listen to Carnatic music?' uncle said to me.

'Not much, but it is kind of nice,' I said. Of course, saying I have no fucking clue what you are talking about didn't seem quite right.

'Mom won two championships at the Tamil Sangam in Kolkata when dad was posted there,' Ananya said, her voice proud.

'But she has stopped singing since we came to Chennai,' uncle said and threw up his hands.

'Why?' I said.

'Various reasons,' Ananya said and gestured at me to change the topic.

'Your aunt is here?' I asked.

'Yes, Shobha athai is in the kitchen. She is dad's elder sister.'

I prayed Shobha aunty didn't have a personality like her brother's. Silence fell in the room. I picked up a snack to eat it. Every crunch could be heard clearly in the room. I had to keep the conversation going. I had read a book on making friends a while ago. It said take an interest in people's work and keep bringing their name into the conversation.

'So, you have worked all over India, Mr Swaminathan?' I tried.

'A few places, until I became stuck here,' he said.

'Stuck? I thought you like Chennai, your hometown,' I said.

Uncle gave me a dirty look. I wondered if I had said something inappropriate.

'I'll get Shobha. Let's eat dinner soon,' uncle said and left the room. I wanted to ask Ananya about her father, but I wanted to grab her first.

'Don't,' Ananya said as she sensed my intentions.

'What?'

'Don't move. Keep a three-feet distance,' she said.

'Are you mad? There is no one here.'

'Not here? My mother is singing in the next room for God's sake.'

'That's singing?'

'Shut up,' she giggled. 'And I'd suggest you learn a bit of Carnatic music. No, stop, don't get off the sofa.' She gave me a flying kiss and I subsided back into the sofa.

'Dad is having a bad month at the bank,' Ananya whispered. 'He got passed over for promotion. He deserved to head Bank of Baroda for his district but dirty politics happened. And he hates politics.'

I didn't mention the interest with which he read the AIADMK article.

'Where is your brother?'

'He slept already. He wakes up early to study.'

We heard footsteps.

'Be careful with Shobha aunty. Speak minimum,' she said.

'Why?' I said as Ananya's mother came to the living room again. She and her guru walked towards the main door. Aunty had a disappointed expression.

'Illa practice?' the guru mumbled as Ananya's mother spoke to him in Tamil.

The guru shook his head and left.

'What?' Ananya asked her.

'Nothing. Where is your appa and athai? Let's eat,' Ananya's mother said in a serious tone.

Ananya's father and aunt came to the living room. They carried more dishes than their arms were designed for. I stood up to help. 'Hello aunty, can I take something!'

'Wash your hands,' uncle told me and pointed me to the kitchen.

We sat on the floor for dinner. Ananya's father passed me a banana leaf. I wondered if I had to eat it or wipe my hands with it.

'Place it down, it is the plate,' Ananya whispered.

'Radha,' Shobha aunty said in a stern voice as she pointed to her banana leaf. It had specks of dirt on one side.

'Oh, sorry, sorry,' Radha aunty said and replaced it. It wasn't different from Shipra masi finding faults with my mother. Psycho relatives are constant across cultures.

I followed Ananya as she loaded her plate with rice, sambhar, funny-looking vegetables and two kinds of brown powders.

'What's this?' I asked.

'Gunpowder, try it,' she said.

I tasted it. It felt like sawdust mixed with chillies.

'Yummy, no?'

I nodded at Ananya. Everyone first kept neat little lumps of dishes on their banana leaf. Soon they mixed it into a slurry heap.

'Mix more,' Ananya said as I tried to copy my in-laws-to-be.

'You are Ananya's classmate?' Shobha aunty spoke for the first time.

'Yes, at IIM,' I said.

'IIT student?'

I nodded. Ananya had told me that my IIT tag was the only silver lining in my otherwise outcast status in their family.

'Sushila's cousin is also from IIT. Radha, I told you, no? Harish lives in San Francisco.'

'Which batch?' I asked.

'IIT Madras, not your college,' Shobha aunty said, pissed off at being interrupted.

I kept quiet and looked at the various vegetables, trying to recognise them. I said hello to beans and cabbage.

'Harish's parents want to get him married. You have Ananya's nakshatram?' Shobha aunty said.

'No, not yet,' Ananya's mother said.

'What, Swami? Your wife is not interested in finding a good son-in-law?'

I couldn't believe they were discussing all this in my presence. 'Can you pass the rice?' I said, hoping to steer the conversation elsewhere.

'Radha, you must listen to Shobha. She knows best,' Ananya's father said. Indian men slam their wives for their sisters with zero hesitation. Ananya's mother nodded as Shobha aunty started a discourse in Tamil. Ananya's dad and mother also responded in Tamil. It was irritating to watch a regional language movie in front of me.

After five minutes I spoke again. 'Excuse me?'

'What?' Ananya's father said.

'Can you speak in English? I can't follow the conversation,' I said.

Ananya looked at me, shocked. Back off, her eyes said.

'Then learn Tamil,' Ananya's father said.

'Yes sir,' I said meekly.

'Anyway, this doesn't concern you,' he added.

I nodded. I heard various technology companies' and boys' names. I felt like upturning my banana leaf on Shobha aunty's face.

I left soon after dinner. Ananya came outside to help me get an auto. Ananya held my arm as we came on the desolate street.

'I am not talking to you,' I said and extracted my hand from her.

'What?' she said.

We passed by a bungalow with coconut trees in the garden.

'They are planning your marriage. What the hell is nakshtram?' I said.

'It's the astrological chart. They are fantasising. I am not getting married to anyone else but you.'

She held my hand up and kissed it. I extracted it again. I hailed an auto. Ananya would have to negotiate with him in Tamil else I'd have to pay double. 'How am I going to win them over? It is impossible to get through. Sitting with your father is like being called to the principal's office.'

Ananya laughed.

'It's not funny.'

'It is a little. What about my mom?'

'I used to be scared of her pictures in campus. Forget her in real life! Her looks alone kill me.'

'Her pictures scared you?'

'Yes, that is why I never wanted to make love in your room. I'd notice your mother's picture and chills ran down my spine. I'd imagine her saying, *What are you doing with my daughter?*'

Ananya laughed again. 'If we weren't in Mylapore, I'd have kissed you. You are so cute,' she said.

'Cut it out, Ananya, what is our plan? Will you speak to your mother?'

'Mom's stressed out. Her Carnatic teacher refused to teach her.'

'Why?'

'I'll tell you later.'

'Can we meet tomorrow? Outside, please,' I said.

'Meet me on Marina beach at six,' she said.

'I can't do six. My extra-caring boss Bala leaves at eight.'

'I didn't say evening.'

'Six in the morning?' I gulped.

Ananya had already turned to the auto driver.

'Nungambakkam, twenty rupees. extra illai, OK?' she told him.

18

The beautiful sunrise at Marina Beach compensated for the 5 a.m. wake-up call. Hundreds of people took a morning walk along the seashore, which ran down miles.

'Do you know this is the biggest city beach in Asia?' Ananya asked as she met me at the police headquarters building.

'You've told me,' I said.

'Why are you in formals?'

'I go straight to work. Trainees are expected to be there at seven-thirty,' I said, removing my shoes and folding my pants up to walk along the beach.

'To do what?'

'To suck up to the boss, who if you do a good job will promote you to the next level of sucking up. Welcome to corporate life,' I said.

'I am not facing it yet. I have to sell a thousand bottles of ketchup every week. I am so behind my targets.'

'You'd better ketch-up fast,' I said.

'Funny,' she said and punched me. Ananya saw a man with a bicycle. He carried a basket full of idlis. 'Breakfast?' she offered.

'Don't they have toast?'

'Don't grumble,' she said. We took four idlis and sat on a bench facing the water. She spoke about her mother. 'Guruji didn't accept mom. He felt she isn't dedicated enough.'

'But isn't she really good?' I asked, not that I could tell from the shrill cries I heard last night.

'She isn't good enough by Chennai standards. Dad used to be posted in towns outside Tamil Nadu. Mom became a star in the Tamilian community there. Here, she is just OK. Chennai's Carnatic music scene is at a different level.'

I nodded as if I understood.

'My parents came to Chennai with great enthusiasm. But now dad lost his promotion. Pesky relatives visit us all the time. Amidst all this, their daughter wants to impose a non-Brahmin, non-Tamil, Punjabi boy on them. Of course, they will freak out. We have to be patient. I love them, too, Krish,' she said and paused for breath.

A gentle breeze blew on our faces. She laid her head on my left shoulder. I stroked her hair. The sun emerged out of the Bay of Bengal, a soft red at first, turning into a warmer orange. I put my arm around Ananya. In my tie and formal pants, I looked like a salesman with no place to take his girlfriend to make out.

'There is only one way you can get regular access to my home,' Ananya said after staring at the horizon for a minute.

'What?'

'IIT tuitions for my brother. They'd accept anything for that,' she said.

I let go of her and sat up straight. 'Are you crazy? I prepared for the IIT exam eight years ago. I can't teach him.'

'I'm sure you can revise some notes and help him. My parents have to get comfortable with you. Only then can I ask them to seriously consider you.'

I dipped my idli into coconut chutney and ate it. I missed my mother's hot paranthas at breakfast.

'Do you love me?' She wiped a bit of chutney from my lips.

I kissed her. I was kissing her after two months. I didn't release her for a minute. I'd revise IIT chemistry for this chemistry any day.

'*Ai!*' a hoarse voice screamed behind us.

I turned around. A pot-bellied Tamilian cop, looking more villain than police, walked fast towards us. 'What is this?' he said and slammed his stick on the bench. Both of us sprang up. Ananya hid behind me.

'Oh fuck,' she said. 'Get rid of him.'

The cop screamed at me in Tamil. Helpless, I asked Ananya to translate.

'He wants to take us to the police station. He is saying we have some nerve doing all this outside police headquarters.'

'Why do they have police headquarters opposite a beach?' I asked.

'Shut up and pay him off,' she whispered.

I look out my wallet and took out twenty bucks.

'Illa Illa. . . .' the cop continued to shout and grabbed my arm.

I took out a fifty. He looked at me and Ananya. 'Warning,' the cop said as he took the note.

Ananya laughed after the cop left us.

'It's so not funny,' I said as I wore my shoes again and straightened my pants. 'Can we meet at my chummery, please?'

'In a while. I travel out of Chennai everyday and come back late,' she said.

'Weekend?'

'I'll try,' she said. 'You will feed me chicken? I'm dying to have non-veg. And get beer, too.'

'OK,' I promised. My building had vegetarian-only rules, but surely they wouldn't notice if I brought something readymade from outside.

We sat in our respective autos. She spoke to me from her side window. 'And I'll speak to my parents about the tuitions. Twice a week at five?'

'Five in the morning?' Why is everyone so eager to wake up in this town!

'That's when everyone goes for tuitions,' she said and sped off.

I had to wait for two miserable weeks in Chennai until Ananya finally decided to visit me in my chummery for lunch one Saturday. One weekend Ananya's mother fell ill and Ananya had to cook for the family, courtesy a guilt trip from her mother. The food did not come out right, as Ananya's culinary experience is limited to making Maggi in my room and making papads with a clothes iron (yes, it works). This led to another guilt trip from Shobha aunty to Ananya's mother who blamed her for not bringing up her daughter right. That guilt trip percolated down to Ananya, who had to take Shobha aunty jewellery and sari shopping the next weekend.

Meanwhile, I had visited Brilliant Tutorials and bought the IIT exam guides. I couldn't believe how tough the course materials were. The only reason I managed to study them in the past was because that distracted me from my parents' fights. I revised chemistry to prepare for my first class.

I also went to my Sardar-ji neighbour to find out the best way to procure chicken and beer.

'Who is coming? Punjabi friends?' he asked.

'Work people,' I said, to stop him from inviting himself.

'Be careful when you take it up in the lift,' he said.

As he had told me, I went to the Delhi dhabha in Nungambakkam, less than a kilometre from my house. I triple-packed the tandoori chicken so no smell came out. I went to the government-approved liquor shop, where they had trouble establishing my age. 'Are you over twenty-five?'

'No, but will be soon,' I said.

'Then we can't give you,' the shopkeeper said.

'Even if I pay ten bucks extra a bottle?'

It is amazing how money relaxes rules around the country. The shopkeeper packed the three bottles in brown paper, and I further placed them in a plastic bag, so one couldn't make out the shape.

'What's in it?' the liftman asked me as the bottles touched the ground noisily when I placed the packet on the floor.

'Lemon squash,' I said.

'You should have coconut water instead,' the liftman said.

I nodded and reached my apartment. Ramanujan saw me place the bottles in the fridge. 'What's that?' He wore a lungi and nothing on top apart from a white thread around his shoulder.

'Beer,' I said.

'Dude, you can't get alcohol in this building,' he said.

'My girlfriend is visiting me. She likes it,' I said.

'You have a girlfriend?' Ramanujan repeated like I had ten wives. None of my flatmates had a girlfriend. They were all qualified, well-paid Tamil Citibankers who planned to be auctioned off soon by their parents.

'Yes, from college,' I said.

My other roommates came to the living room. None of them wore shirts. I shut the fridge to avoid further conversation on the beverages.

'She is visiting Chennai?' Sendil said.

'Will she stay here? She can't stay here,' Appalingam said.

'She lives in Chennai,' I said.

The boys looked at each other as to who would ask the bell-the-cat question.

'Tamilian?' Ramanujan asked.

'Yes,' I said, 'Tamil Brahmin.' I added the last two words to let them absorb the shock at once.

'Wow!' all of them said in unison.

'She drinks beer?' Ramanujan said.

'Yes,' I said and upturned the chicken into a bowl.

'And chicken? What kind of Brahmin is this?' Sendil said. 'And dude, don't get non-veg in this house.'

'It's my house, too,' I said.

'But rules are rules,' he said.

People in this city loved rules, or rather loved to follow rules. Except if you are a cop or liquor shop attendant or an auto driver.

'Let it be, Sendil,' Ramanujan said.

'Thanks,' I said and placed the chicken in the fridge. 'And guys, please wear shirts when she is here.'

Ananya came to my place at two o'clock. I greeted her politely in the living room. My flatmates exchanged shy glances with each other as she greeted them. Sendil spoke to her in Tamil. Tamilians love to irritate non-Tamil speakers by speaking only Tamil in front of them. This is the only silent rebellion in their otherwise repressed, docile personality. When she finally entered my bedroom, I grabbed her from behind.

'Can we eat first? I haven't had chicken for a month.'

'I haven't had sex for four months,' I said, but she went out and opened the fridge.

'You have beer too. Superb!' she praised and she pulled out a bottle. She offered it to my flatmates; they declined. We moved the food and beer to my bedroom. I didn't want my friends outside to witness sin as we finished a full chicken and two beers.

'And now for dessert,' I said and came close to her.

'If I burp, don't stop loving me,' she said as her lips came close to mine.

I burped. She slapped me. We kissed and kissed and kissed some more. Our lovemaking was more intense, not only because we did it after a long time, but also because we were doing it in this stuck-up city for the first time.

'Mr Citibanker, there is no train to catch. Slower, gentler next time,' Ananya said as we lay back. I sighed as I entered a semi-trance state. Ramanujan played Tamil music outside the room.

'What, say something? Men just want sex,' she said and kicked my leg.

'Yeah, and that's why I've agreed to teach your brother at five in the morning. You want to see my chemistry notes?' I sat up, wore my clothes and pulled out tutorials from the drawer. 'I read these for four hours last night,' I said.

'So sweet,' she said and came forward to kiss my cheek. 'Don't worry. My parents will soon see how wonderful you are. And then they will love you like I do.'

'They'll sleep with me?' I lay down next to her.

She elbowed me in my stomach.

'That hurt,' I said.

'Good.' She looked into my eyes. Her gaze turned soft. 'I know the tuitions are hard. My parents are weird people. You'll not give up, right?'

'I won't give up.' I stroked her hair.

'This is so amazing, this intimacy. Isn't it even better than the sex?'

'I'm not so sure,' I said and reached a hand to increase the fan speed.

'We never talk. At home, my mom and dad, they hardly talk. We'll talk about the news, the food, the weather. But we never talk about our feelings. I only do that with you,' she said.

I kept quiet. She sat up to wear her clothes. She picked up the pillows from the floor and placed them back on the bed. I pulled her arm and made her sit down with me again.

'How come you don't ask me to run away with you?' she asked.

'You want me to? What if I did ask you to elope?'

'I wouldn't know what to do. I don't want to hurt them. I already have by choosing a Punjabi mate, but I think we can win them over. I want them to smile on my wedding day. That's how I imagined my marriage since I was a child. What about you?'

I thought for a minute. 'I don't want to elope,' I said.

'Why?'

'It's too easy. And that doesn't serve the greater purpose.'

Ananya stepped off the bed and brought back the leftovers. She took the crumbs of chicken and ate them as we talked. 'Greater purpose?'

'Yes, these stupid biases and discrimination are the reason our country is so screwed up. It's Tamil first, Indian later. Punjabi first, Indian later. It has to end.'

Ananya looked at me. 'Go on,' she coaxed mischievously.

I continued, 'National anthem, national currency, national teams – still, we won't marry our children outside our state. How can this intolerance be good for our country?'

Ananya smiled. 'Is it the chicken, is it the beer or is it the sex? What has charged you up so much? Flatter me and say it is the sex. C'mon say it,' she said.

'I'm serious Ananya. The bullshit must end.'

'And how are we making it end?'

'Imagine our kids.'

'I have, several times. I want them to have my face. Only your eyes,' she said.

'Not that, think about this—they won't be Tamil or Punjabi. They will be Indian. They will be above all this nonsense. If all young people marry outside their community, it is good for the country. That is the greater purpose.'

'Oh, so the reason you sleep with me is for the sake of your country,' she said.

'Well, in some ways, yes.' I smiled sheepishly.

She took a pillow and launched an attack on my head. And then, for the sake of my country, we made love again.

'Open up, Krish,' Ramanujan's worried voice and loud bangs on the door woke me from my nap.

19

Ananya was sleeping next to me and my head hurt from the beer. Ramanujan continued to slam the door.

'What?' I opened the door.

'I've been knocking for five minutes,' Ramanujan said. 'Come out, the landlord is here.'

'Landlord?'

'Yes, be nice to him. It's the last chummery in Nungambakkam. I don't want to be kicked out.'

'What happened?' I asked.

'Come out first.'

I shut the door and wore the rest of my clothes.

'Ananya,' I said.

'Baby, I'm sleepy,' she said, trying to pull me back into bed.

'My landlord is here,' I said. She didn't respond even though I shook her maniacally.

'Your appa is outside,' I said.

She sprang up on the bed. 'What?'

'Come out. My landlord is here,' I said.

I went to the living room. My flatmates sat on the dining table. Mr Punnu, our sixty-year-old landlord, gravely occupied the largest chair. His face had a permanently tragic expression.

I sat next to him. No one spoke.

'Hi guys,' Ananya came out after five minutes. 'You want tea? I'll make some.' She started to walk towards the kitchen.

'Ananya, I will see you later,' I said.

Ananya looked at me, shocked. She tuned into the mood on the dining table. 'I'll leave now.' She picked up her bag.

Mr Punnu stood up after Ananya left the house. He sniffed hard. He peeped into my room. 'Chicken?' he frowned.

I didn't respond. Beer bottles lay on the bedside table.

'Ladies?' he said.

'She works in HLL,' I said, having no clue why I had to mention her corporate status.

'Chicken, beer, lady friends—what is going on here?' he said.

Fun, I wanted to say but didn't. Those three things are what men live for anyway.

Everyone kept quiet. I wondered who had sneaked. My flatmates were no friend material, but somehow I didn't expect them to be such schmucks. Maybe the watchman did it.

'I didn't expect this from you boys,' Punnu said in a heavy Tamil accent.

'It's my fault. I brought the chicken and beer for my girlfriend,' I said.

'Girlfriend?' Punnu said as if I spoke in pure Sanskrit.

'She is my batch-mate. A nice girl,' I said.

Mr Punnu didn't seem impressed.

'She's Tamil Brahmin,' I said.

'And you?'

'Punjabi,' I said and my head hung low a little by default.

'How is she a nice girl if she is roaming around with you?' Mr Punnu asked.

He had a valid point. I decided to change the topic. 'Mr Punnu, this is not a boarding school. We are all professionals and what we do in our own home. . . .'

Mr Punnu banged his fist on the table. 'This is my home,' he pointed out.

'Yes, but you have leased it to us. Technically, we have a right to not let you into the property.'

Mr Punnu looked aghast. Ramanujan had to save the situation. 'He doesn't know, Mr Punnu. He is new here. We should have told him it is a veg building and no alcohol.'

'Not even a drop,' Mr Punnu said. 'I have not touched it all my life.'

Mr Punnu looked like he had touched neither wine nor a woman all his life, but badly needed to.

'Apologise,' Ramanujan told me.

I glanced around. Tamils gathered around me like the LTTE. I had no choice. 'I'm sorry,' I said.

'No ladies from now on.' Mr Punnu wagged a finger.

'And beer and chicken?' I said.

'That wasn't allowed from before anyway,' Sendil said. Everyone around me nodded as they felt the warm fuzzy feeling of having set rules on how to live their life.

I wondered where I'd take Ananya the next time.

20

'I am good at chemistry. I need help in physics,' Manjunath, nerd-embryo and Ananya's younger brother, spoke with the energy of a rooster. His eyebrows went up and down as he spoke, in sync with the three rows of ash on his forehead.

I had come for my first class. Ananya had left for Madurai the night before for a weeklong sales trip. My head hurt from waking up early. Ananya's mother had sent coffee to Manju's room. It didn't help.

Neither did the fact that I had only read up chemistry.

'Let's revise it anyway,' I said and opened my sheets.

'Hydrocarbons?' he said as he saw my notes. 'I've done this three times.'

I offered him a problem and he solved it in two minutes. I tried a harder one, and he did it in the same time. A tape played in the next room. It sounded like a chorus of women marching towards the army.

'M.S. Subbulakshmi,' Manju said, noticing my worried expression. 'Devotional music.'

I nodded as I flipped through the chemistry book to find a problem challenging enough for the little Einstein.

'Every Tamilian house plays it in the morning,' he said.

I wondered if Ananya would play it in our house after we got married. My mother could have serious trauma with that sound. The chants became stronger with every passing minute.

'What is IIT like?' he asked.

I told him about my former college, filtering out all the spicy bits that occurred in my life.

'I want to do aeronautics,' Manju said. At his age, I didn't even know that word.

He took out his physics textbook after an hour. He gave me a problem and I asked for time to solve it. He nodded and read the next chapter. The tutor was being tutored.

I passed the rest of the hour learning physics from Manju. I stood up to leave. I reached the living room where Ananya's dad was making slow love to *The Hindu*. Ananya had instructed me to spend as much time with her father as possible. I waited for ten minutes until he finished his article.

'Yes?'

'Nothing,' I said. 'I finished the class.'

'Good,' he said and flipped another page.

'How's the bank, uncle?'

He glanced up from the newspaper, surprised. 'Which bank?'

'Your bank.' I cleared my throat. 'How is your job?'

'What?' he said, stumped by the stupidity of the question. 'What is there in job? Job is same.'

'Yes, sure,' I said.

I stood for another five minutes, not sure of what I should do. I couldn't compete with *The Hindu*, and a fresh one came every day.

'I'll leave now, uncle,' I said.

'OK,' he said.

I had reached the door when he called out, 'Breakfast?'

'I'll have it in office.'

'Where is your office?'

'Anna Salai,' I said.

'That's on my way. I leave at eight-thirty. I can drop you,' he said.

I realised eight-thirty would mean I'd reach an hour later than my boss. It didn't work for me. But the lift also meant I could be in this house for another two hours and be in the car alone with my father-in-law-in-courtship.

'That's perfect. I have to reach at the same time,' I said.

'Good,' he said and went back to his paper again.

We sat for breakfast at seven-thirty. Ananya's father went to the temple room to pray, and came back with the customary three grey stripes on the forehead. I wondered if I should go pray too, but wasn't sure how I'd explain the three stripes in office along with my lateness.

We had idlis for breakfast, and Ananya's mother put fifty of them in front of us. We ate quietly. Ananya had told me they never spoke much anyway. The best way to fit in was to never talk.

'More chutney?' Ananya's mother's question (and my shaking my head) was the only insightful conversation we had during the meal.

Uncle reversed his Fiat from the garage. He peeked out to look at me several times. I wasn't sure if he wanted to avoid me or make a direct hit.

'Sit,' uncle said. I went around the car to sit next to him. Sitting with my girlfriend's father in a car brought back traumatic memories. I took deep breaths. This is not the same situation, play cool, I said to myself several times.

Uncle drove at a speed of ten an hour, and I wondered what reason I'd give to my boss for not coming to office two hours ago. Autos, scooters and even some manual-powered vehicles like rickshaws came close to overtaking us.

I wanted to talk but couldn't think of any trouble-free topic. I opened my office bag with the dubious 'Citi never sleeps' logo and took out my research reports to read. Dot com stocks had lost 25% last week. The analysts who had predicted that these stocks would triple every hour now claimed the market had gone into self-correct mode. Self-correct – it sounded so intelligent and clever it sort of took the pain away from people who had lost their life savings. It also made you sound dumb if you'd ask why didn't the market self-correct earlier? Or the more basic, what the fuck do you mean by self-correct anyway?

I had two clients who had lost ten lakh each coming to visit me today. With my IIMA degree I had to come up with a sleight of hand to make the losses disappear.

The car came to a halt near a red light.

'You wrote those reports?' uncle asked.

I shook my head. 'It's the research group,' I said.

'Then what you do at the bank?' he was more rhetorical.

'Customer service,' I said, not sure how anything I did was service. Asking people to give you their money and scraping away at it wasn't service.

'Do you know how to write those reports?' he said.

The cars behind us began to honk. The Fiat didn't start instantly. Uncle made two attempts in vain.

'Illa servicing quality,' he cursed at his car as he pulled the choke. I kept the reports inside as I became ready to push the car. Fortunately, the car started at the third attempt.

'I can write them, why?' I said, answering his earlier question.

'Nothing. Stupid joint venture my bank has done. Now they want us to submit a business plan. And that GM has asked me.'

'I can help,' I screamed like a boy scout.

'Rascal,' he said.

'Huh?'

'That GM Verma. In my thirty years at the bank I haven't done any report. Now I have to make a pinpoint presentation as well.'

'Powerpoint presentation?' I asked.

'Yes, that one. Intentionally rascal gave me something I don't understand,' uncle said.

'I can help,' I said. Maybe I had found a way to bond with uncle.

'No need,' uncle said, his voice serious. He realised he had opened up more than he should have.

'You get off here,' uncle said and drove to a road corner. 'Citibank is hardly hundred metres.'

I stepped out of the car. I said thanks three times and waved him goodbye. He didn't respond. He put his hand on the gear-shift.

'Don't meet Ananya too much. We are simple people, we don't say much. But don't spoil her name in our community,' he said.

'Uncle, but. . . .'

'I know you are classmates and you are helping Manju. We can be grateful, we can feed you, but we can't let Ananya marry you.'

I stood at the traffic intersection. Autos blared their horns at each other as if in angry conversation. It was hardly the place to convince someone about the most important decision of your life.

'Uncle, but. . . .' I said again.

Uncle folded his hands to before pressing the accelerator. The car started to move. *Fuck, how do I respond to folded hands?* I thought. Uncle drove past me. Like a defeated insurance salesman, I lifted my bag and walked towards the bank.

21

'Welcome sir, welcome to State Bank of India,' Bala said. His tone couldn't hide his anger, thereby ruining the sarcasm of his lines. He sat on my desk, waiting for this exact joyous moment when he could squash me.

'I'm really sorry, my auto met with an accident,' I lied.

'Your chummery servant said you left at five,' he said.

'You called my chummery? It's only nine. Isn't that the official time anyway?'

'No, this is Citibank. Not a public sector bank,' he said.

'So, people who work here cannot have a life,' I mumbled.

'What?'

'Nothing. Ms Sreenivas is coming at ten today,' I said.

'And you haven't prepared for it. Have you read the reports?'

'Yes, I have. But the tricky part is she is down ten lakh. And that is because she believed these reports. So no matter how well I read these reports, she won't trust them. Can I sit on my chair?' I asked.

Bala stared at me, shocked by my defiance. I took my seat. 'You told me to push these stocks,' I said, 'and now our clients are down. Ms Sreenivas is an old lady. She will panic. I want you to be prepared.'

'Prepared for what?'

'That she, and some other clients too, could move funds elsewhere.'

'How? How can they? This is Citibank,' Bala said.

'Because even as the Citi never sleeps, we make our customers weep.'

Ms Sreenivas' panic mode was entertaining enough to attract bankers from other groups to come to our area. First, she spoke to me in Tamil for two minutes. When she realised I didn't know the language, she switched to English.

'You, you said this will double. It's down seventy percent-aa,' Ms Sreenivas said.

'Actually madam, the market went into self-correction mode,' I said. I now understood the purpose of complex research terms. They deflect uncomfortable questions that have no answer.

'But I've lost ten lakh, ten lakh!' she screamed.

'Madam, stock market goes up and down. We do have some other products that are less risky,' I said, capitalising on her misery to sell more.

'Forget it. I am done with Citibank. I told you to do a fixed deposit. You didn't. Now I move my account to Vysya Bank.'

My sales rep brought several snacks and cold drinks for her. Ms Sreenivas didn't budge.

'Madam, but Citibank is a much better name than Vysya,' I said.

'Give me the account closing documents,' Ms Sreenivas said. We had no choice. First hour in office, strike one. The TV in the reception showed the CNBC channel. Internet stocks had lost another five percent that day.

In the next two weeks, our most trusting customers, hence the most gullible ones to whom we had peddled companies that did nothing more than make a website, lost a total of two crore. My own customers' losses were limited to the two ladies, as I could never sell those companies well anyway. Bala, however, with his empire of smart people who rip off rich people, had to answer country headquarters in Mumbai.

'I have seven complaints,' the country head of the customer service group said in a conference call.

'Sir, it is just an overreaction to the volatility,' Bala said.

'Don't quote from the research report. I've read it,' the country head said.

The call ended. Bala's face had turned pale. The bosses had decided to visit the Chennai branch. I first thought I imagined it, but it was true; Bala shivered a little at the news. Mumbai said we shouldn't have marketed Internet stocks to individual investors, let alone housewives, in the first place. Of course, they had never complained when the commissions kept coming in. But now five customers had closed their accounts and one customer had sent a letter all the way to the CEO of Citibank in New York.

At my weekly sales meeting, I told my sales reps not to sell Chennai customers anything apart from fixed deposits, gold and saris.

'Sir, we don't sell saris,' one of my reps clarified.

'Sorry, I was trying to be funny. We don't sell gold either, right?'

'We do. Gold-linked deposit, sir,' she said.

Yes, I didn't even know my group's products. Actually, I didn't even know why I was doing this job. I nodded and smiled. In customer service, you need to smile more than a toothpaste model.

'Is it true that Ms Sreenivas lost ten lakh?' another of my lady customers walked into the bank. She chuckled, and sat close to the sales rep to get the full lowdown. Too bad we couldn't give her the details due to confidentiality reasons. We couldn't offer returns, but at least we could have given gossip. Maybe that could lure customers.

'Krish, come here,' Bala came to me like a petrified puppy at seven in the evening.

I had packed my 'Citi never sleeps' bag to go back home and sleep. We had our bosses coming in two days. I had spent the last few nights making presentations for them. It was the crappiest, most thankless job in Tamil Nadu. No matter how wonderful I made my slides, the numbers were so bad, we'd be screamed at anyway. Last night I had reached home at three and then woke up again at five to teach brother-in-law dearest. I didn't want Bala, I wanted a pillow.

'Bala, I. . . .' I stopped mid-sentence as he had already turned towards his cabin, expecting me to follow him.

I went into Bala's office. He shut the door as softly as possible. He drew the blinds and put the phone off the hook. Either he wants to fire me or molest me, I thought.

'How is it going?' he whispered, quite unnecessarily as people had already left for the day.

'Fine. I sent you the presentation. You approved, right?' I said. He had given me an OK in the afternoon. The last thing I wanted was another night out.

'Yeah, that's fine. Listen, buddy, I need a favour from you.'

Bala had never called me buddy. The room smelt coconutty and fishy. The coconut came from Bala's hair, the fish from his unspoken intentions.

'What favour?' I asked without smiling.

'See Krish, this job, my career, it is everything to me. I have given my life to this bank.'

I nodded. *Come to the point, buddy*, I thought.

'And you, as you will admit, aren't into it as much as me. Don't take it the wrong way.'

He was hundred percent right. But when someone tells you to not take it the wrong way, you have to take it the wrong way. Besides, I had spent the last three nights working hard with only ATM guards for company. I deserved better.

'That is hundred percent false,' I said. 'I'm dying from work. I do whatever you want me to do. I sold that crap Internet. . . .'

'Easy, easy,' Bala shushed me.

'There is nobody here. We are not planning a James Bond mission that we have to whisper,' I said.

Corporate types love to pretend their life is exciting. The whispers, fist-pumping and animated hand gestures are all designed to lift our job description from what it really is – that of an overpaid clerk.

'I'm not doubting your hard work. But see, in corporate life, we have to look after each other.'

'What? How?' If he didn't come to the point in two seconds, I would slap him. In my imagination, I already had.

'I am your boss, so I can look after you anyway. But today you have a chance to look after me.'

I kept quiet.

'The country manager is coming. They will ask how the Internet stocks sales to housewives came about. I have to take the heat anyway. But if you could. . . .'

'Could what?' I prompted, just to make the scumbag say it. He didn't.

'You want me to take the blame?' I hazarded a guess.

He gave a brief nod.

'Wow, that's unbelievable, Bala. I'm a trainee. Why will they believe me anyway?'

'You are from IIMA. It is conceivable you had a big say from early on.'

'And if I say it, my career is fucked.'

'No, you are a trainee. I have to recommend your promotion. Consider that done anyway. But if I am held responsible, I don't get a promotion, ever.'

'You are responsible,' I stared into his eyes.

'Please, Krish,' Bala said.

The boss-subordinate relationship had changed. Bala begged me for help. I realised the power I could hold over him if I gave in. I could come to office like sane people. I could leave early. I could snooze at my desk. OK, so maybe my career at the Citi overpaid clerks' club would get affected. So what?

I could have said yes then, but I wanted him to grovel some more. I kept quiet.

'The country manager as it is doesn't like me. He is North Indian. He will forgive you but not me,' Bala said. I wondered if he would cry. I could have enjoyed the show longer but I also wanted to go home and rest.

'I'll see what I can do.' I stood up.

'Is that a yes?' Bala said, his eyes expectant.

'Good night, sir,' I said, emphasising the last word.

22

My father never calls me. I have no idea why he did that night. I wanted to sleep before the misery of tuitions and office began all over again. But at eleven that night, Ramanujan knocked on the door.

'What?' I called out. Since the day Ananya had visited, I hardly spoke to my flatmates.

'There's a call for you.'

'Who is it?' Even Ananya never called me this late.

'Your father. Can you ask him not to call at this hour?' Ramanujan yawned.

I froze at the mention of my father. I prayed my mother was OK. Why would he call me? 'Hello?'

'Am I speaking to my son?'

I found his addressing me as his son strange. We had never had a one-on-one conversation for the last three years.

'It's Krish,' I said.

'That's my son only, no?'

'If you say so,' I said.

Silence followed as two STD pulses passed.

'I'm listening,' he said.

'To what?'

'To whatever my son has to say to me.'

'There isn't anything left to say. Why have you called so late?' I said in an angry voice.

'You sent your mother your first salary cheque?'

'Yes,' I said, after a pause.

'Congratulations,' he said.

'Is mom OK? I hope you are not calling me for some guilt trip of yours. Because if mom is not OK. . . .' I said, separating my words with pauses.

'Your mother is fine. She is proud of you,' he said.

'Anything else?'

'How's life?'

'It's none of your business,' I said.

'Is this the way to speak to your father?' he shouted.

'I don't speak to you,' I said, 'in case you didn't notice.'

'And I am trying to increase communication,' he said, his voice still loud.

I could have hung up the phone right then, but I didn't want him to take his anger out on my mother. I kept quiet as he ranted about how I had let him down as a son. He didn't say anything he hadn't in the last twenty years. I also knew that once the monologue started, it would take a while to stop. I put the phone on the table and opened the fridge. I took out an apple and a bottle of water. I went to the kitchen, cut the apple into little pieces and came back. I had two bites and drank a glass of water. Squawks came from the phone receiver.

After finishing half the apple, I picked up the phone.

'You have no qualities I can be proud of. These degrees mean nothing. Just because you send your mother money, you think you can boss around.

I think a person like you. . . .' he was saying when I put the phone down again. I picked it up again after I finished the apple.

'I said, are you listening?' His voice was trembling.

'I am,' I said. 'Now it is late. Your bill must also be quite high. May I go to sleep?'

'You have no respect.'

'You said that already. Now, can we sleep? Good night,' I said.

'Good night,' he said and hung up. No matter how mad they are, army people still believe in courtesies. I am sure Indian and Pakistani officers wish each other before they blow each other's brains off.

I came back to bed. I didn't want my father's chapter in my life again. No father is better than a bad father. Plus right now I had to deal with another father, who had folded his hands to keep me away from a daughter I so badly wanted to be with. And I have Bala and loser flatmates and psycho landlord and horrible sambhar smells everywhere in this city. A dozen random thoughts spilled out in my brain right before going to bed. These thoughts swam around like clumsy fishes, and my poor little brain begged—*guys, I need some rest. Do you mind?* But the thoughts didn't go away. Each fish had an attention deficit disorder. The Bala thought showed visions of me jabbing him with something sharp. The Ananya's dad thought made me think about a dozen post-facto one liners I could have said when uncle folded his hands—*But I love her, sir; But you should get to know me, uncle; You realise we can run away, you* Hindu-*reading loser.*

Some people are lucky. They lie down, close their eyes and like those imported dolls your Dubai relatives give you, go off to sleep. I have to shut fifty channels in my brain, one click at a time. One hour later, I shut the final thought of how I'd admit I taught housewives to play with radioactive stocks.

23

'Ready?' Bala jollied me with coffee in the morning. Yes, Mr Balakrishnan, branch head of customer services, brought me coffee in a mug. Too bad he didn't carry it in a tray.

'Doesn't take much preparation to present yourself as stupid,' I said and took the coffee. I noticed the mug had become wet at the bottom. Bala picked up a tissue from my desk for me. I could get used to this, I thought.

We met in the conference room two hours later. Bala loaded up the presentation. True to character, he had removed my name from the title slide. Like all banking presentations in every department of every bank in India, it started with the 1991 liberalisation and how it presents tremendous opportunity for India.

'As you can see, the IT space has seen tremendous volatility in the last three months,' Bala said, pointing to a graph that only went down.

Our country head, Anil Mathur, had come on the first flight to Chennai. His day had started bad as he couldn't get a business class seat last minute and had to rub shoulders with the common people. His grumpy expression continued to worsen during the presentation.

Anil was forty years old and seen as a young turk on his way up. Citi thrived on and loved the star system. People introduced him as 'This is Anil, MD. He is a star performer'.

Again, there is nothing starry to do in a bank anyway. It is another thing Citi invented to reduce the dullness of our jobs. However, when Anil entered the room, some Chennai bankers' eyes lit up, much like the auto driver who saw Rajni's poster.

'And that in short, has led to the circumstances we are in today,' Bala said as he ended his hour-long speech. I couldn't believe he tagged his talk as short.

Anil didn't respond. He looked around the room. Chennai trainees avoid eye contact anyway, especially when it comes to authority. He looked at Bala and Bala looked at me. I nodded; I'd be the suicide mission today.

Anil's cell-phone rang. He took it out of his pocket. His secretary had called from Mumbai.

'What do you mean wait-listed for business class? I am not coming back like I did this morning sitting cramped with these Madrasis.'

Apart from me and Anil, everyone in the room was offended. However, since Anil is the boss, everybody smiled like it was a cute romantic joke.

Anil stood up with his phone. 'And why do I have a Honda City to pick me up? Tell them I am eligible for BMW if they don't have Mercedes . . . yes, of course, I am,' he said and hung up the phone.

He let out a huge sigh and rubbed his face. It is a tough life when you have to fight for basic rights every day.

'OK, focus, focus,' he said to himself and everyone in the room straightened their backs.

'Sir, as I was saying. . . .' Bala started again. Anil had a flight back in four hours. I guess Bala hoped if he kept presenting, time would run out for Anil to ask tough questions.

'Bala, you have said a lot,' Anil said. 'All I care about is why have you lost seven big customers in a month. In every other market we have grown.'

All of us studied the floor.

'Two crore? How can retail customers lose two crore? They come to save their money in the bank, not lose it,' Anil said. Such truisms had led him to become the star in the jargon-filled bank.

'Sir, as you know, those losses have come from Internet stocks,' Bala said, his voice pleading.

'So, whose big idea was it to sell these ladies net stocks?' Anil asked.

'Sir,' Bala said and looked at me. Everyone turned to me. I had become guilty by collective gaze.

'You are?' Anil asked.

'Krish, sir,' I said.

'You are from Chennai?' Anil said, puzzled at my accent that didn't match the rest of the table.

'No, I'm from Delhi.'

'Punjabi?'

I nodded.

Anil didn't answer. He just laughed. The sadistic laugh of seeing a fish out of water gasp for life. 'What happened? HR screwed up?' Anil said. His phone rang again. The secretary confirmed business class and a BMW pickup at the airport. Anil asked her to make sure it is a 5-series at least.

'Remember the Tata Tea deal we did with BankAm? I came back with that idiot MD from BankAm and the car company sends me a Toyota and a 5-series for him. Can you imagine what I went through?' Anil emphasised again. The secretary confirmed she wouldn't make him slum it in a car that cost less than an apartment. Calmness spread in the room as Anil's mood improved.

'Where was I?' Anil said and looked at me. He laughed again. 'Which college are you from?'

'IIMA,' I said.

'Salute, sir,' Anil said and mock-saluted me.

I didn't brag about my college, you asshole, I wanted to say. He got the name out of me.

'I went to IIMC. I was on the waitlist for IIMA but they never called me. I guess I am not as smart as you,' Anil said.

I had no clue how to answer that question. Another trainee in the room was from IIMC and he introduced himself. They hi-fived before Anil turned to me again.

'But who cares, I became the country manager and many of your IIMA seniors didn't,' Anil said and winked at me.

Obviously you still care, you obnoxious, insecure prick, I said to myself even as I smiled. What would life be without mental dialogue.

'So, you had the idea of selling Internet stocks to housewives?' Anil asked after he touched down from his gloat-flight. 'And Bala, you didn't stop him.'

'Sir, I always try to encourage young talent. Plus, IIMA, I thought he'd know,' Bala said, picking on Anil's resentment against my bluest of the blue-blooded institute.

'IIMA, yeah right,' Anil said. 'You have cost the bank more business than you can ever make back in five years.'

I wondered if I should cancel my deal with Bala. Even the personalised coffee didn't seem worth it.

'What about monitoring? Bala, you didn't monitor when the losses started?'

'I was getting more business, sir,' Bala said.

We had a lunch-break. I didn't join the group. One, I had to prepare for IIT trigonometry for the class tomorrow with brother-in-law. Two, I didn't need any more slamming. And three, the food was South Indian special, which I had begun to hate by now and I was sure Anil would too.

Post-lunch, Anil wrapped up the meeting. 'I want good customer numbers. Either bring those customers back or win new ones, I don't care. And please have better food next time.'

'We will, sir, we are working super hard,' Bala said.

The other trainees nodded. Apart from the IIMC guy, they hadn't spoken a word during the entire meeting.

'I can tell you, this Internet debacle will lead to layoffs across the bank. And if we see Chennai at the bottom, literally and figuratively, there will be layoffs,' Anil said and horror showed on all faces at his last word.

'And you, HR error,' Anil said and tapped my shoulder. 'You need to buck up big time.'

The BMW came to the branch to take Anil and our anxieties away. Bala came to my desk after we had come back to our seats. 'Thanks, buddy. I owe you,' he said.

'Big time, buddy, big time,' I said.

24

I figured it must be a special occasion when I heard excessive frying sounds from Ananya's kitchen. I had completed two months of tuitions and Manju had become smarter than the kids in the Complan and Bournvita ads. I could bet one month of my after-tax, PF and HRA salary that Manju would crack IIT, medical or any draconian entrance exam known to man. Most of it was his own work, and my waking up at five had little to do with it.

'What's going on,' I said and sneezed twice. The pungent smell of burnt chillies flared my nostrils.

'Special cooking for special guests,' Manju said, while continuing to solve his physics numerical.

'Who?'

'Harish, from the bay area,' Manju said.

'Harish who?'

Another fryer went on the stove. This time smells of mustard, curry leaves and onions reached us. If this was one of those prize-winning Indian novels, I'd spend two pages on how wonderful those smells were. However, the only reaction I had was a coughing fit and teary eyes.

'You are rhumba sensitive,' Manju said and looked up at me in disgust. He stood up and went to the door. 'Switch on the exhaust fan, amma,' he screamed and shut the door.

Ananya's mother continued to tackle the contents of the fryer. 'OK, you go for bath. They will come anytime,' Ananya's mother said and went to max volume, 'Ananya! Are you ready?'

'Who is Harish?' I asked again as Manju refused to look up from his problem.

'The nakshatram matched no, so they are here. OK, so g is 9.8 metres per second squared and the root of. . . .' Manju drifted off to the world he knew best, leaving me alone to deal with my world, where a boy was coming to meet my girlfriend to make her his wife.

I yanked Manju's notebook from him.

'Aiyo, what?' Manju looked at me shocked.

'What's the deal with Harish. Tell me now or I'll tell your mother you watch porn,' I said.

Manju looked stunned. 'I don't watch porn,' he said in a scared voice.

'Don't lie to me,' I said. Every boy watches porn.

'Only once I s . . . saw a blue film, at my friend's house, by mistake,' he stuttered.

'How can you watch it by mistake?'

'It belonged to my friend's dad. Please don't tell amma.'

His face, even his spectacles looked terrified. I closed his books. 'Tell me all about Harish. How did this happen?'

Manju told me about Harish, the poster boy of the perfect Tamilian groom. Radha aunty had pitched Harish for the last two years. He fit every criteria applied by Indian parents to make him a worthwhile match for Ananya. He was a Tamilian, a Brahmin and an Iyer (and those are three separate things, and non-compliance in any can get you disqualified). He had studied in IIT Chennai and had scored a GPA of 9.45 (yes, it was advertised to the Swamis).

He went on to do an MS with full scholarship and now worked in Cisco Systems, an upcoming Silicon Valley company. He never drank or ate meat or smoked (or had fun, by extension) and had a good knowledge of Carnatic music and Bharatnatyam. He had a full half-inch-thick moustache, his own house in the San Francisco suburbs, a white Honda Accord and stock options that, apart from the last three months, had doubled every twelve minutes. He even had a telescope he used to see galaxies on the weekend (I told you he had no fun). Manju was most excited at the prospect of seeing the telescope and thought it reason enough for his sister to marry that guy.

'He said you can actually see the colours on the rings of Saturn,' Manju said, excited.

'You spoke to him?'

'He called. Couple of times,' Manju said.

'Ananya spoke to him?'

'No. He used to call when she wasn't at home. Anyway, until the nakshatram matches, the boy and girl are not allowed to talk.'

'Nakshatram what?' I asked. The list of Tamilian hoops one needs to jump before getting married seemed infinite.

'Horoscope. It is a must. If they don't match, boy and girl's side don't talk. But they have matched for akka and him.'

I thought about my own family. The only nakshatram we think about is the division of petrol pumps when we have to see the girl.

'You are a science whiz kid who wants to see Saturn rings. And you accept that people whose horoscopes don't match shouldn't talk?' I said.

'That's how it is in our culture,' Manju said, his hands itching to get to his workbook. I gave him back his notes.

'And he is coming now?' I said.

'Yes, for breakfast. And please, don't snatch my notebook again.'

'I am sorry,' I said and stood up. I wanted to have a showdown with Ananya about this. Surely, she'd have known a bit more about his visit. But for now, I wanted to get out.

'Bye Manju,' I said as I turned to leave.

'Krish bhaiya, can I ask you one thing?' he said.

'What?' I said.

'Can something bad happen if you watch blue films?'

I stared at him.

'I won't, I promise. I just wanted to know,' he said.

'If you just watch them?'

'Just watching . . . and,' he said and hesitated, 'and if you do something else afterwards.'

'Why don't you ask your appa?'

'Aiyo, what are you saying?'

'You could become blind,' I said with a serious face.

'Really?' he said, 'how is that possible?'

'Be careful,' I winked at him and left.

'Welcome, welcome,' the greetings had started at the entrance even before I could leave the house.

A crowd had gathered at the main door—Ananya's dad and mom, Shobha athai, three other Kanjeevaram-clad aunties and two random uncles in safari suits became the welcome party. They received Harish like an astronaut who had returned from the first Indian lunar mission. The only time grown-ups get excited about young people is when young people are getting married and the old people control the proceedings. I had come to Ananya's house several times, and I had received a welcome no better than the guy who came to collect the cable bill. But Harish had it all. Aunties looked at him like he was a cuddly two-year-old, only he was fifty times the size and had a moustache that could scare any cuddly two-year-old. He wore sunglasses, quite unnecessary at seven in the morning, apart from showing off his sense of misplaced style. He had come with his parents, a smug Tamilian family who walked into the room with their overachiever in shades. Fortunately, he removed them when he sat on the sofa.

Ananya's father noticed me with a confused expression.

'Uncle, I was leaving,' I said. 'Sorry. I came for Manju's tuitions.'

'Had breakfast?' he asked.

'No,' I said.

'Then sit,' he said. The firmness in his voice made me obey instantly. I wanted to wriggle out of it, but a part of me wanted to see the drama unfold. Uncle's attention shifted to the new guests. Maybe he had made me stay intentionally. To show me what Ananya deserved and what I could never be. I perched in a corner chair like a domestic servant who is sometimes allowed to watch TV.

The taxi driver came in to ask for his bill and Harish's dad stepped outside to settle it. They couldn't agree on the price and their argument began to heat up. Harish's dad bargained for the last five rupees even as Harish's mother casually mentioned another of their son's achievement. 'MIT calling him, requesting him to do Ph.D. at their college.'

All the ladies in the room had a mini orgasm. Marble flooring is to a Punjabi what a foreign degree is to a Tamilian.

'But his Cisco boss said, nothing doing. You cannot leave me,' Harish's mother said. Harish kept a constant smile during the conversation.

Manju came into the room and called me.

'What?' I asked, dreading another physics problem.

I went into his room. Ananya sat on his bed, wearing a stunning peacock blue sari – the same colour she wore as the day I had proposed to her.

'Go, your groom is waiting,' I said.

'Manju, leave the room,' she said.

Manju had already sat down to study again. 'Aiyo, where should I go?'

'Go and meet the guests. Or help Amma in the kitchen,' Ananya said in a no-nonsense way.

Manju went to the living room with his physics guide.

I turned away from Ananya.

'I'm sorry,' she said.

'Who the fuck invented the word sorry? How can there be just one word to answer for anything one does. Tomorrow you could marry Mr Sunglasses outside, and then say sorry. What am I supposed to say?'

'Don't overreact. I am doing it to fob off Shobha aunty. I still have the final say. I'll say no.'

'Why didn't you tell me?'

'Because this is not important. You saw the petrol pump girl, didn't you?'

'But I told you later. And it wasn't a formal thing. My mother went to visit Pammi aunty.'

'And neither is this formal. My parents said Harish is only coming for a casual visit.'

'Oh, so people match horoscopes casually?'

'It is the first step. And Shobha aunty did it. Krish, listen. . . .'

'Ananya!' a Tamil-accented scream filled the room.

'I love you,' she said, 'and I have to go now.' She brushed past me to the door.

'Why are you wearing this stunning sari?' I placed my hand on the bolt to stop her.

'Because my mother chose it for me. Now, can I go or do you want appa to come here?'

'Let's elope,' I said.

'Let's not give up,' she said and stood up on her toes to kiss me. The taste of strawberry lip-gloss lingered on my lips.

I came outside after five minutes. The hubbub over Harish had settled down a little. The men opened their newspapers. The women gave each other formal smiles like ballet dancers. The groom took out his latest Motorola Startac mobile phone, checking messages. Ananya's mother served her standard fossilised snake snacks. No one spoke to each other. In a Punjabi home, if a similar silence occurred, you could assume that something terrible has happened—like someone has died or there is a property dispute or someone forgot to put butter in the black daal. But this is Ananya's home protocol. You meet in an excited manner, you serve bland snacks and you open the newspaper or exchange dead looks.

My re-entry made everyone notice me. Ananya's mother seemed surprised. Ananya sat next to her and faced Harish's parents. I occupied my corner chair.

'Manju's tutor,' Ananya's mother said. Everyone looked at me, the tutor who came to teach in a corporate suit.

'He is Ananya akka's classmate,' Manju said, restoring some status to me.

'You also went to IIMA? I have many colleagues who are your seniors,' Harish said.

'Really? That's nice,' I said. I wanted to shove the spiral snacks up his moustache-covered nose, but I kept a diplomatic smile.

Ananya's father spoke to Harish's father in Tamil. 'Something something Citibank Chennai posted something. Something something Punjabi fellow.'

Everyone nodded and felt relieved after my credentials of being a Punjabi made me a safe outsider.

'Talk, Ananya,' Ananya's mother whispered to her.

'How long are you here for?' Ananya asked as her bangles jingled. She really didn't have to wear the bangles.

'Two weeks. Then I have to go for our annual conference to Bali,' he said.

'Bali?' one of Ananya's aunts said.

'Bali is an island in Indonesia, an archipelago. It is eight hours flying time from here via Singapore,' Harish's mother said.

Everyone nodded as they absorbed the little nugget of knowledge before breakfast. Ananya's family loved knowledge, irrespective of whether they ever used it.

We moved to the dining table, or rather the dining floor. Ananya's mother had already kept the banana leaves. I found them a little greener than usual, perhaps my jealousy reflected in them.

Aunties loaded up Harish's leaf.

'This is too much,' Harish said, pointing to the six idlis on his leaf. 'Does anyone want one?' He picked up an idli and placed it in Ananya's leaf.

'Wow!' all the aunties screamed in unison.

'See, how much care he is taking of her already. You are so lucky, Ananya,' an aunt said as I almost tore a piece of banana leaf and ate it.

I saw the bowl of sambhar in the middle. I wondered if I should pick it up and upturn it on Harish's head. *She can take her own idlis, idiot, why don't you go drown in Bali,* I thought.

Harish thought it really funny to shift everything he was served to Ananya. He transferred parts of the upma, pongal, chutney and banana chips from his leaf to hers. *Really Harish, did nobody teach you not to stretch a bad joke too far? And all you aunts, can you please stop sniggering so as to not encourage this moron?*

'We must decide the date keeping in mind the US holiday calendar,' Shobha aunty said and I felt she was moving way, way too fast.

'Easy, aunty, easy,' Ananya said.

Thanks, Ananya madam, that is so nice of you to finally impart some sense to these people. 'You OK?' Manju offered an idli to me. I had spent two months with him. He could sense the turmoil in me.

'I'm good,' I said.

The breakfast continued. And then Ananya's mother did something that paled all the idli-passing and date-setting comments. She began to cry.

'Amma?' Ananya said as she stood up and came to her mother.

Amma shook her head. Manju looked at her but didn't stop eating. The uncles pretended nothing had happened.

'What, Radha?' Suruchi aunty said as she put a hand on Amma's shoulder.

'Nothing, I am so happy. I am crying for that,' she said in such an emotional voice even I got a lump in my throat. All the other aunts had moist eyes. Harish's mother hugged Ananya's mother. I looked at Ananya. She rolled her eyes.

'How quickly our children grow up,' one aunt said, ignoring the small fact that along with the children, she'd grown into an old woman, too.

I'm going to get you all, I will, I swore to myself as I went to wash my hands.

25

'Why don't you tell them! This gradual strategy is obviously not working,' I said as I opened the menu.

We had come to Amethyst, a charming teahouse set in an old colonial bungalow. It is one of the few redeeming aspects of the city. Set in a one-acre plot, the bungalow is on two levels. Outside the bungalow there are grand verandahs with cane furniture and potted plants with large leaves. Waiters bring eclectic drinks like jamun iced tea and mint and ginger coolers along with expensive dishes with feta cheese in them. It is a favourite haunt of stylish Chennai ladies and couples so madly in love, they feel a hundred bucks for jamun mixed with soda was OK.

'I'll have the Jamun iced and chicken sandwich, and some scones and cream, please.' Ananya said.

'And some water, please,' I said to the waiter.

'Still or sparkling, sir?' the waiter said.

'Whatever you had a bath with this morning,' Krish said.

'Sir?' the waiter said, taken aback, 'tap water, sir.'

'Same, get me that,' I said.

'I have told them, of course. They don't agree,' Ananya said, as we reverted to our topic.

'Is Mr Harish history?'

'Finally, though it will take years to make Shobha athai OK again. She is like – tell me one thing wrong with Harish.'

'He can't get a woman on his own,' I said.

'Shut up, Krish,' Ananya laughed. 'You know how I finally closed it?'

'Did you tell him about me?'

'Sort of.'

'Sort of?' I said, my voice loud. 'I am not Mr Sort Of. I am The Guy.'

'Yeah, but I can't tell him exactly. How would he feel? My boyfriend sat with me when he came to see me.'

'Imagine how I felt. Anyway, what did you tell him?'

'He asked me, rather hinted, about my virginity.'

'He did not! I will kill that bastard,' I said, my face red.

Ananya laughed. 'Jealousy is a rather enjoyable emotion to watch,' she observed.

'Funny.'

'He just said . . . wait let me remember. Yes, he said, are you still pure or something,' she giggled.

'What a loser. What is he looking for – ghee?' I asked.

Ananya laughed uncontrollably. She held her stomach as she spoke. 'Wait, you'll die if I told you my response.'

'And that is?'

'I told him – Harish, if there is an entrance exam for virginity, you can be sure I won't top it,' Ananya said.

'You did not! And then?'

'And then the Cisco guy hung up the phone. No more Harish, finito. Radha aunty said now Harish also doesn't like me. Yipee!'

The waiter brought us our drinks. The contents looked like water after you've dipped several paintbrushes in it. The jamun tea tasted different, though different doesn't translate into nice. Amethyst is about ambience, not nourishment.

'Ananya, we need to bring this to closure. I'm not getting traction with your parents. Manju maybe, but others barely acknowledge me.'

'You will. In fact, that's why I called you here today. You have a chance to score with dad.'

'I can't. I told you he folded his hands at me.'

'He is dying doing his presentation. No one in Bank of Baroda has ever made a business plan. He doesn't know computers. It is crazy.'

'I offered help. He said no.'

'He won't say no now. I could help him but I am travelling most of the time. And if you help him, it may work.'

'*May*, the key word is *may*. Can be replaced just as easily with *may not*,' I said.

'Try,' Ananya said and placed her hands on mine. It was probably the only restaurant in Chennai she would try such a stunt. Here, it looked sort of OK.

'First your brother, then your father. If nothing else, I'll be your family tutor,' I said as I sipped the last few drops of my tea.

'And my lover,' Ananya winked.

'Thanks. And what about your mother? How can I make her cry in happiness like the purity-seeking Harish?'

Ananya threw up her hands. 'Don't ask me about mom,' she said. 'One, she gives me a guilt trip about Harish everyday. And two, Chennai has put her in her place about her Carnatic music abilities. She has stopped singing altogether. And that makes her even more miserable, which creates her own self-guilt trip, which is then transferred to me and the cycle continues. Even I can't help her with this. Work on dad for now.'

I nodded as Ananya paused to catch her breath.

'Thanks for bearing this,' she said and fed me a scone dipped in cream. I licked cream off her fingers. Little things like these kept me going.

'Easy, this is a public place,' she said.

She pulled her hand back as the waiter arrived with the bill. I paid and left him a tip bigger than my daily lunch budget.

'Hey, you want to go dancing?' she asked.

'Dancing? You have an eight o'clock curfew. How can we go dancing?'

'Because in Chennai we go dancing in the afternoon. Let's go, Sheraton has a nice DJ.'

'At three in the afternoon?'

'Yes, everybody goes. They banned nightclubs, so we have afternoon clubs.'

We took an auto to the Sheraton. I am not kidding, a hundred youngsters in party clothes waited outside in the sunny courtyard. The disco opened in ten minutes. Everyone went inside and the lights were switched off. The bar started business. The DJ put on the latest Rajni Tamil track. The crowd went crazy as everyone apart from me registered the song.

Ananya moved her body to the music. She danced extremely well, as did most others trained in Bharatnatyam while growing up.

'Naan onnai kadalikaren,' she said 'I love you' in Tamil. I took her in my arms.

I looked around at the youngsters, doing what they loved despite everyone from their parents to the government banning them from doing so.

Yes, if there can be afternoon discos, Punjabis can marry Tamilians. Rules, after all, are only made so you can work around them.

'Uncle, Ananya told me you are having trouble with your business plan.'

Uncle braked his car in shock. We never spoke in the Fiat. We had a ritual. I read my reports, he cursed the traffic and the city roads. In twenty minutes, we reached the traffic signal near Citibank where he dropped me. I thanked him, he nodded, all without eye contact. Today, one week after my Amethyst date, I had made my move. Ananya had gone to Thanjavur on work for five days, and her mother joined her on the trip to see the temples. Ananya had told me it would be the perfect time to offer help. Her father wouldn't suspect I wanted to come home for Ananya. Plus, more important, he could actually take help from me and keep face as his wife and daughter won't be there to witness.

'Why is she telling you all this?' His hands clenched on the steering wheel.

'Actually, I had helped my boss make a business plan,' I lied.

'Really?' His expression softened and he looked at me.

'MNC banks make presentations all the time,' I said.

Uncle released the brake as the car moved again.

'Do you want me to sit down with you?' I offered as we reached closer to the Citibank signal.

'You take tuitions for Manju already. Why are you helping us so much?'

I thought hard for an answer. 'I don't have anyone in Chennai. No old friends, no family,' I said.

His eyebrows went up at the last word.

'Of course, you are also not family,' I said and his face relaxed again. 'But it is nice to go to a home.'

I had reached my signal. I opened the door slowly, to allow him time to respond.

'If you have time, come in the evening. I will show you what I have done.'

'Oh, OK, I will come tonight,' I said as uncle drove off. The Fiat left behind a fresh waft of carbon monoxide.

26

'I think it is a great idea,' Bala said. We sat in our priority banking group team meeting. Mumbai had proposed a 'raise spirits' dinner event for our private clients across India. Despite the economic slowdown, they had approved a budget for all major centres. Chennai needed it most, given the adventure banking we had subjected our clients to.

'So, we need to brainstorm on which event will work best for Chennai customers,' Bala said.

'An art exhibition,' one executive said.

'Again, we are selling something,' another executive said. 'The focus should be on fun.'

'A fashion show,' said the earlier executive.

'Too bold for our market,' came the counter response.

The discussion continued for ten minutes. All ideas from movie-night to inviting a Kollywood celebrity to calling a chef to prepare an exotic cuisine were discussed.

However, for some reason, none of the ideas clicked. I felt quite useless having nothing to say. But I didn't know what would work for Chennai customers apart from giving them their money back.

'Krish, what do you think?' Bala asked, breaking my daydream of walking hand-in-hand with Ananya in a peacock blue sari.

'Huh?' I said, and realised everyone had turned to me.

'Would you like to contribute?' Bala said. Even though he had cut me slack, on occasion the repressed boss in him came out.

'Music, how about music? Say a musical night?' I suggested.

Excited murmurs ran across the room. Finally, we had an idea without any strong negative opposition. However, within music there were a dozen ideas.

'Kutcheri, let's do a kutcheri,' said one.

'What's that?' I said, turning to Saraswati.

Saraswati was a conservative Tamilian agent who spoke only once a year and never waxed her arms. (I admit the latter point is irrelevant but it is hard not to notice these things.)

'Kutcheri is a Carnatic music concert,' Saraswati made her point and drifted back to being part of the wall.

'Hey, I thought we wanted the evening to be fun,' I said.

'Carnatic music can be fun,' said Ravi, another supervisor.

Yes, as much fun as wailing babies in a crowded train, I wanted to say but didn't. Political correctness is a necessity in Chennai, especially when everyone hates you for being an outsider anyway.

I turned to Bala. 'We want to raise spirits. Isn't Carnatic music too serious? Why not have an evening of popular music. Good popular music.'

'A.R. Rahman, can we get A.R. Rahman?' said one person.

'Or Ilaiyaraaja,' said another.

Bala shook his head and waved his arms to say 'no'. 'We can't do such big names. The budget is not that high. And these people attract the press. Last thing you want is some customer telling the press about their losses and us wasting money on such concerts. Mumbai will kill me.'

After two hours of further deliberation that took us to lunch break, we made a few decisions about the event. The concert would be held in Fisherman's Cove, an upmarket resort on the city outskirts. We'd have three to five singers of reasonable fame, provided we kept to the budget of two lakh.

'All set then,' Bala said as we ended the meeting at six in the evening. I realised I had to leave. After all, I had a big date with the big daddy tonight.

27

'So, this is almost done?' I clicked through the slides. Uncle had given me a CD of his work. I had uploaded it on my laptop. The unformatted slides had paragraphs of text, no bullet points and font sizes ranging from eight to seventy-two.

'Yes, I spent three weeks on it,' he said.

We sat at a work-table in the living room. Manju studied inside. No one else was at home. Ananya's father and I hunched close together to see the laptop screen.

'These have no figures, no charts, no specific points even. . . .' I said, trying to be less critical but truthful as well.

'Figures are here,' uncle said as he opened his briefcase. 'I still have to learn that feature in Powerpoint.'

He took out three thick files with dirty brown covers and two hundred sheets each inside.

'What's this?'

'Our last year business data,' he said.

'You can't put it all,' I said. 'When is this due?'

'That rascal Verma wants it in a week,' uncle said.

The rate at which Ananya's dad was going, he couldn't deliver it in a year.

'One week? This is only past performance data. Don't you have to make a plan for next year?'

'I was going to do that, soon.' He swallowed hard.

I kept my left elbow on the table and my palm on my forehead. I flipped through the slides in reverse to reach the first.

'What?' he said. 'Anything wrong in what I've done?'

I turned to him and gave a slight smile. 'No, a few finishing touches left,' I said.

'So, how do we do it?'

'Let's start by you telling me what exactly you do at the bank. And then take me through these files.'

I shut the laptop. For the next three hours I understood what a deputy district manager does at a public sector bank. Actually, there is a lot of work, contrary to my belief that government bank staff did nothing. However, a lot of the work is about reporting, approvals and maintaining certain records. It is more bureaucracy and less business.

I yawned as he finished explaining how the staff-recruiting process works in his Egmore district. I looked at the wall clock. It was nine-thirty.

'Sorry, I didn't even ask you for dinner,' Mr Swaminathan said.

'It's OK, keep going. I'll wash my face,' I said and pulled back my chair.

I came back from the bathroom and uncle had brought two steel plates and a bowl of lemon rice. He put the bowl in the microwave to heat the food. 'Sorry, I can't give you proper dinner tonight. I told the maid to make something simple,' he said.

'It's fine,' I said as I took the plates off him. I went to the kitchen. I picked up the curd and water. I saw the spoons but decided not to take them.

'Manju?' I asked as I returned to the table.

'He ate already. He wakes up at four so he has to sleep now,' uncle said.

We ate in silence. For the first time in their house, I felt welcome. Sure, they'd given me breakfast and a lift to work three days a week. However, today was different. Uncle refilled my plate when I finished and poured water for me. We continued to work after dinner until he couldn't keep his eyes open.

'It's eleven-thirty, I'd better go,' I said. I shut down my laptop and stacked all the papers together.

'Yes,' uncle said as he looked at his watch. 'I didn't realise this would be so much work.'

I came to the door and outlined the agenda.

'Here's the plan,' I said. 'Tomorrow we make a structure, so we at least have a title for all fifty slides that need to be there. The next day we will put the text. Day after we will start on the figures and charts.'

We came out of the house.

'It's late. I will drop you?' uncle said.

'No, there are autos on the main road. Good night uncle, tell Manju I will see him day after.'

'Thank you, Krish,' uncle said as he waved me goodbye.

'Anytime,' I said.

28

I spent the next three evenings in the company of Mr Swaminathan. The Bank of Baroda Egmore district business plan had become the focus of my life. I brought some of uncle's work to my own office and worked on it in the afternoon.

'What are you working on?' Bala said as we met near the common office printer where I had come to collect a printout of uncle's presentation.

'Personal research,' I said as I clenched the sheets in my hand and ran back to my desk.

It is uncanny, but I could tell Ananya's call from the phone ring.

'Hi hottie. How is it going?'

'Did you know Bank of Baroda had no ATMs four years ago, but now there are over a dozen ATMs in Egmore alone,' I said as I opened the twelfth slide of the presentation.

'What?' she said.

'And in two years, there will be thirty,' I said.

'What are you talking about?'

'I am working on your dad's presentation, in my office,' I said and swivelled my chair to turn away from the monitor.

'That's why you are such a sweetie,' she said.

'I am stealing a talented MBA's time paid for by Citibank. I could go to jail for this,' I said.

'How exciting! My lover goes to jail for me,' she chuckled. 'Manju told me you are there every evening until late. And today you took Manju's morning tuitions, too. Take care of yourself.'

'I'm fine. I rest in office. And the presentation should be done tonight.'

'Cool. How's the bonding with appa?'

'Well, it is pretty business-like. But let's just say, I saw him smile. I bit a whole chilli at dinner and ran to the kitchen. When I returned, he smiled for three whole seconds and I created it.'

'With my dad, that's huge,' Ananya said. 'He didn't smile in any of his wedding pictures.'

'Well, he had to marry your mom,' I said.

'Shut up,' Ananya said.

The peon came to me to say Bala had tried my extension and couldn't reach. I told Ananya to hold.

'Tell him I am with a prospective new client. Inviting them to the concert,' I said. The peon nodded and left.

'Concert?' Ananya said.

'It is a private client event. At Fisherman's Cove,' I said.

'Fisherman's Cove is nice. Can I come?' she said.

'Only if you have ten lakh to spare,' I said.

'Sure, my husband will send the cash,' Ananya said.

'Yeah, right after I execute my bank robbery. OK, now should I humour you or make sure your father doesn't get laughed at in five days?' I said.

'Daddy first,' she said. 'I am back in three days.'

'How is Thanjavur?'

'Temples, Tamilians and a temperamental mother. Care?' she said.

'Maybe next time. What's causing the temperamentalness?'

'Me, me and only me,' Ananya said and laughed, 'as is always the case.'

'Really? What's your crime now?'

'I don't have time for her. Which is true, as I'm all over the district in meetings the entire day. Of course, she also feels saying no to Harish is like declining the Nobel Prize. And so, that's the dinner appetiser. Main course is a lecture on how I've abused my privilege of being allowed to study further. Dessert is usually tears. I have to go to Pondicherry next week. No way I am taking her.'

'You *have* to go?'

'Just a day trip.'

'Hey, isn't Fisherman's Cove on the way to Pondicherry?' I asked.

'Yes, why?'

'Good, I should take the initiative and check out the venue. I'll come with you that day,' I said. Anything to get out of office.

'Oh, cool,' she said.

The peon came again.

'Yes,' I turned to the peon after asking Ananya to hold.

'Sir is asking which client?' peon said.

I looked around. Outside the office window there were several hoardings. I saw one for fireworks.

'Standard Fireworks, Sivakasi. OK?' I said.

The peon nodded.

'Bye sweetie, am I disturbing you?'

'Yeah, but what is life without being disturbed by the right people,' I said.

'Thank you. Love you,' Ananya said.

'I love you, too' I said and hung up the phone. The peon stood in front of me, his eyes big after my last line.

'Why are you still here?' I said.

'Sorry, sir,' the peon said and left.

I left my office early to finish the presentation at uncle's house. We had come to the end with only final formatting left. I passed a CD store in Mylapore. Some music would be nice while I completed the presentation, I thought. I went in.

'What you want, sir?' the shopkeeper said.

I scanned the shelves filled with Tamil CDs in psychedelic covers resembling crime novels. 'What non-Tamil CDs do you have?' I asked.

He shook his head in disappointment. 'Non-Tamil you go to Nungambakkam, sir.' But the shop attendant looked through his collection to find something.

'OK here,' he said as he took out three CDs.

The first CD was non-stop Hindi remixed hits. It had girls with cleavage on the cover. I had to reject it. The second was a romantic love-songs collection that had a heart-shaped cover. The third CD was nursery rhymes in English.

'Give me the love songs,' I said.

The shopkeeper made the bill as I scanned a section on Carnatic music.

'Any good Carnatic music CDs?' I said.

'Good meaning what, sir?' he said as he wrapped my red-coloured CD.

I looked at the Carnatic covers. Most of them had middle-aged Tamilian men and women on them. 'Do you have any greatest hits collection in Carnatic?' I said.

The shopkeeper looked puzzled. I threw up my hands in despair. 'I have no clue. I want to get started,' I said.

'North Indian?' he said.

I nodded.

'Then why you want to learn Carnatic music?'

I didn't answer.

The shopkeeper gave me two CDs. One had a woman holding a tambura on the cover. The other had the picture of an old man. The entire text was in Tamil. I flipped it around.

'T.R. Subramanium nice,' said an elderly lady who had just walked into the shop and noticed my CDs.

'Yeah, my all-time favourite,' I said as I kept the CDs in my bag and walked out of the shop.

I reached Ananya's place at 6.30. Uncle already sat at the table. He wore reading glasses and made corrections on a printout of the presentation. He had kept hot vadas on the table with red, green and white coloured chutneys.

'Take one. It is a famous shop near my office. I brought them for you,' uncle said.

I looked at him as I picked up a vada. We made eye contact for the first time ever since I had known him. I noticed that if you ignored the wrinkly face and reading glasses, he had the same eyes as Ananya.

'So today, no matter how late it gets, we finish this,' I said as I opened the file.

Uncle nodded. He pulled his chair close to mine to see the screen.

'OK, so let's go through each slide. I will format as we go along,' I said.

I went through the first five slides in an hour.

'Uncle, do you mind if I put some music on? This formatting is quite tedious,' I said. I opened the CD player in my laptop.

'Play it on the stereo,' uncle said and pointed to the hi-fi system kept in the living room display cabinet. I took out the CDs from my office bag.

Uncle walked up with me to connect the system. He fiddled with the wires as I noticed a one-litre unopened bottle of Chivas Regal whisky kept next to the stereo system.

I took my chances and asked him. 'You like whisky?'

'No, just a little peg sometimes when I have a cold. Harish gave me this big bottle. It will last me years,' he said.

I kept quiet.

'You know Harish? The boy who came to see Ananya.'

I nodded.

'Really good boy,' he said.

Uncle switched the stereo on. I gave him the heart-shaped CD in my bag.

Uncle turned it around in his hands a few times.

'That's all the Mylapore shop had,' I said in a sheepish voice.

'What are the others?'

I showed him the other two CDs.

'T.R. Subramanium and M.S. Sheela? Who did you get this for?'

'For myself.'

'You understand Carnatic music?'

'No, but I want to learn. I've heard it is the purest form of music,' I said.

Uncle shook his head. I wondered if my reason had not come across as real. He put the CDs back in my bag. 'Sometimes, I wish I had never encouraged Radha in Carnatic music. It has only given her pain.'

I nodded, not sure of how I should respond. Uncle was talking personal for the first time. It is amazing how much closeness two men with a laptop in a closed room can achieve in five days.

We sat back at the table as I worked on the sixth slide. Mandy Moore's romantic track filled the room.

I wanna be with you
If only for the night
The lyrics were a little odd for a work date between a fifty-year-old Tamilian and a twenty-four-year-old Punjabi boy, but better than the silence. I enjoyed putting the textboxes, tables, charts and lists in their right place and making each slide look slick. Uncle read each point and checked the figures. The song continued.

To be the one who is in your arms
Who holds you tight
The CD played itself over three times before I reached the halfway mark. We paused for dinner at ten. Uncle went to the kitchen and came back with tomato rice in two plates.

'You must be bored of South Indian food?' he said.

'No, I am used to it now. Feels like home food,' I said.

'Good,' he said. He went to the display cabinet.

I had made it to the category of 'good' though still not 'really good' like Harish, I thought.

'The presentation is under control now. You want a drink?' uncle said.

'Sure,' I said.

Uncle took out two glasses from the crockery rack in the display cabinet. He told me to get a spoon and ice from the kitchen. He opened the bottle.

'Five spoons for me is enough,' he said as he made his drink. 'How about you?'

'We don't use spoons to measure alcohol,' I said. I was a little agitated. One week of working my ass off and still Harish was the 'really good' boy. Fuck you, Harish, I am going to have your Chivas Regal. I poured the golden coloured liquid four fingers thick.

'What are you doing?' he exclaimed.

'Making myself a real drink. Cheers,' I said and lifted my glass.

'Actually, Radha stops me from having more,' uncle said and took the bottle from me. He tilted it and made his drink level with mine.

'Cheers,' he said, 'and thank you. You IITians are very smart. What a presentation you have made.'

'You are welcome,' I said.

We finished our dinner and first drink by ten-thirty. I brought the whisky bottle next to the laptop. I poured a second drink for myself and offered it to uncle. He didn't decline. The song changed to *Last Christmas*.

Uncle went to the stereo and increased the volume. 'I gave you my heart,' uncle sang in sync with the song and snapped his finger. He came back and sat down.

I had witnessed an amazing sight. A Tamil Brahmin had set himself free probably for the first time. If I didn't have the presentation to make, I'd have loved to observe him more. All I remember is that in the next two hours, we reached the last slide and the one-third mark on the whisky bottle.

'And thank you,' I said as I read the last slide. 'Here we go, it is done.'

I saved the file.

'Save it twice,' uncle said.

I saved it again and checked the time. It was 1 a.m. In three hours, Manju would wake up.

'All ready to present it?' I asked.

'Present? Me? No, no, Verma will present this. My job was to complete this and it's done.'

'Uncle,' I said my voice firmed by the whisky, 'you have to present. What's the point of slaving over this for weeks if you don't get to present.'

'I have never operated that projector,' uncle said.

'There's nothing to it. Your IT will set it up. And you press the forward button to move to the next slide.'

'I don't know.' He turned quiet.

I closed my laptop and shook my head. 'This is unbelievable. The presentation is in such good shape. Your country manager will be there. And all you want to do is sit in a corner. Verma will take all the credit.'

'Really?' he said.

'That's what all bosses do, without exception,' I said.

'Bloody North Indian fellow,' uncle said.

I stood up to leave.

'Sleepy?' he asked.

'Not as much as you. You sleep at ten, right?' I said.

'This has woken me up,' uncle said, pointing me to his drink. 'Want another one?'

'Uncle, I have to find an auto. It's late.'

'Why don't you just stay here?' he said.

'Excuse me?' I said.

'Yes, I'll give you a set of nightclothes. Mine should fit you,' he said.

I had past-life trauma of wearing my girlfriend's father's clothes. This can't be a good idea, I thought.

Before I could respond, uncle had poured us another round of drinks.

'Change the music if you want,' he said.

I rifled through Ananya's tapes in the drawer. I found a Pink Floyd album and couldn't resist. The alcohol demanded Floyd.

The long, trippy opening note of *Shine On You Crazy Diamond* played in the room.

Uncle tapped a foot gently to the slow beats. I wondered if he would be able to handle so much alcohol. I longed to smoke. *No, don't think about smoking,* my mind advised. *Don't think about being with Ananya. Think about the worst-case emergency plan. What if uncle threw up or fainted? How do you call an ambulance in Chennai? How would you explain it to Ananya's mother?*

However, uncle seemed to be having a good time. He sat on the sofa and put his legs on the table. 'One thing Verma told me I will never forget,' he said.

I nodded.

Verma said, 'Swaminathan, do you know why they made you deputy GM and sent me to become GM?"

'Why?' I said, too drunk to show restraint.

'He said it was because South Indians are top class number two officers, but horrible in number one positions.' Uncle shook his head as he took a big sip. Even in his drunkenness, I could sense his pain. I didn't know what to say.

'Do you agree?' he asked.

'Oh, I don't know. My boss is South Indian,' I said.

'Yes, but you have just started. Maybe he is right. We hate the limelight. I know I should present this, but I don't want to.'

'Why?'

'Because knowledge is not for showing off. If I do good work, people should notice me. I cannot go sell myself like that shameless Verma.'

I nodded, more to tell him I listened than in agreement. There is no better source of wisdom than two drunk men.

'Right?'

'Depends,' I said.

'On what?'

'Did you feel bad when they didn't make you GM?' I said.

Uncle looked at me for a few seconds. He leaned forward from the sofa to come near me. 'Let me tell you one thing. What is your name?' he said.

Obviously, I was not anywhere close to getting close to him. 'Krish,' I said.

'Of course, sorry, this whisky . . . Anyway, Krish, I had offers. Ten years back I had offers from multinational banks. But I stayed loyal to my bank. And I was patient to get my turn to be GM. Now, I have five years to retire and they send this rascal North Indian.'

'You did feel bad,' I said.

'I still feel horrible. I haven't even told this to my wife. I am drinking too much,' he said.

'It's OK. The point is, if you feel horrible then you need to do what it takes to get to be number one. And. . . .' I stopped myself.

'What? Say it,' he said.

'And if you don't have marketing skills, then better admit that than take a moral high ground about knowledge. You've done good work, let the world know. What the hell is cheap or shameless about that?'

Uncle didn't respond.

'I'm sorry,' I said, composing myself.

'No, you are right. I am useless,' he said, his voice quivering. I became worried he'd cry.

'I didn't say that. We made this, right?' I pointed to my laptop.

'You think I should present? Will I be able to?' he asked.

'You will kick ass,' I said.

'What?'

'Sorry, I said you need ice?'

He shook his head.

'You'll be fine. Tell Verma you will present this. Don't give him a copy.'

'I'll fight with him?'

'Yes, if you call it that,' I said. 'And make sure from now on, people know about the work you do. Look at Bala, my boss. He copies the country manager on everything. Bala briefed the country manager about the food menu for this stupid local concert we are having next month. You definitely have to get noticed, you don't have to do the work. That's how corporates work, everyone knows it.'

Uncle nodded and fell deep in thought. I checked the time: 2 a.m. I couldn't control a yawn.

'OK, we should go to bed,' uncle said and stood up. 'Wait.' He came back with a lungi and vest. 'Here, will this do?'

You got to be kidding me, I wanted to say, but said, 'Perfect.'

Uncle showed me the guestroom. I sat down on the bed with the nightclothes in my lap.

'What do you want to be? MD at Citibank?' uncle asked me as he reached the door to leave my room.

'A writer,' I said.

'Excuse me,' he said and his tired body became alert again.

'MD, country manager, I don't care, It's not me,' I said.

'Will you leave the bank?'

'Not immediately. I'll save for a couple of years first.'

'And after that? What about your parents? Are they OK with this?'

'We'll see. You should sleep, uncle. You have a presentation to make tomorrow,' I said.

Uncle switched off the main light and left. I went to the bathroom and struggled with my lungi. Finally, I used a belt to tie it around my waist and lay down in bed. My back was resting after eighteen hours; I let out a sigh of relief.

Uncle knocked on my door. He came inside and switched on the light again.

I sat up on the bed in one jerk. 'What?'

'Water,' uncle said as he left a bottle next to my bed. 'Drink up, or you will have a headache in office tomorrow.'

'Thanks,' I said.

'You OK with that lungi? You need help?'

'No, I am fine,' I said and clutched my belt and modesty close to myself.

'Good night,' uncle said as he switched off the light again.

'Good night, sir,' I said and cursed myself for the next ten minutes for calling him sir.

29

'Three lakh!' Bala flipped during the concert steering committee meeting. Yes, one of the great value additions from Bala is to make everything sound important. He created the CSC, or the Concert Steering Committee. It sounded so important, I could almost put it in my resume.

But right now, we had a problem. Everyone kept silent as the person in charge of the singers gave her report. 'You want three celebrity singers, sir,' said Madhavi, a fat agent with spectacles who looked like a cross between a school prefect and an ICU nurse.

'But how can they get paid so much?' Bala said. Somehow, Bala felt only he deserved a job that paid far in excess of the work involved.

'They come with a band, sir, and back-up singers,' Madhavi said.

Everyone in the room nodded.

Bala shook his head. 'Why do we need back-up singers? The main ones will crash or something?'

Nobody laughed.

'Back-up means chorus, sir,' Madhavi said.

Bala remained unimpressed.

'Chorus are those people who say aa aa aa in love songs, sir,' said Renuka, another agent.

'I know what chorus is,' Bala said as he banged his fist on the table. 'But this is too much.'

'We can cut the food,' said one agent. He got more dirty looks than an eve-teaser in a bus. He retracted his suggestion.

'Why don't we get some lesser known singers?' I asked.

'But this is a Citibank event. If we get B-grade singers and tomorrow HSBC does an event with A-grade singers, we are screwed,' Bala said.

'Sir, the venue. . . .' one agent who had never spoken in a meeting in his entire career was shot down mid-sentence.

'Has to be five-star,' Bala said.

'Who is the top singer of the three?' I said.

'Hariharan,' said one agent.

'No, it is S.P. Balasubramanium,' said another.

War broke out between the normally peaceful Tamilians. When it came to music, they could kill.

'No match, Hari is no match for SP,' Madhavi shouted emotionally.

'Suchitra? You forgot Suchitra?' another agent said.

Bala stood up. Like all corporate meetings worldwide, even this one had ended without a conclusion. 'All I am saying is, we can't afford to pay this much. The venue, food and advertising are already costing four lakh,' Bala said.

'Advertising?' I asked.

'We are giving a half-page ad in *The Hindu*,' Bala said.

The agents closed their files to leave.

'Isn't it an invitation-only event?' I said.

'Exactly, the ad will say so. Only our customers will have the invites. However, the ad will ensure their friends and relatives feel jealous.'

'That's the Citi advantage,' I said.

'Exactly.' Bala patted my back.

'So, dad's happy, huh?' I quizzed Ananya inside the auto.

'You bet. Dad only talks about the presentation at dinner every day. And now he's in Delhi, to make the same presentation in head office. Can you believe it?' Ananya said.

'Wow!' I said as we reached our destination.

We had come to Ratna Stores in T. Nagar to buy steel plates for my chummery. I needed four, this place had four million of them. Seriously, every wall, roof, corner, shelf and rack over two floors was covered with shiny steel utensils. If direct sunlight fell in the store, you could burn like an ant under a magnifying glass. I wondered how the store kept track of its inventory.

'How do you ever choose?' I said to Ananya as we neared the plates section.

Ananya demonstrated the desired width with her hands to one of the attendants.

'Seriously, thanks for helping dad. I think he likes you now,' she said.

'Not as much as he likes Harish. I drank his whisky though.'

'What?' Ananya said.

I told Ananya about our drinks session.

'You wore his what to bed?' she said, shocked at the end of my story.

'Lungi,' I said as I paid at the cashier's counter. 'What's so surprising? It is quite comfortable.'

Ananya raised her eyebrows.

'I did it for you.' I looked into her eyes.

She moved forward and even though one could see our reflection in five hundred frying pans around us, she kissed me. All the Tamilian housewives in the store turned to us in shock.

'Ananya,' a lady's voice came from behind us.

Ananya turned around. 'Fuck, Chitra aunty,' Ananya said, lifting a large steel tray to hide her face. It was too late as the woman had started to come towards us.

'Chitra who?' I said.

'Chitra aunty lives in my lane. She sings Carnatic music with my mother,' Ananya said from behind the tray.

'I bought Carnatic music CDs, too,' I said.

'What?' she said.

'Never mind, hello aunty,' I said as Chitra aunty came next to us.

'Krish,' Ananya said. 'Colleague.'

'Really, what kind of colleague?' Chitra aunty asked bossily.

'I have to go,' I said and lifted my plates. 'We need these before dinner.'

Ananya called me late at night, after I had eaten in the new steel plates.

'All OK?' I said.

'Sort of,' Ananya said. 'She is going to tell my mother. They have this rivalry anyway. Guruji accepted her but not my mother.'

'And then?'

'Nothing, I'll tell my mother she is exaggerating. Am I mad enough to smooch someone in Ratna Stores?' she said.

'You are,' I laughed.

'Yes, but only you know that.'

'I don't want to ruin what I've built with your dad,' I said.

'It's mom you have to worry about now. Manju and Dad are OK.'

'How?'

'I don't know. I told her you are coming over for dinner tomorrow.'

'Why?'

'The stated reason is to thank you for helping dad. We can tell her about our visit to Ratna Stores before Chitra aunty. Of course, we'll skip a few bits.'

'You shouldn't have kissed me there. Why did you do it?'

'Because I couldn't help it, you are irresistible sometimes,' Ananya said.

My heart stopped for a second at Ananya's response. Alright Mrs Swaminathan, if your daughter can't resist me, there is no way you can either.

30

'Excellent presentation, that is what the board told Dad in Delhi. Now they've asked all zonal offices to make similar ones,' Ananya said in an excited voice.

We sat on the floor for dinner. Ananya's mom kept quiet as she stirred a bowl of rasam. She offered it to me without a word.

'You OK, mom?' Ananya said.

'Did you go to Ratna Stores with him?' Ananya's mother said, pointing to me.

'Oh shit, Chitra aunty had to tell you the next morning,' Ananya said, her hand busy mixing the rice and daal.

'Akka, don't use bad words at the dinner table,' Manju said.

'Manju, you eat. I am talking to mom here,' Ananya said.

'He's right. We don't talk like that in this house. We don't do the things you do either,' Ananya's mother said as she vented some of the anger on the rice in her leaf. She mashed and smashed it with all the vegetables extra hard.

'What have I done, mom? Krish wanted steel plates. How would he know where to go? I took him to Ratna Stores.'

'And you do cheap things in the store?' Ananya's mother said.

'What cheap things, mom?' Manju said.

'Manju, can you leave the room? Go read your physics book,' Ananya bade.

'But I've already revised physics today,' Manju said.

'Then study maths or chemistry, for God's sake. Go.' Ananya's stern glance did the trick. Manju picked up his banana leaf and took it to his room.

'Something something cheap something. . . .' Ananya's mother said as Ananya interrupted her.

'Mom, Krish doesn't understand Tamil. Please, speak in English,' Ananya said.

Ananya's mother gathered herself and spoke again. 'Why are you sending your brother away, when you are ready to be cheap in public?'

'I didn't do anything cheap.'

'Chitra is lying?'

'I gave him a little kiss.'

'Kissing!' Ananya's mother said as if Ananya had mentioned us snorting drugs.

'Mom, stop hyperventilating. He is my boyfriend. You understand?'

'You are my daughter, do you understand? You are spoiling our name in the community, do you understand? I brought you up, educated you, made sacrifices for you, do you understand?'

I don't know if mother and daughter understood anything, but I understood it was time for me to go. I stood up.

'Where are you going?' Ananya demanded of me.

'To wash my hands,' I said, showing her my curd-filled hands as proof.

'Even *my* hands are messy. Stay with me,' Ananya ordered.

'You don't know what I have to bear because of you,' Ananya's mother said. In one movement she stood up, gathered her leaf and composure and left the room.

Ananya let out a huge sigh.

'I liked the rasam, nice and tangy,' I said.

'You said you owe me big time,' I said. I sat in Bala's office. He kept both his elbows on the desk and ran all ten fingers through his oily hair.

'But how can I?' Bala said.

'You said you were over budget. I have a singer for you, free.'

I played with the paperweight in his office. Alone with him, I behaved his equal.

'Who?' he said.

'Radha Swaminathan, upcoming singer.'

'Really? Never heard her,' Bala said.

'She is still in the underground scene. She has trained in Carnatic music.'

'But this is a popular music concert. We'll have dancers to complement the singers.'

'Bala, popular music is cakewalk for Carnatic singers. You know that.'

'Is she good? Have you heard her sing?'

'Sort of.'

'Sort of?'

'Yes, I have. It'll be fine. Plus you have Hariharan and S.P., can't go too wrong.'

Bala stood up and walked towards his window.

'Is she hot?' Bala said, 'like good-looking?'

'She is my girlfriend's mother. I find the daughter pretty.'

'What?'

'I have to do this Bala. I am hitting all-time lows with her. If I don't do something drastic, I can kiss my girl goodbye forever. They've got a Cisco guy lined up, pure as fresh coconut oil.'

'Your girlfriend is Tamilian?'

'Yes, Brahmin, so you can deal with it for once.'

'Iyenger or. . . .'

'Iyer, does it matter?'

'No,' Bala said and came back to his seat. 'Now I know why you came to Chennai.'

'Apart from the fact that I was dying to work with a financial wizard like you,' I said.

'What?'

'Nothing, now, are you doing it?'

'What?'

'Finalising the singers, Hariharan, S.P. and new talent Radha.'

'What will the agents say? We have a committee.'

'Everyone in the committee works for you. They are your drones.'

'But still,' Bala said, deep in thought.

'You decide,' I sighed. 'I have work. I haven't cleaned up my mailbox in ages. I still have those emails of yours asking me to push those Internet stocks. I should delete them, right?'

Bala started at me as I turned to leave. 'Look, it is not personal,' I said, 'but this is about my future kids.'

31

'Aunty, may I come in?' I said.

Ananya's mother looked at me through the mesh door with sleepy eyes. She wore a nightie; I had disturbed her afternoon nap.

I had told my agents I would be out for a late lunch. Before coming to their house, I stopped at Grand Sweets and packed two kilos of Mysore pak.

Aunty opened the door. I came inside. She went inside to change her clothes. I flipped through *The Hindu* until she returned.

'Uncle's back?' I asked.

'He came last night.' She yawned. 'But he is in office now.'

'Sorry to wake you up,' I said and passed her the box of sweets.

'What's this?'

'I wanted to apologise for the dinner that night.'

Aunty kept quiet and looked at the coffee table.

'I am sorry about the Ratna Stores incident. I assure you, nothing cheap happened,' I said.

'Chitra is a loudmouth,' she responded. 'She would have told the whole of Mylapore by now.'

'I can understand. We have people like that in Punjabis as well. People who love to interfere in other people's lives.'

Aunty ignored me. She went inside to keep the sweets in the fridge. She came back with a glass of water and their family dish of hard, brittle spirals that didn't taste of anything.

I took one. My tooth hurt as I tried to bite it. I took the spiral out of my mouth and faked I had taken a bite by pretending to chew. We had an awkward minute of silence.

'Aunty, I wanted to show you this,' I said and opened my bag. I took out the Carnatic music CDs and gave them to her.

'T.S. Subramanium? Whose is it?'

'Mine.'

'What?'

'I'm trying to develop a taste. I'm learning, but it's hard. There's the swara, the raga, the shruti.'

'You know about shruti?'

'Only the basics. I am not an expert like you.'

She returned my CDs and gave a wry smile. 'In Chennai I am a nobody. Even Chitra is better than me. Though people say she knows the corporator of Chennai, who asked Guruji to take her on. The corporator is in charge of the kutcheri venues, so Guruji had to oblige her. Can you imagine how shallow she is?'

'There have to be other gurus,' I said.

'I was ready for an advanced one. Anyway, I am sorry I overreacted that day.'

'No, no, you don't have to apologise. I came to apologise. And for a little request.'

'Request? What are you requesting me? You young people do whatever you want, anyway.'

'No this isn't about Ananya and me. This is about our Citibank concert.'

Over the next half an hour I explained the upcoming event. I told her about the Fisherman's Cove venue, the who's who of Chennai that we expected to be present, the popular music concert for two hours divided between three singers, and that I wanted her to be one of them.

'Me?' she echoed, shocked.

'Yes,' I said.

'I've never sung popular music,' she said.

'You have a trained voice. Switch on MTV and see the latest chartbusters. Three Kollywood, three Bollywood. You are done.'

'Why me?' she asked, still bewildered.

'Actually, we are desperate. We need three singers and we found only two. My boss gave me the job of finding the third singer. So, my appraisal depends on you.'

'Who are the other two singers?'

'They are a bit known. So, the third one has to be fresh to balance things out.'

'Who?'

'Hariharan and S.P. Balasubramanium,' I said.

Aunty's mouth fell open. She stood up and left the room. I followed her into the kitchen. 'Aunty, it is no big deal. It isn't a public concert.'

Aunty answered by placing a frying pan on the stove and pouring oil in it. Once the oil heated up, she tossed in mustard seeds and curry leaves. A pungent smell filled the kitchen. I coughed twice.

'See, this is what I do all day. I cook, I don't perform. I am an amateur. I can't even sit in front of Hariharan and S.P., let alone share the same stage.'

'It's a fun night, not a competition. They sing after you.'

She tossed chopped onions in the pan. My eyes burned along with my throat. 'Aunty, have you ever performed on stage before?'

'No. OK, yes, a couple of times in the Tamil Sangam events where Ananya's father was posted. But this, five-star hotel, high-society, Hariharan. . . . You've got Hariharan, why do you need me?'

'Only professionals will make it too commercial. We want to give our clients a family feel. A casual vibe will be nice,' I said.

Aunty shook her head. I continued to convince her until she had prepared the evening dinner of tomato rasam, lemon rice and fried bhindi. I had followed the recipe and could now make rasam from scratch. However, I still didn't have her on board.

'Why are you doing this? I accepted your apology, didn't I?'

'That's not why I am doing it.'

'Then why?' She covered the dishes with plates.

'I am doing it because I think you are a good singer.'

'How do you know that?'

'Because Ananya told me. She also said you've trained all your life. And I believe her.'

She looked at me.

'Don't tell me the idea doesn't excite you. Not even a little?' I said as we came back to the living room.

'Of course, it is a huge honour, but I can't.'

'Don't say you can't. C'mon, we will keep it a surprise. We won't tell uncle. We won't even tell Ananya if you want.'

We sat down on the sofa. I noticed the whisky bottle, the level was the same as I had left it.

'OK, here is the deal. You give a tentative yes now. You prepare the songs when Ananya and uncle are not at home. If on the day of the concert, you want to back out, let me know the night before and I will manage. If not, give it a shot. Deal?'

'I will chicken out at the end,' she promised.

'I'll take a chance. Please,' I said.

She took ten seconds, but she gave a brief nod at the end.

I sprang up the sofa in excitement. 'Cool, your practice starts now,' I said and picked up the TV remote and put on MTV.

'What are these songs?' she said as the screen showed two hundred South Indian dancers dancing on the Great Wall of China.

'I'll let you figure it out. And now, I better get to work,' I said, 'The Citi never sleeps, but the Citi shouldn't bunk office, too.'

I fist-pumped as I left Ananya's house.

32

People close to you have the power to disturb you the most. I should have torn my father's letter. I ended up reading it thrice.

Son,

I am omitting the 'Dear' as I am not sure I can address you as that anymore. I knew you are on the wrong path the day you lost respect for your father. I am sure you remember that day. You have broken all contact with me since.

I have learnt you are involved with a girl in Chennai. I don't know the details. I can only deduce so much from your mother's conversations with her useless relatives.

We should choose the girl for you, not you. For you are on the path to becoming a man of low character. Such are the values given to you by your mother and her siblings that you may not even know how disgraceful your actions are.

That you chose to hide your actions from me only reinforces that at some level you are ashamed of them as well.

Unfortunately,
Your father

I changed my sleeping position for the tenth time. I wanted to sleep, but felt more alert than anytime in office. *Forget it, he only wants to provoke you,* I said to myself again. *Go to sleep, now! –* I scolded myself. The funny thing about sleep is you can't instruct it to happen. Your mind knows the facts and repeats them to you – *it is late, only five hours when you have to wake up again, you need the rest.* Your mind also has a million options on what it can think about; the stars in the clear moonless sky, the beautiful flowers at the Nungambakkam flower shop, the smell of incense in Ananya's house, your best birthday party. There are positive thoughts somewhere in people's heads all the time. But somehow, even one negative thought will crowd them out. Maybe it is an evolutionary mechanism so we can focus on the problem at hand rather than rejoice in all things wonderful. But it makes life a bitch, as good memories have to make space for the next pain in the neck item. And what does one gain by losing sleep? I hope our genes mutate ASAP so we can evolve out of this.

Memories of that day my father referred to kept coming back. *What drama is he going to do when I tell him my marriage plans?* I thought. *Go to sleep, idiot, only four hours to wake up,* my mind scolded me.

My brain refused to relax. I sprang out of bed at two and called home.

'Hello?' my mother said in a sleepy voice.

'Sorry, it is me.'

'Krish? Everything OK?' she sounded panicked.

'Yes,' I said.

'What happened?'

'Dad sent a letter. I'm quite disturbed.'

'Oh, really? What did it say?'

'Not important. He knows about Ananya.'

'Your friend, no? Yes, so what?'

'Mom, she is not just a friend. I want to marry her.'

'Oh Krish, don't start this so late at night. A girlfriend is fine, do whatever you want in Chennai. But why are you forcing her on us?'

'I am not imposing, I am telling you about my choice of life partner,' I said, my voice loud.

'Stop screaming.'

'I'm sorry.'

'If you have the guts, shout at your father.'

'I don't speak to him at all. You know I don't care.'

'Then why is that letter bothering you?'

I kept silent.

'Hello?' my mother said after five seconds.

'I'm here,' I said, my voice soft.

'Are you OK?'

I held back my tears as I spoke. 'I'm lonely, mom. I don't need this from dad.'

'Tear the letter and throw it.'

'I am battling Ananya's parents here anyway. This is such a strange city, I am welcome nowhere. And now you think I am imposing on you,' I said and couldn't control myself. I held the phone tight and cried.

'Stop Krish, don't,' my mother said.

I composed myself and used my left leg to open the fridge. I took out a bottle of water and drank it. 'What do I do?' I said after I regained composure.

'Come back. Why don't you apply for a transfer back to Delhi?'

'I only came here six months ago.'

'Say you have family issues. Tell them I am sick.'

'Mom, please.'

'Leave your job if you have to. We'll find another one. There is a Canara Bank right across our house.'

'Mom, I'm in Citibank. It is an MNC.'

'Fine, we will look for a multinational. Swear on me you will ask for a transfer. Don't be trapped in that city with horrible black people.'

'Mom, they are not all bad.'

'I don't care. Apply for a transfer or I will send a letter to your boss. I will say I am an old woman and you have to consider my plea on humanitarian grounds.'

'Mom, swear on me you will never do anything like that,' I said and smiled at her choice of words inspired by Indian government offices.

'Then you do it.'

'I will, mom. I have to finish a few things first. I am almost there,' I said and regained my composure.

'OK, you fine now?' she said.

'Yes, I am good.'

'Good. And don't take any nonsense from these Madrasis, give it back to them. They get scared fast.'

'OK, mom.'

'And don't get serious about that girl.'

Already too late for that, mom, I thought. 'Good night, mom,' I said.

'I love you. Good night,' she said and hung up.

I came back to my bed and tossed the letter in the bin. I felt light after speaking to my mother and drifted off to sleep in five minutes. What would the world be without mothers?

33

'Bike?' Ananya beamed when I went to pick her up on a black Yamaha RX 100.

'Bala's,' I said.

Ananya sat pillion in a maroon salwar kameez, using her white dupatta to cover her head and face. She looked like a member of Veerappan's gang.

Pondicherry is a hundred and forty kilometres away from Chennai, down the East Coast Road, or ECR, running along the Bay of Bengal.

Fisherman's Cove falls on the way, twenty kilometres outside Chennai city.

We left Ananya's office at Anna Salai. She sat behind me and held the sidebars tight. By the time we left the city at Lattice Bridge Road, she switched from gripping the sidebars to my shoulders. We took the Old Mahabalipuram Road, which led us to the ECR.

'This is beautiful,' I said as the sea became visible.

'I told you.' Ananya planted a kiss on the back of my neck.

We halted at Fisherman's Cove where I met the catering manager briefly. Everything seemed under control for the Citibank event. We left the resort and came on the ECR again. An hour of driving later, we passed Mahabalipuram. It had stunning rock-cut temples next to the sea.

'Wow, these are amazing temples,' I said as the wind swept back my hair.

The ECR ended an hour after Mahabalipuram. The roads became narrower. We passed several little towns with long names and sprawling paddy fields. At a few places, I had to stop to make way for bullock carts, village schoolkids and goatherds. We reached Pondicherry around noon, and my first reaction was disappointment.

'This is it?' I asked as I reached the main chowk in town. It was like any other small town in India, dusty and noisy with Cola ad signs painted on uneven walls.

'The nice part is inside, the French quarter and the Aurobindo Ashram,' Ananya said as I negotiated a sharp bend in the road along with fifty other two-wheelers and four trucks.

The only French I saw was an underwear billboard with the brand Frenchie.

'Drop me here,' Ananya said as we passed Cuddalore road, where HLL has one of its factories.

I had three hours to kill in this Malgudi town as Ananya had an extended lunch meeting. We had agreed to meet at the L'Orient hotel at four for coffee.

I drove out of the factory compound and followed the signs to the Aurobindo Ashram on Rue de la Marine. The Ashram building resembled a quiet hostel by the sea. I came to the reception. More foreigners than Indians thronged the ashram lobby.

A forty-year-old Western woman in a sari and beaded necklace sat at the counter. 'What are you looking for?' she asked me.

Maybe, because I was in an ashram, or because the way she said it, I suspected deeper meaning in her question. I looked at her. She had blue eyes with wrinkles around them. 'I've come for the first time,' I confessed.

She gave me Ashram brochures. Another person came and bought meal tickets.

'Can I get lunch here?' I asked.

'Yes, at the Ashram Dining Hall,' she said and showed me the coupon booklet. I bought one for myself.

'Come, I'm going there,' she said, walking out with me from the reception. We walked along a lane adjacent to the ashram. The dining hall was half a kilometre away. She told me her name was Diana and that she came from Finland. A former lawyer, she now found more satisfaction as a volunteer at the ashram than helping Nokia secure patents.

'I work for Citibank,' I said. I had the urge to tell her about my dream of being a writer, but didn't think I knew her well enough.

'Are you a seeker or here as a tourist?' She handed me my coupon.

'Seeker?'

'Yes, if you wish to seek your path. Or if you seek answers to a specific problem.'

'Frankly, I came with a friend who had some work here. I wanted a day away from office.'

Diana laughed. We reached the dining hall and picked our stainless steel plates. We entered the eating area where everyone sat on the floor. Lunch was simple – organic brown rice, yellow daal and a carrot and peas subzi.

'OK, so I seek an answer. How do I get it?'

'Well, the answers are within us. People stay in the ashram for a few weeks to introspect, they attend satsang and ask questions of one of the gurus. How much time do you have?'

'I need to meet my girlfriend for coffee in two hours. Then head back to Chennai.'

Diana smiled and shook her head. 'That's a pretty stiff deadline to sort out life's unresolved answers.'

'Maybe I shouldn't even try then,' I said.

'Wait, see that gentleman there,' she said and pointed to a seventy-year-old man in white robes who sat two rows ahead of us. 'He is a guru. Maybe I can introduce you to him.'

'No, no, please don't,' I said.

'Why not? If he is busy, he will say no.'

'Pranam Guruji,' Diana said and touched his feet. I followed suit and he blessed us. 'Guruji, this is my friend. His name is,' Diana said and paused.

'Krish.'

'Yes, he has only two hours. But he wanted to seek answers to some problem,' Diana said.

'What do you have to do in two hours?' Guruji asked, his voice calm.

'He has to meet his girlfriend,' Diana said, excitedly stressing on the last word.

'And surely, the girlfriend is more important than the problem,' Guruji smiled.

'Actually, she is the problem,' I said.

Diana threw me a puzzled look.

'Not her. But my family, her family,' I said. 'It's OK. I know it is very little time.'

'Send him to my house in fifteen minutes,' Guruji said and left.

34

I hovered at the open door of Guruji's house before walking in.

'Come in, Krish,' Guruji said. He sat on a day-bed in his living room. I had thought I'd be roaming around French cafés in Pondicherry. I had no idea I'd end up in a guru's house. The tiny house had sparse wooden furniture.

'You may find it strange to be here. But I'd like to think we were destined to meet,' Guruji said.

'Do you read minds?' I wanted to know.

'I read people. Your nervousness is obvious. Sit,' he said and stroked his white beard.

I sat cross-legged on the floor, facing him.

'What is bothering you?'

'My girlfriend is Tamilian, I am Punjabi. Our families are against our marriage. I am doing whatever I can, but it is stressful.'

'Hmmm,' Guruji said. 'Close your eyes and speak whatever comes to mind.'

'I love her,' I said, 'and we make each other happy. But if our happiness makes so many people unhappy, is it the right thing to do?'

I rambled for some more time; Guruji didn't make any sound. Since my eyes were closed, I had no idea if he was even around anymore. 'She is my future,' I concluded.

'Is that all?'

'You are there?' I countered.

'Are you sure this is the only problem that is bothering you?'

'What do you mean?'

'There is a lot of . . . pain in you, unresolved issues. Before you build a future, you must fix the past.'

'What are you talking about?' I opened my eyes. Guruji's eyes were shut.

'Close your eyes,' Guruji said.

'I have,' I said and shut them again.

'What keeps you awake at night?'

I kept quiet.

'Do you take a long time to go to sleep?' he probed.

'Yes,' I said.

'What kept you awake lately?'

'Various things. There is work, which I am not exactly excited about. There's uncertainty about Ananya. There's my father.'

'What about your father?'

'It's complicated,' I said.

'And a heavy load, isn't it?'

I sighed deeply.

'Let it go,' Guruji said.

'I can't. I don't want to. I haven't even talked about it.'

'I'm listening,' Guruji said. He bent forward and placed his palm on my head. I felt a new lightness. I felt transported to another world. It was as if my soul had disowned my body.

'Guruji, don't make me do it,' I begged, not wishing to revisit the pain that awaited me.

'Go on, I'm listening,' Guruji said.

35

Three years ago

My father came home at midnight. I had waited for hours. I didn't have time, I had to talk to him tonight. He refused dinner with a wave of his hand and sat on the living room sofa to take off his shoes.

'Dad?' I said, my voice low. I wore shorts and a white T-shirt. The T-shirt had a tiny hole at the shoulder.

'What?' he turned to me. 'Is this what you wear at home?'

'These are my nightclothes,' I said.

'You don't have proper nightclothes?'

I changed the topic. 'Dad, I want to talk about something.'

'What?'

'I like a girl.'

'Obviously, you have time to waste,' he said.

'It's not like that. She is a nice girl. An IIT professor's daughter.'

'Oh, so now we know what you did at IIT.'

'I've graduated. I have a job. I'm preparing for MBA. What's the problem?'

'I don't have a problem. You wanted to talk,' he said, not looking at me.

'The girl's father is taking her abroad. They'll get her engaged to someone else.'

'Oh, so her father doesn't approve of it.'

'No.'

'Why?'

I looked at the floor. 'We had some issues with him, me and my friends.'

'What issues? Disciplinary issues?'

'Yes,' I said.

'Shocking. The son of an army officer has disciplinary issues. All the reputation I have built, you'll destroy it.'

'Those issues are history now.'

'Then why does he have a problem? Does your mother know about this?'

'Yes,' I said.

'Why hasn't she told me? Kavita!' my father screamed.

My mother came to the room, woken from a deep sleep. 'What happened?'

'Why was I not informed about this girl earlier?' my father screamed.

'He told me only a few weeks ago,' my mother said.

'And you hid it from me, bitch,' my father said.

'Don't talk to mom like that,' I said in reflex. I would have said more, but I needed him today.

My mother broke into tears. This wasn't going well at all.

'Dad, please. I want your cooperation. If you meet her father, he may reconsider.'

'Why should I meet anyone?' he said.

'Because I love her. And I don't want her to go away.'

'You are distracted, not in love.'

'Leave it, Krish, he won't listen. See how he talks to me. You don't know how I lived when you were in hostel.'

My father lunged menacingly towards my mother. He raised a hand to hit her. I pulled my mother behind me. 'Don't,' I said.

'Who do you think you are?' He slapped me hard on my right cheek. I sat down on the dining room chair.

'Leave us and go. Why do you even come back?' My mother folded her hands at him.

'Don't beg, mom,' I said, fighting a lump in my throat. My father had made fun of me earlier for crying. To him, only weak men cried.

'Look at his voice, like a girl's,' my father mocked. He gave me a disgusted glance and went to the bathroom to change.

'Go to sleep, son,' my mother said.

'He is sending her away next week,' I said.

'What girl have you involved yourself with? You are so young,' my mother said.

'I am not marrying her tomorrow.'

'Is she Punjabi?' my mother asked.

'No,' I said.

'What?' she said, shocked as if I'd suggested she wasn't human.

'Will you meet her father, once?'

My father came out of the bathroom. He had heard my last sentence.

'Don't you dare go anywhere, Kavita,' my father said, his eyes wild.

I stared back at him.

'Go to your room,' my father said.

I came back to my bed. I heard noises in my parent's room. I couldn't sleep. I woke up and came towards their room. I'd heard enough arguments of my parents throughout my life to care, but I placed my ear at the door, anyway.

'He is growing up,' my mother said.

'With all the wrong values. What does he know about girls? He is my son, he is from IIT, see what deal I get for him at the right time.'

There it was, for all my father's principles, I was his trophy to be sold in the market to the highest bidder.

'You are responsible for bringing him up like this,' my father screamed at my mother. I heard the sound of a glass being smashed against the wall.

'What have I done? I didn't even know about this girl. . . .'

Slap . . . slap . . . my father interrupted my mother. I banged the door open as I heard a few more slaps. I saw my mother's hand covering her face. A piece of glass had cut her forearm.

My father turned to me. 'Don't you have any manners? Can't you knock?'

'You don't teach me manners,' I said.

'Go away,' he said.

I shook my head. I saw the tears on my mother's face. My face burned with rage. She had lived with this for twenty-five years. I did know why – to bring me up; I didn't know how she did it.

My father lifted his hand to hit me. Automatically, I grabbed his wrist tight.

'Oh, now you are going to raise your hand against your own father,' he said.

I twisted his arm.

'Leave him, he won't change,' my mother panted.

I shook my head at her, my eyes staring right into his. I slapped his face once, twice, then I rolled my hand into a fist and punched his face.

My father went into a state of shock, he couldn't fight back. He didn't expect this; all my childhood I'd merely suffered his dominance. Today, it wasn't just about the broken glass. It wasn't only that the girl I loved would be gone. It was a reaction to two decades of abuse. Or that's how I defended it to myself. For how else do you justify hitting your own father? At that moment I couldn't stop. I punched his head until he collapsed on the floor. I couldn't remember the last time I revelled in violence like this. I was a studious child who stayed with his books all his life. Today, I was lucky there wasn't a gun at home.

The insanity passed after five minutes. My father didn't make eye contact with me. He sat on the floor, and massaged the arm I had twisted. He stared at my mother, with a 'see, I told you' expression.

My mother sat on the bed, fighting back her emotions. We looked at each other. We were a family, but pretty much as screwed up as they come. I took a broom and swept the broken glass into a newspaper sheet. I looked at my father and vowed never to speak to him again. I picked up the newspaper with the glass pieces and left the room.

36

'That's it, Guruji,' I said, the tears now dry on my face. 'I've never shared so much with anyone.'

The sound of the sea could be heard, the waves asymmetrical to my tumultuous thoughts.

'Open your eyes,' Guruji said.

I lifted my eyelids slowly.

'Come, we will go to the balcony behind,' Guruji said.

I followed him to a terrace in the rear of the house. The sea breeze felt cool even in the hot sun. I sat on one of the two stools kept outside. He went inside and came back with two glasses and a book.

'It's coconut water. And this is the Gita. You've heard about the Gita?'

'Yes,' I said, 'sort of.' I took a sip of the coconut water.

'What have you heard?'

'Like it is the ultimate book. It has all of life's wisdom. You have to work and not worry about the reward. Right?'

'Have you read it?'

'Parts of it. It's nice, but a little. . . .'

'Boring?'

'Actually, no, not boring. Hard to follow and apply everything.'

'I'll give you just one word to apply in your life.'

'What?'

'Forgiveness.'

'Meaning? You want me to forgive my father? I can't.'

'Why not?'

'Because what he did was so wrong. He has ruined my mother's life. He has never loved me.'

'I am not saying he did the right thing. I am asking you to forgive him.'

'Why?'

'For you. Forgiving doesn't make the person who hurt you feel better, it makes *you* feel better.'

I pondered over his words.

'Close your eyes again,' Guruji said. 'Imagine you have bags on your head. They are bags of anger, pain and loss. How do they feel?'

'Heavy,' I sighed.

'Remove them from your head one by one,' Guruji said. 'Imagine you are wearing a thick cloak that is wearing you down. Pardon the hurt others have caused you. What they did is past. What is bothering you today are your current feelings that come from this load. Let it go.'

Strange as Guruji's metaphors were, I felt compelled to obey the imagery in my mind. My head felt lighter.

'And surrender to God,' he went on. 'You don't control anything or anyone.'

'I don't understand,' I said.

'Do you control your life? Your life depends on so many internal organs functioning right. You have no control on them. If your lungs don't cooperate, if your kidneys fail, if your heart stops, it is all over. You'll drop dead now. God has chosen to give you the gift of life, surrender to him.'

He kept me in meditation for the next few minutes.

'And now, you are free to go,' Guruji smiled.

I opened my eyes. The sharp afternoon sun shone on Guruji's face. He went inside and brought a small cup with grey ash. He dipped his index finger in the ash and marked my forehead.

'Thank you,' I said as he blessed me with his hand on my head.

'You are welcome,' he said. 'Anything else I can help you with?'

'Yes, which way is Hotel L'Orient?'

'Oh that,' Guruji laughed, 'It is on Rue Romain Rolland. One kilometre from here.'

I reached L'Orient at four. Ananya was waiting at the entrance. The hotel is a renovated heritage building and was originally the Education Department Office when the French had colonised Pondicherry. Now a ten-room boutique property, it had a small restaurant in the indoor open patio. We ordered coffee and a slice of ginger cake with custard sauce.

'Isn't this place lovely?' Ananya breathed in deeply.

I nodded, still deep in thought.

'So, tell me, what did you do? And what's with the tilak on your forehead?'

'I hit my father.'

'What?'

'A long time ago. Remember, how I would always avoid talking about my father in campus?'

'Yes, and I never pushed after that,' she said. 'But what are you saying?'

I repeated the story of that night.

She looked at me, awestruck

'Oh dear, I didn't know your parents were like this.'

'I never told you. It's fine.'

'Are you OK?' she said and moved her hand forward to hold me.

'Yes, I am fine. And I met a Guruji, who gave me good advice.'

'What? Who Guruji, what advice?' Ananya said.

'I don't know the Guruji. It doesn't matter. Sometimes in life you just meet someone or hear something that nudges you on the right path. And that becomes the best advice. It could just be a bit of common sense said in a way that resonates with something in you. It's nothing new, but because it connects with you it holds meaning for you.'

I explained with such intensity, Ananya became concerned.

'Are you OK, baby? I shouldn't have left you.'

'I'm fine. I'm glad I had time. I feel better.'

'I love you,' she said, brushing floppy hair off my face.

'I love you, too,' I said and clasped her hand tight.

Our order arrived, she cut the cake in two pieces and passed my half to me. I wanted to change the topic. She read my mind.

'So, tell me about this Citibank event. There is a concert?'

'Yes,' I said, 'only for clients though.'

'Do I get to come?'

'Of course, I'll get passes for your family.'

'Who is performing?'

'S.P. Balasubramanium, Hariharan and. . . .' I paused.

'Wow, those are big names. Who else?'

'Some new singer.'

'Cool, I'm sure mom and dad will love to come.'

I nodded. I spoke after a few more sips of coffee. 'I've tried enough, Ananya. I want to go back.'

I told her about my conversation with my mother about transferring back to Delhi.

'What do you mean?' she said, wiping my milk moustache.

'I can't work in Chennai forever. I'll give it a few more weeks, and then I'll tell your parents to take a call on me.'

'Weeks? What if they say no?'

'Then we'll see. I've surrendered everything to God anyway.'

'What?'

'Nothing, let's go. I want to hit the road while there's still light.' I picked up my helmet.

37

'Aunty, sorry to bother you, but the concert is next week,' I said over the phone.

I had called Ananya's mother from my office in the afternoon. I had the design of the newspaper ad in my hand.

Citibank Priority Banking is pleased to invite its clients
To an enchanting musical evening at Fisherman's Cove
Featuring maestros:
S.P. Balasubramanium
Hariharan
And new talent, Radha
The concert will be followed by dinner.
By invitation only.
(For passes, contact your customer rep or any of the branches.)
Note: New account holders who open an account before the concert will also get invites.

I hated the last line as it was too blatant. However, Bala insisted on it.

'Hello, aunty? You there?' I said.

'What have you trapped me in?' Ananya's mother wailed.

'You are practising, right?'

'Yes, but. . . .'

'But what? Have you done any *Kaho Na Pyaar Hai* songs? Those are hot,' I said.

'Yes, I have. Film songs are easy. It is . . . my confidence.'

'You'll be fine. I am sending the ad to the newspaper today. Your name is in it, without surname as you insisted. It will come on Sunday, the day of the concert.'

'Don't, don't put my name. What if I decide not to come?' she asked with a touch of panic.

'It's fine. There are plenty of Radhas in Chennai. Nobody will know which one did not show up,' I said.

'I'll let you down,' she said.

'You won't,' I said.

'Until when can you remove my name from the ad?'

'Saturday. Don't think like that, please,' I said.

'OK, still wanted to check,' she said.

'Fine, and practice the *Ek Pal Ka Jeena* song. It is number one on the charts,' I said.

'I said take my name out,' Ananya's mother called me on Sunday morning at 6 a.m.

'You saw the ad already?' I rubbed my eyes. I picked up *The Hindu* from under the chummery entrance door. I opened *Metroplus*, the Sunday supplement.

'Yes,' she whispered. 'What is this?'

She had called when uncle had gone for a bath. Ananya hadn't woken up and Manju huddled in his room with his best friends – Physics, Chemistry and Maths.

'I couldn't do it,' I said, and made up a story. 'The newspaper told me *Metroplus* goes to press two days before. Only the main paper can be changed until the night before.'

'So, what are we going to do now?'

She had called me the previous morning to get her name removed. However, I never called the newspaper to change the ad wordings.

'Nothing, we'll just say Radha fell ill,' I said.

She kept silent. 'Won't it make you look bad?' she enquired after a pause.

'Yeah, won't be the first time though. I'll manage. Anyway, all of you will come for the concert, right?' I said.

'OK listen, if I do have to perform, where and when do I have to report?'

My heart started to beat fast. She was going to do it. 'Aunty, everything is well organised. We have a room next to the concert garden that will act as the greenroom. Come there three hours early, by four. OK?'

'Yes,' she said.

'Thanks, aunty,' I said.

'I should thank you. I haven't told anyone at home yet.'

'Good, make an excuse and leave the house. See you.'

38

'Which one should I wear?' Ananya's mother asked, sitting on the king-size bed of the cottage we had converted into a greenroom. The make-up artists, sound engineers and the staff of Hariharan and S.P. had already arrived. The main singers would come only at the last minute. However, Radha had come early and laid out three Kanjeevaram silk saris for me to choose from.

'They are all beautiful,' I said.

The first was purple and gold, the second yellow and gold and the third orange and gold.

'Touch-up, madam?' the make-up man came towards Ananya's mother.

'I should leave the room,' I said. Even though we had half a dozen people around, I felt awkward watching my potential mother-in-law applying mascara.

'I'm so tense, I can't choose,' she said, wiping sweat off her forehead.

The make-up man applied foundation on Ananya's mother's cheeks. I tried not to look.

'Take the orange, nice and bright.'

'That's my wedding sari. I've hardly worn it since that day.'

'Tonight's quite special, too.'

'How's the purple?'

'That's beautiful, too,' I said.

The make-up man sprayed water on her forehead and wiped it.

'I'll be outside. I'll see you on stage.'

She closed her eyes and folded her hands to pray.

I came outside and checked the food arrangements. I called Ananya at six to make sure they left on time.

'You are going to kill me,' Ananya said.

'Why?' I said.

'Mom is not coming.'

'Why?' I said, careful to sound upset.

'She said my grandmother fell ill in Thirukudayur. She left after lunch.'

'Where is Thirukudayur?'

'Six hours from Chennai. She won't be able to make it.'

'What about you guys?'

'We are almost ready. I wanted to wear my mom's nice orange Kanjeevaram sari but I can't find it. I hope she has not lost it. She wouldn't take it with her, hardly the occasion.'

'Leave soon, Ananya, I can't promise good seats otherwise,' I said.

'OK, OK, bye,' she said and hung up.

Bala arrived at 6.30 with Anil Mathur, the country manager. Anil had flown down from Mumbai. Bala had ensured that a Mercedes brought Anil straight to the venue. Bala tailed him like a Tamil villain's sidekick, showing him the arrangements and taking credit for the entire event.

'And this is the bar. And see the Citibank banner behind. I put a big ad in *The Hindu* today. Number one newspaper here,' Bala said.

I greeted Bala. He ignored me and continued to walk.

'Hey, you are the Internet fiasco guy,' Anil noticed me.

'Good evening, sir,' I said. I had become the poster boy for loserdom in the bank.

'Aren't you the only Punjabi stuck here?' he laughed. 'I think that's enough punishment. No, Bala?'

Bala guffawed, even though the joke was on him, rather his city.

'Looking to move back?' the country manager said.

'I'll talk to you about it, sir,' I said.

'You let me know first,' Bala finally acknowledged me. 'I'll help him, sir.'

The country manager patted my shoulder and walked away.

Ananya arrived with her father and brother at 7.15. 'Are we late?' she asked breathlessly. She wore a peach chiffon sari with a skinny silver border. She had accessorised with a silver necklace and matching earrings.

'Yes, but the concert hasn't started yet. Come,' I said. I led them to one of the several round tables laid out in the garden. I chose one near the stage.

'Food is that side, and uncle, the bar is that way,' I said.

'I don't drink,' uncle said, looking at Ananya.

'Sure,' I said.

Clients filled each of the ten seats on all eighteen tables. One or two bank agents sat at every table with their clients. I had made Ananya's family sit on the staff table, comprising primarily of junior Chennai Citibankers. Bala and the country manager had a separate table with the biggest clients, those with assets of five crore or more. I felt sorry for these clients. Frankly, I'd rather not be rich than face the agony of having dinner with senior bankers.

The lights dimmed at 7.30. Conversations stopped at the round tables as Bala came on stage. He wore a shiny cream silk shirt under his suit and resembled a pimp in training.

'Welcome everyone, what a delightful evening! I am Bala, regional manager for the Priority Banking Group,' he said and wiped the sweat off his face.

'Your boss?' Ananya whispered to me.

I nodded.

'What's with the shirt?'

'Shsh,' I said. Manju and Ananya's father listened to Bala with full attention.

'I want to welcome someone special,' Bala said.

The crowd cheered as they expected Hariharan or S.P. to take the stage.

'Please welcome Mr Anil Mathur, country manager and MD, Citibank India,'

The crowd let out a collective sigh of disappointment.

Anil came on stage and realised that no one cared about him. He attempted a joke. 'Hello everyone, who would have thought some of our biggest clients will come from the land of dosas and idlis?'

The crowd fell so silent, you could hear the waves on the adjacent beach. Ananya looked at me shocked. I shrugged my shoulders. I had no control over this.

Anil realised the joke didn't work and attempted a rescue. 'You see in Bombay, idli and dosa are seen as simple snacks,' Anil said.

'He's digging himself in deeper,' Ananya said.

'Yes, luckily he has only five minutes.'

Anil realised his sense of humour only worked with people who worked under him. He switched to what bankers do best, present boring powerpoint slides with growing bar charts.

'So you see, when we came to Chennai, we started with a tiny footprint and now we are a giant. From a mini idli we have become a paper dosa,' Anil said, gesturing with his hands to show the relative sizes of the two dishes.

'Please, someone stop him,' Ananya groaned.

'We can't. He is the boss,' I said.

Anil finished his speech and the staff applauded hard. The clients waited in pain as two clueless but confident research analysts spoke about global corporate outlook for the next ten years.

'If we assume a seven percent GDP growth rate, the picture is like this,' the analyst said. Nobody questioned how the seven percent assumption came about, but after that, the analyst had enough charts to show what happens if the growth rate is indeed seven percent.

We ended the presentations at 8.30. People started to get restless as Bala came on stage again. 'Not another banker,' you could almost hear them think.

'And now, for the music concert we have a separate MC, Miss T.S. Smitha,' Bala said.

The crowd applauded as the extra busty Smitha came on the stage. She wore a low-cut blouse, a tad too deep for Citibank sensibilities.

'Welcome, ladies and gentlemen,' Smitha said, holding the mike in her hand. 'Are you having a good time?'

Nobody responded.

'What is she wearing?' Ananya said. Our whole table heard and sniggered.

'It is a little provocative, I admit,' I said.

'Her cleavage is so big, she can use it to hold the mike. Hands-free,' Ananya whispered to me.

'Shut up, Ananya,' I said, suppressing a smile.

'We have three talented singers tonight,' Smitha said. My heart beat fast. 'We are all, of course, waiting for the maestros. But the first singer is the new, very talented, Radha. Please welcome her on stage.'

The crowd applauded as I craned my neck to see the stage. Ananya's mother arrived on stage in the orange sari.

'It's mom,' Manju noticed first as he stood up.

39

'What?' Ananya's father stood up as well.

Ananya looked at the stage and then me in quick succession. 'Krish, what is. . . .'

'Shsh, pay attention,' I placed a finger on my lips.

Radha took the mike.

'Mom!' Manju screamed.

Ananya's mother looked towards us and smiled.

'What are you going to sing for us first, Radha?' Smitha asked coyly.

'*Ek pal ka jeena* from *Kaho Na Pyaar Hai*,' Ananya's mother answered shyly.

The crowd roared and clapped as introductory music began for the song.

Radha aunty sang well; I noticed several clients tap their feet or nod their heads to the music. Tamilians can tell good singers from bad, like Punjabis can judge butter chicken in a jiffy. Nobody in the audience looked disapproving.

'How did Radha come here?' Ananya's father spoke after recovering from the shock.

'Obviously, Krish arranged it, dad. Can't you guess?' Ananya said.

'She never told me,' uncle said. But his eyes glinted with pride.

'Mom is singing so well,' Ananya said to Manju, who nodded and reached out for the various snacks ferried by waiters.

Ananya bent forward and kissed me on my cheek. Her father didn't notice, as his eyes were transfixed on stage. A few agents did, and I smiled in embarrassment.

'Ananya, this is an office event,' I whispered.

'Of course, that's why my mother is on stage,' she said as she played footsie with me.

Her mother switched to the latest Tamil hit number from Rajni's movie. The crowd's excitement rose further. The song was a slow ballad, and required a lot of voice modulation. Claps ran through the crowd as Ananya's mother manoeuvred a tough range of notes.

'Lovely, beautiful!' Ananya's father said in reflex as Ananya's mother switched three octaves in one line.

Ananya's mother sang four more songs to finish her act. Each song ended with enthusiastic applause.

Smitha came on stage again.

'That was wonderful, Radha. And before you leave, I'd like to invite the next singer, Mr S.P. Balasubramanium, who has a few words to say about you.'

The crowd rose to its feet and applauded as one of South India's greatest singers took the stage. Radha aunty folded her hands and bowed to him.

S.P. said, 'Good evening, Chennai, and thank you, Citibank. Before I begin, I want to praise Radha for her wonderful singing. The songs were popular, but I can see she has a strong classical base. Do you sing often, Radha?'

'No, first time like this.'

'Well, you should sing more. Shouldn't she, Chennai?'

Everyone banged their tables in support. Ananya's mother bowed to everyone. As she straightened, her eyes were filled with tears.

'So, you will?' S.P. said as he pointed the mike to Radha.

'Yes, I will. Also, sir, I want to say that today is the happiest day of my life. I've shared the stage with you.'

The crowd clapped. Radha aunty fought back her tears as she left the dais.

'And I thought her happiest day was the day I was born,' Ananya muttered as she continued to clap.

The evening progressed with S.P. and Hariharan casting their spell on the crowd. For everyone else, the main act had just begun. For me and Ananya's family, the main act was over.

Ananya's mother joined us at the table after ten minutes.

'You were wonderful,' a lady at the next table said to Ananya's mother.

Ananya's father exchanged shy glances with his wife. S.P. sang *Tere mere beech mein* from *Ek Duje Ke Liye*. I looked at Ananya. Our struggle resembled that film's story. I only hoped our end wouldn't resemble that movie's climax.

An hour into the concert, Bala came to my table.

'Krish, come with me. I want you to meet Mr Muruguppa, famous jeweller,' Bala said.

'What?' I said.

'Come, he wants to open a ten-crore account. Give him some bull on Citi. I have to drop Anil at the airport.'

'Sir, I have guests,' I said as Ananya noticed my dilemma.

'It's fine, we will manage. Dinner's over there, right?' Ananya said.

'Oh, so she is the one?' Bala said and turned to Ananya. 'Tamil teria?'

'Let's go, Bala,' I said.

I met Mr Muruguppa, a fat, jovial, fifty-year-old.

'Punjabi? Tamil ille?' he said and gave me his card.

'No. So you are the jewellery king?'

'What king? Emperor! We are the biggest in Chennai.'

'Sir, regarding your account,' I said as I noticed Ananya's family from a distance. They laughed together over dinner. Several people came up to congratulate Ananya's mother. The time to strike was not far way.

'Mr Muruguppa, actually, I may need some jewellery myself,' I said as I led him to the dinner table.

40

'Oh, trust me, she is on a different planet since that day. No need for dinner to thank her,' Ananya said over the phone.

We were in our respective offices. I had just invited Ananya's family for dinner.

'But we didn't even pay her for the concert. That's the least I can do,' I said.

'You have done a lot,' Ananya said.

'Trust me, the dinner is important,' I said.

'Really? What's up?'

'You'll find out next Friday at Raintree. See you all at eight,' I said.

The Raintree restaurant is located in the Taj Connemara hotel, on Binny Road off Anna Salai. The outdoor restaurant is snug under a canopy of trees of the same name. Fairylights adorn the branches of the trees and candles light up the tables. Apart from Amethyst, it is the one other oasis in the city.

I sat with Ananya's family at one of the outdoor tables, my trouser pockets heavy.

'This is stunning,' Ananya said as she looked up at the little lights. She wore a white fitted dress with sequins that reflected in the semi-darkness.

'You've never come here before?' I said.

'No we haven't. Right, dad?'

Uncle shook his head even as he admired the foliage right above us. Uniformed waiters served us a welcome drink of coconut water with fresh mint. They left the menu cards on our table. The restaurant specialises in Chettinad food, named after a region south of Tamil Nadu. The cuisine is known for its intense spices and flavours, along with a large range of non-vegetarian preparations.

'Sir, for cocktails, I'd recommend Kothamalli Mary,' the waiter said.

'Kotha-what?' I asked.

'It is like a Bloody Mary, sir, tomato juice and vodka, but with Chettinad spices.'

I looked at uncle. He looked reluctant to nod for alcohol in front of his wife.

'I want one,' Ananya said.

Ananya's mother gave her a sharp look.

'C'mon, just one cocktail,' Ananya said.

I opened the menu. I couldn't pronounce the tongue-twister names of the dishes. Specials included kuruvapillai yera and kozhi melagu Chettinad. I didn't bother reading the rest.

'You know this food better, please order,' I said.

Ananya's parents looked at the menu several times.

'It's too expensive,' Ananya's mother said.

'It's fine,' I said. 'Ananya, please.'

Ananya took the menu and ordered for everyone. We ordered kozhakattai, masala paniyaram, adikoozh, kandharappam, seeyam and athirasam. Of course, I had no clue what went into those dishes; I figured at least one of them would be edible. The waiter also suggested we order idiyaappam, rice noodles bunched up like a bird's nest.

'How is the IIT preparation, Manju?' I asked after the waiter left.

'Good, I came tenth in the Mylapore mock IIT test,' Manju said.

I nodded. 'So, any more singing offers?' I said to aunty.

Aunty smiled. 'Don't embarrass me. But I did find another guruji who has a modern approach to Carnatic music.'

I turned to Ananya's dad. 'How's the bank, uncle?'

'Good, your presentation is still being talked about.'

The food arrived; spicy, tangy and delicious.

'This is great,' I said as I had the masala paniyaram, a tastier cousin of the idli and shaped like a ball.

The Raintree staff brought a trolley with ten chutneys to choose from.

'I swear, Delhi needs to taste this. We haven't gone past the paneer masala dosa yet,' I said as I took a spoonful of the tomato tamarind curry with idiyappams.

'You like it? I can make it at home,' Ananya's mother said.

I realised that the right moment was near. Maybe at dessert, I told myself. We scanned the dessert menu. Ananya's father chose coconut ice-cream. The deep love for this fruit among South Indians is inexplicable. The ice-cream arrived in an actual green coconut shell.

'Superb,' Ananya's father said, a signal I took as *ready, get-set, go.*

'I want to talk about something important,' I said.

Ananya's father looked up from his ice-cream.

'If it is OK?' I amended.

Uncle nodded. Ananya's mother looked at Ananya and me.

'Manju, you too,' I said. He kept his face so close to the ice-cream bowl, his spectacles were smeared.

I had everyone's attention. 'Hi,' I cleared my throat. 'Uncle, aunty, Manju, I came here six months ago. It is no secret why I chose Chennai as my first posting. However, I cannot stay here forever. I met Ananya almost three years ago, and apart from our first fight, I've loved her every day since that day.'

Ananya took my hand in hers from under the table.

'And we thought our love is enough reason for us to get married. We thought our parents will meet at the convocation and things will be smooth. Well, we were wrong.'

The waiter came to collect the ice-cream plates. I told him to come five minutes later.

'We could have run away. We could have forced our decision on you. However, Ananya told me she had this dream of both sets of parents smiling on our wedding day. And so, I want to see if we can do that. Also, I didn't think we had done anything wrong that we had to run away.'

Ananya's parents kept a deadly silence. Either they were listening carefully or the ice-cream had been too cold.

'And ever since I came to Chennai, I have tried to be accepted by you. I don't expect you to love me like you do Harish, but at least you can accept me.'

Ananya's mother wanted to talk. I signalled her to wait. 'And while you may not love me, I don't want you to merely tolerate me either. Somewhere in the middle lies the acceptance I am talking about.' I slid my right hand inside my trouser pocket and collected the four mini boxes with my fingers.

'Keeping all that in mind, considering your daughter's happiness and taking a view of what you know of me,' I said and paused to breathe. I took out the four little red boxes and kept them on the table. The boxes said 'Muruguppa Jewellers' on top. I opened the four boxes. Each had a gold ring. I stood up from my chair and kneeled on the floor.

'I, Krish Malhotra, would like to propose to all of you. Will all of you marry me?' I said and held the four boxes in my palm.

Ananya's parents looked at her and me in quick succession. Manju's mouth was open, the coconut ice-cream very visible inside.

Ananya's father gestured to Ananya on what to do.

'After you, mom and dad,' Ananya said, 'and Manju, you too.'

Manju picked up his box. 'Nice, real gold?' he asked.

I nodded.

'Argentum, atomic number seventy-nine,' Manju said as he held the ring in his hand.

'Uncle?' I prompted. My knees had started to hurt on the concrete floor.

'If you promise to take care of my daughter,' Ananya's father said, 'then it is a yes from me.' He bent forward and picked up his box.

Ananya hugged her father. 'Thanks, dad,' she said, 'I love you.'

Ananya's father blessed her with a hand on her head.

Ananya's mother said, 'It is not that we don't like you. But our communities. . . .'

'Mom, c'mon,' Ananya interrupted her.

Ananya's mother took a minute to respond. 'I know he will take care of you. But will Krish's parents treat my daughter with respect?'

'We'll work on that, too,' I said, aware another challenge awaited me in Delhi. 'If they do, then?'

'Then it is a yes from me,' Ananya's mother said.

'Yay!' Ananya cheered. Aunty took her ring and Ananya planted a kiss on her mother's forehead.

'Akka, you haven't picked yours,' Manju said as the mother-daughter affection continued. When they separated, both had tears in their eyes.

'Oh, of course, where is it?' Ananya picked up her ring.

I came back to my seat.

'Sir, did you enjoy your meal?' the waiter said as he cleared the plates.

'You bet I did,' I said, tipping him more than the bill that night.

41

'I will miss you,' Bala said as he handed me my transfer papers in his office.

'I wish I could say the same,' I said. Bala's chin dropped. 'I am kidding, cheer up. I won't be there to blackmail you anymore,' I said.

Bala had agreed to make my case with Anil Mathur for the same reason. My transfer to Delhi took two months to execute. I wanted to be home soon. After all, I had finished my Chennai job. Of course, we had a few more battles to win. Ananya would have to deal with the full force of Punjabiness. However, life is best dealt with one disaster at a time.

Operation Delhi would have to be quick. Ananya convinced her bosses to send her to Delhi for a week. After all, every HLL manager must have North India exposure, Ananya had argued.

Ananya's parents came to drop us at the airport. Ananya's mother worried about Delhi, given its status as the worldwide capital of eve-teasing.

'Mom, the HLL guest-house is safe. I won't be out much,' Ananya said.

Ananya's dad had his own concerns. 'Remember, we have said yes. But you are not married yet. Don't embarrass us,' uncle said to me as he bid us goodbye.

'Of course, uncle,' I said, trying to figure out what he meant. No sex, I guess.

Ananya and I went inside the terminal. She grabbed my arm as her parents melted out of sight. The flight took off. I brought out my notebook to explain the next stage to Ananya – Operation Delhi.

'So, I have to agree with your mom, whatever she says. Like whatever,' Ananya said, twenty minutes into the flight and thirty thousand feet high in the sky.

The plane passed through an area of turbulence.

'Yes, never disagree,' I said, tightening my seat-belt, 'and the timing of your trip could not be better. My cousin sister Minti is getting married next week. You'll come to the wedding, meet everyone, bingo, done.'

Ananya lifted the armrest to hold my arm tight. 'I'm sure I'll be fine with you.'

'See, you have to win over my mother. My father won't agree ever, so he is not part of the equation. Make mom happy, OK?'

'Lower the armrest, it is not safe,' the flight attendant said in a strict voice as she passed the aisle.

When you are part of a couple, you don't realise how cheesy your affections are to the outside world.

'Who does she think she is?' Ananya huffed.

'My mother?'

'No, the airhostess. What's with the thick red lipstick? Is she a flight attendant or an item girl?'

I don't know why women love commenting on other women's appearances. I never noticed the bald man next to me, who snored through the flight.

'Focus, Ananya. You are dealing with a Punjabi mother-in-law here. You have never seen anything like this,' I said.

'Can't wait,' Ananya said, sarcasm dripping from her mouth like the airhostess's lipstick.

Act 4:
Delhi reloaded

42

'Let go of my elbow,' I said.

'Why?' Ananya said.

'I see my mother.'

Mother waited at the arrivals area. She stood among ten thousand drivers holding placards with every Punjabi name possible. There were no more Venkats and Ramaswamis, only Aroras and Khannas.

When people land at Chennai airport, they exchange smiles and proceed gently to the car park. At Delhi, there is a traffic jam of people trying to hug each other to death. My mother hugged me tight, and even though it was over the top, I liked it. No one had hugged me like that in Chennai for the last six months (apart from Ananya, of course, but that's a different category of affection). We walked towards the auto stand. Ananya greeted my mother but it went unnoticed.

'You ate?' my mother asked me the most important question.

I nodded.

'What did they serve?' I noticed she was ignoring Ananya completely.

'Paneer masala and rice,' I said. 'Mom, you've met Ananya, remember?'

My mother gave Ananya a fake smile and turned back to me. 'No rotis?'

'Mom, Ananya has a one-week stint in her Delhi office.'

'Where will she stay?' my mother said, her voice concerned.

'At the company guest-house,' Ananya said.

'Yes, but she only joins them day after, on Monday. I thought it will be a good idea if she came home for the weekend.'

'Whose home?' my mother asked, aghast.

'Our home,' I said. I removed my bags from the trolley at the auto stand.

My mother turned silent. I paid the money at the pre-paid stand.

We fit ourselves and our bags tight into the auto. I sat in the middle, with Ananya on my right and my mother on the left.

'All set for Minti's wedding?' I said.

'What a boy Minti is going to marry!' my mother said.

'Really? Is he good?' I said.

'Oh yes, so good-looking. White as milk,' my mother said, 'and guess the budget of the wedding?'

I shrugged.

'Rajji mama is spending five lakh on the parties alone. Plus they have a big surprise gift for the boy for the sagan.'

'What's the boy's name?' I said.

Ananya didn't participate in the conversation. She turned her face to the scenery outside. Her hair blew in the breeze and a few strands caressed my face.

'I forget his real name, but everybody calls him Duke.'

'Duke? Like British royalty duke?' I said.

'Yes, he is an engineer from a donation college. Now he works in Escorts Software. And his parents are so nice,' my mother said. 'Every occasion they have met your mama-ji, they bring something for me. They've already given me three saris.'

'Amazing,' I said.

'You should see how they give respect. The boy touches my feet every time he meets me.'

I nodded. I wanted to end the topic. But my mother was in full form. 'I asked Rajji mama why he is spending so much. You know what he said?'

'What?' I said.

'He said "didi, where do you get good boys these days?" So, I said, if Duke is getting this, what will Krish get?'

I kept quiet. My mother continued anyway. 'He said if Duke's budget is five lakh, yours should be ten lakh, gifts separate.'

'Thanks for pricing me,' I said.

'I am just saying. . . .' my mother said.

We remained silent for the next five minutes. My mother shifted in her seat due to lack of space.

'You could have booked a car. I would have paid,' I said.

'I didn't know you'll bring extra baggage from Chennai,' my mother said.

I showed Ananya the guest-room. She kept quiet as she took out fresh clothes to take into the bathroom.

'Hey, I'm sorry about my mother. She's all talk. Good at heart.'

'Even murderers are good at heart. I thought you had told her about my coming.'

'I wanted to give her a surprise,' I said.

'Fuck off,' Ananya said as she pushed me out of the room.

My father had gone for a business meeting. Ever since he left the army, he had tried different ventures. These included a property dealership, a security agency and a freight forwarding agency. None of them worked. According to him, unscrupulous partners or corrupt officials had led to their failure. According to me, it was his short temper and inability to come out of his army officer mode. When you are used to a hundred people saluting you every day, it is difficult to suck up to uneducated builders to allow you to sell their house. However, my father kept jumping from one disaster to the next, which kept him out of the house most of the times. Some even said he had a mistress somewhere, though I doubt another woman could survive him.

Ananya hadn't left her room ever since she came. My mother went for her evening stroll at 6 p.m.

'What are you doing inside? Come out, mom's gone for a walk.'

She opened the door, her face still upset.

'Should we make love?' I winked at her.

'Don't test your luck, Mr Malhotra, I shall turn violent.' She pushed me aside and came to the living room. She switched on the TV.

'What's with this attitude, Ananya? You are supposed to win my folks over,' I said.

'You can win over normal people. Not rude, insensitive people who insult guests,' she said.

'So you will stay inside that room and sulk?' I switched the TV off.

'I don't know what to do,' she said.

'If you listen to me, you will be able to navigate her.'

'I am all ears,' she said dryly.

'Dinner,' I said.

'Dinner what? Do you guys talk about anything but food? What was that? She asked what they served us on the plane? Like the first thing when you landed.'

I opened the fridge and took out two Frootis. I gave her one.

'She is going to come back from her walk and prepare dinner. Offer to help her, it is a good start.'

'Help her?' She poked a straw into the Frooti with more force than necessary.

'You know, make a dish or two. Or if you want to bowl her over, make the dinner tonight.'

'What? Are you crazy, I've never made full dinner.'

'Really?' I slurped noisily at my drink.

'Don't "really" me. Did you ever learn to cook?'

'No, but I studied all the time.'

'I went to IIMA, too.'

'Yeah but,' I said and paused.

'Yeah but, what? I am a girl, so tough luck, baby. There's the kitchen,' she said and tossed the Frooti carton on the table.

'Ananya, I am suggesting ways to win over my mother. You said you will do whatever it takes.'

'Fine, can I have another Frooti? I am famished.'

I gave Ananya another tetrapack. The doorbell rang. Ananya stood up to go to her room.

'Stay,' I said as I opened the door.

43

My mother came back with two plastic bags full of vegetables. I helped her carry them into the kitchen. She opened the fridge to keep the vegetables inside.

'Who had the Frootis?' my mother said.

'I had one. And Ananya also.'

'Three Frootis are missing. She had two?' she said.

I kept quiet.

We came to the living room. My mother brought a giant cauliflower, a plate and a knife with her. She started cutting little florets with the knife, using her thumb as a base.

'Aunty, can I help?' Ananya said.

'With?' my mother said.

'With dinner,' Ananya said.

'Yeah, mom, why don't you let Ananya make dinner today?' I suggested with a hearty smile.

Ananya glared at me. To help is one thing, to prepare a whole meal another. Still, if Ananya had to make an impression, she had to more than wash the vegetables.

My mother looked at Ananya.

'Sure, aunty, why not? It will be fun,' Ananya said.

Mom shrugged and passed the plate to Ananya. 'Krish likes gobi aloo. I thought we will also make black daal, bhindi, raita and salad. Nothing much, simple dinner.

'Mom,' I said, to stop her from increasing the menu.

'The dry atta is in the drum below the gas stove. Knead some for the rotis,' my mother said. 'Yes, Krish?'

'Nothing. You want to cook together so it is faster?' I said.

'She can make it if she wants to. I am not that hungry. Let it take time,' my mother said and switched on the TV.

Ananya cradled the cauliflower in her lap like a newborn child. She couldn't cut it like a pro, with the knife and thumb action. She cut florets one at a time, using the knife like a saw.

My mother sniggered. I gave her a dirty look. 'I have a headache. I'll rest in my room. Call me when dinner is ready,' my mother said and left.

'Ananya, you want help?' I said.

'Leave me alone,' Ananya said, her gaze deep into the cauliflower.

'Use your thumb, like this,' I said and mocked the action with my hand.

Ananya tried. Two florets later, she cut herself. 'Ouch!' she screamed.

'What happened?'

'Nothing,' she sniffed. 'Nothing, go rest with your mother.'

'Is that blood?' I said. 'You are hurt!'

'It's OK. I said I will do what it takes. What's a little blood?'

'This cut is not my mother's fault,' I said.

'Shut up and get me a band-aid. And bring the bhindi from the fridge,' she said.

An hour later we had cut the gobi, bhindi, onions, garlic, ginger, tomatoes, cucumber and green chillies required for the various dishes. Until you do it yourself, you don't realise the effort your mother puts into every meal.

We went to the kitchen. I took out the atta in a bowl.

'I have no clue how to knead this,' she said.

'It's OK, I've seen my mother do it. Let me try,' I said and poured water into the bowl.

'And you fry the onions in . . . this?' Ananya pulled out a kadhai from the utensil shelf.

'Yes, please,' I said and switched on the gas. I opened the box of spices. She didn't know how to use them.

'Remember the five constant spices in every Punjabi dish – salt, turmeric, red chillies, coriander powder and garam masala,' I said.

Ananya cooked the vegetables while I worked the atta. I had to refill the atta twice due to too much stickiness. A pungent smoke rose in the kitchen. Both of us had a coughing fit.

'What did you do?' I said.

'I . . . don't . . . know.' Ananya coughed uncontrollably.

My mother came into the kitchen. 'What are you doing?' She ran to the stove and lowered the flame. 'Who cooks on such a high flame? See, the spices have burnt.'

Ananya backed off from the stove.

'And you? What are you doing here?' my mother said.

'I . . . I came because of the burning smell,' I said.

'And your hands fell into the atta?' she said, pointing to my dough-smeared palms and fingers.

I kept quiet.

'See, this is how she will use you after marriage. She can't even make rotis.'

Ananya exited the kitchen. I wanted to go after her, but with mom present, it didn't seem like a good idea. I threw up my atta-filled hands in despair.

'She is South Indian, mom, how can you expect her to. . . .'

'You said she wants to make dinner. OK, tell her to make dosas if she wants. Can she make dosas?'

'Yeah, I am sure. But you need a grinder. . . .'

Ananya came back into the kitchen. 'No, aunty, I can't make dosas,' Ananya said. 'And I can't make a roti either. In fact, I am terrible at cooking anything.'

'Apart from cooking schemes to trap my boy,' my mother said.

They exchanged battlefield looks. Ananya left the kitchen in disgust.

'Mom!' I said in frustration.

'What? What else is this?' my mother said. 'You are under her spell. You bring her home. You knead atta for her. You give her two Frootis I had brought for guests. You are so worried about her. What about me?'

'What about you, mom?'

'What is she doing here?'

'Mom, she can hear you.'

'See, you only care about her. Go, be with her.'

My mother rearranged the plates in the kitchen. She threw the old spice mixture and made a new one as I left.

'Get me to the guest-house, I want to leave,' Ananya said, her face wet with tears.

'No,' I said and wiped her tears. 'No, you can't.'

'I can't do this,' she said. 'I thought convincing my parents would be enough. You said your mother is sweet. Sweet? If your mom is sweet, then Hitler is a cuddly toy.'

'Take a shower, Ananya,' I said. 'Let's all eat dinner together.'

We sat down for dinner. My mother served me. Ananya took the food herself.

I chose a safe topic. 'What are the important ceremonies for Minti's wedding?'

'I have to go every day,' my mother said, chewing her food. 'There is a puja, then a sangeet. Of course, the important ones are the sagan and the marriage, next Friday and Sunday. You'll come, no?'

'Sagan and marriage, of course. I'll bring Ananya, too.'

My mother gave me a dirty look. She didn't want to talk about it with Ananya present.

'Don't avoid the topic, mom. I've brought Ananya here so you and the family get to know her.'

'I already know she can't cook dinner,' my mother said.

'I'm sorry, aunty,' Ananya said. I didn't expect it but felt relieved that Ananya apologised.

'It's fine, you modern girls are like this. That is why I want Krish to marry. . . .'

'Mom, I want to marry Ananya,' I said, 'in case it is not clear.'

My mother placed the piece of roti back on her plate and pushed her chair back to get up.

'Mom, please wait. I want to talk,' I said.

'Why should I talk? You will do whatever you want anyway. Go to the temple right now and get married.'

'Aunty, we want you to be happy about it,' Ananya said.

'Well, I am not. You can't force me to be happy. Everyone is praising Minti's mother for her choice. I've suffered for years to bring my son up. Why can't I have the same happiness? I want a lavish wedding, I want the girl's parents to respect me, I want the girl to be approved of by my brothers and sisters.'

'They will like Ananya! She is intelligent, educated. . . .'

'She is South Indian,' my mother said, cutting me.

'So what? Let's see what your brothers and sisters say about Ananya. This wedding is a perfect excuse.'

'And who will I say she is?' my mother asked grimly.

'Say she is Krish's classmate who's never seen a Punjabi marriage ceremony and wanted to come,' I said.

My mother kept quiet. She picked up her roti and began to eat again.

'Aunty, I am sorry I came unannounced. I thought Krish had told you.'

'He never tells me anything. He is so careless,' my mother said.

'I agree, he doesn't communicate well,' Ananya said.

'See,' my mother said to me.

Even though they were ganging up against me, I let it pass. I wanted them to bond in any way possible.

'The daal is excellent, aunty, you must teach me how to make it,' Ananya said.

'Then why are you eating like a squirrel? Take a proper helping,' my mother said.

'I'll speak to Minti,' I put in. 'I'm sure she will have no problem if I bring a friend.'

'Only as a friend,' my mother said.

'Thanks, mom,' I said and hugged her.

'Your dad never gave me anything. You don't deprive me of what I deserve,' my mother said.

'Where's uncle?' Ananya said.

'Who knows?' my mother said. 'He'll be back late. You'll see him in the morning. You are sleeping in the guest-room and Krish in his room, right?'

'Of course, mom,' I said, 'how else?'

My mother finished dinner. Ananya offered to do the dishes. My mother said the maid would arrive in the morning but Ananya insisted. My mother went to her room.

'OK, Miss Brand Manager, you sure you don't need help?' I said as I leaned against the kitchen wall.

Ananya applied Vim on the dishes with a wire mesh. 'No, I don't want to be accused of trapping the Prince of Punjab again,' Ananya said and mercilessly scrubbed a kadhai.

'Let me dry the dishes,' I offered.

'Go away, I beg you,' she said as she pushed me out of the kitchen.

44

'Good morning, uncle,' Ananya said as she came into the living room in her night-suit. It was seven-thirty in the morning. My father, bound to his army habit, had showered and changed. He looked up from his newspaper. He didn't respond.

'I'm Ananya, Krish's friend.'

'Good,' my father said and went back to his newspaper. He kept calm. I knew he'd blow his lid when Ananya left. I came to the living room and ignored him.

'Ananya, get ready. We should leave before the peak-hour traffic.'

'Where are you going?' my father said.

I didn't answer. My father stood up and went to the kitchen.

'Is this the way to behave?' I heard him scream at my mother.

'What happened?' my mother said as I kept one ear to the kitchen.

'I asked him where is he going, he didn't answer. And who is that girl?'

'He is going to drop Ananya to her guest-house and go to office. Why?' my mother said.

'Why can't he say it? And why didn't you tell me we will have a visitor in the house.'

'I didn't know,' my mother said.

'You are lying again,' my father screamed.

Ananya looked terrified.

'Welcome to my world,' I said, 'now let's get the hell out of here.'

I came home from work and found a deadly silence in the house. Obviously, my father was home. He sat at the dining table with my mother.

'Krish, your father wants to talk to you,' my mother said.

'Tell him I don't want to,' I said.

'He said he won't come for Minti's wedding if you don't speak to him,' my mother said. Weddings on my mother's side of the family were when we needed my father the most. My mother wanted to portray a sense of normalcy. If my father showed his face, it prevented tongues wagging for weeks. I had no choice. I went and sat opposite him.

'So, now that you have resorted to blackmail, what do you want to talk about?' I said.

'It's not blackmail. When my family doesn't talk to me, why should I. . . .' he said.

'Whatever. What is it?' I said.

'Who is that girl?'

'Ananya Swaminathan,'

'How do you know her?'

'She is a classmate from college and my girlfriend.'

'See Kavita,' my father said, 'and you said she is only a friend.'

'You talk to me, why do you have to take it out on her,' I said.

'What is the purpose of her visit here?' my father said.

'She came on a work assignment. Minti invited her to the wedding. Do you have a problem?'

'You will not choose a girl for marriage. I will choose for you,' my father said.

'You want to sell me. And while you are out there negotiating me, what's my going rate?'

'Kavita, this boy. . . .'

'This boy is right here. Talk to me.'

'I am not coming for Minti's wedding,' my father announced.

'Please, don't do that. Krish, talk properly,' my mother pleaded.

'No mom, we won't take him. We'll tell them he is sick, mentally.'

'Watch your mouth,' my father said and raised his hand.

'I dare you,' I said and stood up. I went to my room but could hear them.

'I won't come for the wedding, Kavita,' my father said. The sound of a clattering plate, presumably shoved away on the dining table.

'Do whatever you want, all of you,' my mother said.

I lay in bed. I wondered why we even stayed together as a family. I never thought I would, but I missed Chennai. Sure, people there didn't really connect with me, but at least nobody could jab my insides. I thought of calling Ananya but I didn't want to dump my mood on her. Questions darted in my mind. *Am I even doing the right thing by bringing Ananya into this family? What impression will she have of me? Will she change her mind about me?* Watching my mind's stupid daily pre-sleep thought dance, I tossed and turned in bed all night.

45

Minti's sagan ceremony took place at the Taj Palace Hotel in Dhaula Kuan. Frankly, it was a big deal for our clan. We had seen some over the top weddings, but never before did an engagement ceremony happen at a top end five-star hotel. Rajji mama had taken his one-upmanship among the relatives right to the top by booking the Taj.

The banquet hall entrance had a sign.

The Talrejas welcome you
to SAGAN ceremony of their:
Most lovely daughter
Manorama (Minti)
With
Dashing Gentleman
Dharamveer (Duke), B. Tech

'Don't laugh,' I said to Ananya, suppressing my own smile.

'I can't help it,' she grinned. She adjusted the drape of her bottle green and gold sari for the fifth time.

'Welcome-ji, welcome,' Rajji mama gave my mother and me hugs in quick succession.

We came inside the banquet hall, which held two hundred people. The main stage had two ornate chairs stolen from a king's palace. Alongside, there were seventy-five boxes of sweets and five giant baskets of fruits.

Most of the women stood at the chaat and juice counter. All the men stood at the bar. I helped my female cousins access vodka by giving them my glass, which they poured into their juice.

'So, there is Rajji mama, Lappa mama, Shipra masi and your mother – in that order, right?' Ananya said.

'Yes, and since my mother is the youngest, she needs validation from all of them to do anything in life,' I said.

'Fine, let me understand first. Minti and Rohan are Rajji mama's children,' Ananya said and took out a notepad. 'And who is the girl you gave the vodka to?'

'That's Tinki, and she has a younger sister Nikki, both in college. They are Lappa mama's children. And Shipra masi has a son and a daughter, Bittu and Kittu. That's it, my mom only has me.'

'OK, OK,' Ananya said as she finished taking notes.

'Krish, come here,' my mother screamed. She stood next to the stage.

'Let's go,' I said and pulled Ananya's hand.

Ananya hesitated at first, but came along. My mother sat with an eighty-year-old lady who wore a gold necklace. It had a pendant bigger than the Olympic gold medal.

'She is Swaran aunty, my masi,' my mother said.

My grandmother had died a couple of years ago. Swaran aunty was the senior-most family member who was brought out at weddings and other auspicious occasions to bless everyone.

I bent forward to touch her feet. I signalled and Ananya followed.

'Kavita, teri noo hai?' Swaran aunty said in Punjabi, asking if Ananya was my mom's daughter-in-law.

My mother explained she was a friend.

'What is friend?' Swaran aunty asked me.

'Aunty, you need chaat?' I countered.

'Yes, nobody is getting me anything,' she complained.

I returned with a plate of chaat. Ananya sat next to Swaran aunty and my mother.

'She is Madrasi?' Swaran aunty said in a voice loud enough to belie her age.

'Tamilian,' Ananya said.

'But she is fair complexioned?' Swaran aunty said, genuinely confused. For her years, her eyesight wasn't bad at all.

Shipra masi passed by, looking expensive. Everything she wore—clothes, jewellery, handbag and shoes—contained real gold of varying proportions.

'Shipra, see this, a gori Madrasin,' Swaran aunty screamed.

'Hello Kavita, how are you Krish?'

'Fine aunty, meet my friend, Ananya,'

'Oh, we all know what kind of friend. Yes, she is fair.'

Shipra masi called for Rajji mama and Lappa mama's wives, Kamla and Rajni, respectively.

'Come, see Krish's friend. That Madrasin Kavita told us about,' Shipra masi shrieked.

Rajni aunty and Kamla aunty came over. We exchanged polite greetings. My mother explained how my father had viral fever so he couldn't come. Everyone knew the truth but nodded in total support. Shipra masi even suggested some medicines.

'Ananya Swaminathan, aunty,' Ananya repeated her name to Kamla mami as she hadn't caught it the first time.

'You are so fair. Are you hundred percent South Indian?' Kamla mami asked.

She is also an IIMA pass out and a brand manager at HLL, I wanted to say. But those are things you discuss in Chennai, not at the Taj Palace, Delhi, during the Talreja's sagan ceremony.

'By South Indian standards, she is quite pretty,' Shipra mami added insight.

'I know, otherwise how black and ugly they are,' Kamla mami said.

Everyone laughed, apart from Ananya. She had braved a smile all along, but it disappeared. I moved next to her and gently patted her back.

I didn't want her to react. Smile like a ditz and your chances of being accepted will improve. Sometimes, love is tested in strange ways.

'The boy's side has come!' Kittu, my youngest cousin, came running inside like Amitabh Bachchan had lost his way and rung the doorbell.

'Let's go, let's go,' Kamla mami hauled up all the ladies. The ladies deposited their gold sequined bags with Swaran aunty. Her immobility made her an ideal cloakroom.

'So, what is the surprise gift?' my mother egged on Kamla aunty.

'You will see it soon-ji. But the expense has broken our back. Minti's daddy had to take a loan.'

'It's OK, you have only one daughter,' Shipra masi said as all of them walked out.

Ananya let out a huge sigh after the Punjabi aunty gang left.

'You OK?' I said. 'No, let me guess. You are not OK.'

'I need a drink, let's go to the bar,' Ananya said.

'But stay a few steps away. I'll order the drink,' I said.

We reached the bar. Tinki and Nikki came running to me, their lehngas lifted up to their ankles with their hands.

'Krish bhaiya, get a full glass of neat vodka. My friends from college have come.'

'Why can't the girls take drinks themselves?' Ananya asked.

Tinki and Nikki turned to Ananya, puzzled. At nineteen and seventeen, they looked overdressed in their designer clothes.

'Tinki, Nikki, this is Ananya,' I said.

'Oh, you are the one,' Tinki exclaimed.

'The one who?' I said.

'She is your girlfriend, no, Krish bhaiya?' Nikki said.

I didn't respond.

'You are blushing,' Tinki said, and turned to Ananya. 'I love your earrings. Where did you get them from?'

'Coimbatore,' Ananya said.

'Where is that?' Tinki said.

'Tamil Nadu, that is where I come from,' Ananya said.

'Stupid, didn't you read it in geography?' Nikki scolded her sister and turned to me, 'Your girlfriend is so pretty. And her sari is also so beautiful.'

'Thanks,' Ananya said. 'Both of you look great. I want a lehnga like that.'

I took a full glass of vodka from the bar and poured it into three glasses. I topped the drinks with Sprite and brought it for the girls.

'I don't drink. It's only for the DJ later,' Tinki clarified. 'Anyway I am eighteen now.'

'You went to IIMA, no? You must be so intelligent. Can girls get into IIM?' Nikki said.

'Of course, why not? What's it got to do with being a girl,' Ananya said.

I stepped away from them. The girls talked for the next ten minutes. If nothing else, Ananya had bonded with the younger set of my family. Why was it so much harder to win over the older generation?

'Where are you?' my mother's angry voice cut into my musings. 'The ceremony is about to start.'

I collected the girls and we went to the stage. Minti sat on the floor of the stage with Duke in front of her. A priest sat alongside.

As my aunts would say, Duke was on the healthier side.

'He is fat,' Ananya said flatly.

'Shut up, someone will hear you,' I said.

'Oh, people really are careful about what they say around here,' Ananya said, sarcasm shimmering in her words like the sequins in her blouse.

'C'mon Ananya, they are not even aware they are being offensive. You will like them once you know them.'

'Please, I like your cousins, let me be with them,' Ananya said, her voice defiant from the vodka.

'We like her,' Nikki and Tinki certified as they gave Ananya a hug. Just like men, women too become friendlier after alcohol.

Duke was indeed fair as milk. The chubby cheeks and fair complexion made him look like a solely Cerelac-fed adult. He wore a shiny maroon kurta, of probably the same fabric as one of Ananya's mom's saris. Damn, I was remembering Ananya's mother here. *Focus*, I said to myself.

Minti wore an orange lehnga studded with Swarovski crystals and other precious stones. According to my mother, it cost twenty thousand rupees, while the wedding sari had cost thirty thousand. Ten percent of the wedding budget is bridal costumes, my brain made a useless calculation.

The priest chanted mantras. Minti gestured at her cousins to ask if she looked fine.

Nikki put her right thumb tip and index finger tip together to signify she looked fab. Nikki also put her right middle finger on her forehead to show Minti she needed to adjust her bindi. Minti followed the instruction and fixed her bindi with the left hand even as the priest tied a thread on her right. I learnt three facts about women: a) they never lose track of how they look; b) they help each other out by giving instructions in any way possible; and c) they can multi-task. Of course, my mind couldn't focus on the ceremony. I thought of ways to make my family like Ananya.

Duke pulled out an engagement ring from his kurta pocket. He displayed it for the cameras. A collective sigh ran across the women as they realised it was a solitaire.

'One-and-a-half carats at least,' Shipra masi curated it immediately.

Duke put the ring on Minti's finger and everyone clapped. Minti gave a shy smile as she brought out a ring, a simple gold band for Duke. She put the ring on him.

'She looks so sweet,' Tinki said and the two sisters gave each other hugs, their eyes wet. Women have surplus emotions and they don't need a big trigger to spill them out.

Duke's family waited after the ring ceremony in anticipation. Rajji mama took out a little box from his shirt pocket. He passed it on to Duke. Duke refused three times. Rajji mama insisted until Duke accepted it. Duke opened the black box. It had a key with the Hyundai Motors sign on it.

This time the women and men gave out a collective sigh. Yes, Rajji mama had outdone the solitaire.

'They've given a car,' Shipra masi said, to make it clear in case somebody hadn't got it.

Grown-ups from both sides opened their respective sweet boxes and force-fed the other family. All of us went on stage one by one and congratulated the couple. Minti's parents gave gifts to all of Duke's uncles and aunts. Duke's parents returned the favour. My mother and Shipra masi received a sari each.

'Show me yours,' Shipra masi said to my mother. Fortunately, they found them similar. Duke's parents could not be accused of aunt favouritism.

Rajji mama gloated after everyone complimented him on the masterstroke gift.

'Uncle, start the DJ,' Nikki said to Rajji mama.

Rajji mama nodded towards the dance floor. DJ Pussycats from Rajouri Garden comprised of two fat surds who had waited hours for that signal. They started with dhol beats. All the younger cousins hit the dance floor. The uncles needed a few more pegs and the aunties needed a few more elbow pulls from the younger kids to come and groove.

'They gave a car?' Ananya said in a shocked voice even as Nikki dragged her towards the dance floor.

'Yeah, a silver Santro,' Nikki said, 'come no, didi.'

Ananya went with the girls. Her years of Bharatnatyam training made her the best performer on the floor. She picked up the Punjabi steps fast and even taught my cousins a few improvised moves. She looked beautiful in her dark green Kanjeevaram. Like an idiot, I fell in love with her all over again.

'Have you eaten dinner?' my mother came up next to me.

'Er . . . no,' I said, peeling my eyes away from the floor.

'Then eat fast, we won't get an auto home,' my mother said.

'We will buy a car soon,' I said.

'Like your father will let us have one. Anyway, why should we take? Kamla said we shouldn't buy anything major until you get married. We don't want duplicate items.'

'Mom,' I protested.

'Go fast, the paneer will get over. And tell your friend to eat.'

I waved at Ananya to come eat with me. She panted as she walked with me to the buffet. I put black daal, shahi paneer and rotis on my plate. Ananya took yellow daal and rice.

'That's it?'

'That's all I like,' she said.

There was a commotion at the bar. Duke and his friends were fighting with the bartender.

'What happened?' I asked.

'They are not making the pegs large enough. Duke's friends are upset,' an onlooker said.

Rajji mama intervened. The hotel staff had foreseen that the whisky may run out and so had started doling out smaller quantities. There were no extra bottles of that brand even in the hotel. Rajji mama took out a wad of notes and gave it to the hotel staff. A waiter was sent to the Delhi border to fetch the whisky. Like always, money soothed nerves and everyone became cheerful again.

'This is a wedding?' Ananya said.

'Of course, that's how all weddings are. Why, your side has it different?' I said.

'You bet,' Ananya said.

We bade goodbyes to Rajji mama and Kamla aunty. As I walked out with my mother and Ananya, Shipra masi called me.

'Yes, aunty,' I said.

'Listen, you are our family's pride. Don't do anything stupid. These Madrasis have laid a trap for you.'

'Good night, aunty,' I said.

'See, I am saying it for your benefit. Your mother has suffered, make her happy. You can get girls who will fill your house with gifts.'

I bent down. If all else fails with kin, touch feet.

'What did Shipra masi say?' Ananya asked me.

'She said to make sure Ananya is dropped home safe,' I said as I stopped an auto.

46

I met Ananya at Punjabi by Nature in Vasant Vihar. I should have thought of a better-named venue, given her current mental state. However, the location was convenient and the food excellent.

'What is the point of me attending these family events, I feel so awkward,' Ananya began.

'It's one more ceremony – the actual wedding. Don't worry, tomorrow my aunts will be more used to you. Once my mother sees them accepting you, she is more likely to say yes.'

'I think she wants a set of car keys more than anyone's approval,' Ananya said.

'No, my mother is not like that. She doesn't want the car, but she wants her siblings to appreciate she managed a car. Get it?'

'Not really,' Ananya shook her head.

The waiter came to take the order. We ordered one parantha, which came with enough butter to stop your heart instantly. We ate dinner as we contemplated our next move.

'Sir, would you like to try our golgappas with vodka?' the waiter said.

'What?' Ananya said.

'No thanks,' I told the waiter and turned to Ananya. 'It is a gimmick. Trust me, Punjabis don't do that on a regular basis.'

'I am going back to Chennai in two days,' Ananya said.

'I know. But I will speak to mom, maybe even my uncles, after the wedding. I want to lock this in,' I said.

'What about your dad?' Ananya said.

'He won't agree. We'll have the wedding without him. Aren't mom's side relatives enough?'

'They are more than enough. Each talks more than ten of my relatives. Still.'

'Ananya, you can't get everything in life. Your parents, my mom, relatives—we have enough blessings. My father is not required.'

'You should talk to him though. He's your father,' Ananya said.

'Isn't the food great?' I said as I rubbed butter on my parantha.

47

Minti's final wedding ceremony gave new meaning to the expression over the top. Real elephants and ice sculpture fairies greeted us at the entrance. The boy's side had not yet arrived. Patient ushers waited with trays of flower petals. We shuffled through landscaped gardens with two dozen dolphin-shaped fountains to reach the main party area. The caterer had chosen a world theme. Food stalls served eight cuisines—Punjabi, Chinese, home-style Indian, Thai, Italian, Mexican, Goan and Lebanese—with at least five items in each genre. Apart from these, there were two chaat stalls – one for regular eaters and the other for health-conscious guests. The regular counter served samosas and tikkis, while the health counter had sprouts-stuffed golgappas. My aunts took both, one for taste and another for health.

There were two bars. The first bar had a giant Johnny Walker Black Label magnum cask. All uncles congregated here and waiters kept bringing in a regular supply of paneer tikkas and hara bhara kababs. The second bar was the mocktail bar, nicknamed the ladies bar. It had a large display shelf with two dozen glasses of different shapes and filled with psychedelic fruit drinks.

'Beautiful, Rajji, you have held the family name high,' my mother said, admiring the flower arrangements on the bridal stage.

'These orchids have come from Thailand. Just landed two hours ago from Bangkok,' Rajji mama said.

'Fifty thousand is just the flowers bill,' Shipra masi said. We raised our eyebrows to express suitable awe.

My cousin Rohan came running in to tell us that the baraat had arrived. We went outside and stood next to the elephants to receive them. Rohan gave me a pink turban, something all brothers and close male relatives wore to receive the groom.

'You look cute,' Ananya grinned.

All turbaned men posed for pictures with their equivalent counterparts from Duke's side. I had a picture clicked with Prince, Duke's cousin. Minti's father grinned as he hugged Duke's father for a picture. Duke's father frowned.

'Why is the boy's father so serious?' Ananya said.

'Maybe he is hungry,' I said. We soon found out I was wrong. Duke's family did come inside and sat on the sofas. However, they refused to touch anything to eat.

'One cold drink-ji,' Kamla mami begged Duke's mother, who shook her head.

'We are not hungry,' Duke's father said. Duke, his parents and a dozen close relatives sat on the sofas next to the stage. Half a dozen waiters stood by with trays but the boy's side ate nothing.

'The snacks are not hot, go get fresh ones,' Minti's father screamed at the waiters. His anger was misplaced. The boy's family had not refused food because of its temperature.

'Ask what's the matter. Something is wrong,' Shipra masi said.

'Who will ask?' Rajji mama said, 'They are not saying anything.'

Kamla aunty wore a worried expression. Ten minutes passed.

'What's going on?' Ananya said.

I shrugged. Shipra masi told the younger cousins to move back. She folded her hands and went to Duke's father. He looked the other way.

Ananya and I stepped back a few metres. We could see the elders but not hear them.

My mother and her two brothers folded their hands in front of Duke's parents. Like a landless farmer, they waited for the feudal lords to respond. A few minutes later, one of Duke's aunts spoke to my mother.

My mother nodded as she listened carefully. After Duke's aunt finished, my mother came back to huddle with her siblings.

'This is too much drama, I have to know what's going on,' Ananya said.

I pulled my mother aside.

'It's the Santro,' my mother said.

'What? It doesn't start?'

'Be serious, Krish.'

'Sorry, what happened?'

'Some misunderstanding has occurred. When Rajji gave the Hyundai keys, Duke's parents thought it was Hyundai Accent. But it was a Hyundai Santro. Accent costs five lakh, Santro only three lakh.'

'I thought it was a gift,' Ananya said.

If my mother found Ananya's entry into the family conversation odd, she was too preoccupied to dwell on it.

'Yeah, wasn't it a surprise?' I said.

'What do you think this is Krish? A birthday party? Everyone knows the surprise. Duke's parents had already announced the Accent to their family. They are feeling insulted and cheated.'

It is amazing how people can feel insulted even after being welcomed by elephants.

'Now what?' I said.

'Nothing, they are saying no wedding until Rajji changes the car.'

'Can he?' I said.

'He is already broke doing this wedding. But what choice does he have? He has promised them he will.'

'Then why are they sitting there with sullen faces?' I said.

'They want a guarantee. Duke's father wants the difference in cash right now.'

'Now?' I said.

Ananya's eyebrows went up and stayed there as she didn't know how to react. Shipra masi called my mother again and the elders held animated discussions.

'Is this for real? I am so pissed off,' Ananya said.

'I am as stunned by it as you,' I said.

We went to the ladies bar. I ordered two mocktail daiquiris.

'What are they discussing? Why don't they call the police?' Ananya said.

'Ananya,' I said, 'are you stupid?' I handed her a glass.

'No, I want to send some criminals to jail. Is that stupid?'

'Yeah, if you care about Minti's reputation. Plus, what about all they've spent?' I pointed to the various stalls.

'Oh, and nothing about the little fact that your sister is going to marry into a family of total jerks.'

'This kind of stuff happens. The elders will resolve it,' I said.

'We should be with the family at this time,' Ananya said as she kept her glass down.

We moved back to Drama Venue. Rajji mama had placed his pink turban at Duke's parents' feet. They ignored him. He offered a cheque, Duke's parents refused it. Rajji mama called his friends for cash. No one could come up with such a large amount at such short notice. Meanwhile, new guests were arriving at the party. With them, Rajji mama hid his stress and smiled and hugged all of them. Meanwhile, the ladies came up with a bizarre plan.

'Quick, Kavita, take your jewellery off,' Shipra masi said and removed her own necklace. My mother struggled to remove her bangles. Kamla and Rajni mami took off their jewellery sets as well.

Shipra masi put all the ornaments in a plastic bag and gave it to Rajji mama. 'Give this to them. Tell them to keep it until the car is replaced,' she said.

Rajji mama fell on Shipra masi's feet.

'Are you mad? You are my little brother. Minti is our daughter,' Shipra masi said. All her siblings broke into tears. Duke's father, still sofa-bound, kept looking at us from the corner of his eye.

'Now go,' Shipra masi said.

'I'll check with them first,' Rajji mama said. He went up to Duke's father.

'I can't believe this,' Ananya said.

'Shsh, everything will be normal soon,' I said.

Rajji mama returned after meeting Duke's parents.

'Shipra didi, they've agreed to keep the extra jewellery as security,' Rajji mama said.

Rajji mama collected the bag from Shipra masi.

'Uncle, wait,' Ananya said.

All eyes turned to her. This isn't your business, I wanted to tell Ananya.

'May I suggest something,' Ananya said, 'before you give it to them, Rajji mama.'

'What?' my mother said to Ananya, surprised.

'Aunty, you elders have had so many meetings to resolve this. Can the younger cousins talk to Duke?' Ananya said.

'Ananya, this matter concerns grown-ups,' I said.

'It's Duke's marriage. We should have a word with him,' Ananya said.

'When the jewellery is ready, then why?' Kamla mami said.

'Please uncle, Shipra masi, please. What's the harm?' Ananya said.

Shipra masi sighed her consent.

Tinki, Nikki, Rohan, Kittu, Bittu and us sat in a separate group of chairs ten metres away from the grown-ups. Ananya walked up to Duke's side of the family and identified a twenty-year-old boy. 'Are you Duke's cousin?'

'Yes, myself Pranjal,' he said.

'Good, can you collect all Duke's cousins and bring them to Minti's cousins over there,' Ananya said, pointing to our group.

'What's going on?' Duke's father said.

'Uncle, the younger people want to have a meeting. C'mon, Pranjal, round them up fast,' Ananya said.

'Who is this girl?' Duke's mother said.

'I'm their family friend,' Ananya said and turned to the groom, 'Duke, can you join us?'

Duke gave Ananya a puzzled look. Ananya continued to stare at Duke until he became uncomfortable and stood up. She asked him to follow her.

'Krish, call Minti here,' Ananya said.

'Minti?' I squeaked.

'I'll get her,' Tinki said and ran inside.

48

We made a circle of a dozen younger cousins along with Minti and Duke. The elders gave us suspicious looks from far, keen to know what was going on but Ananya made sure all younger cousins had their backs to the elders.

'We shouldn't have allowed this,' Duke's mother said.

'Of courseji, two minutesji,' Rajji mama said, agreeing to everything Duke's parents said.

'Hello everyone,' Ananya stood up to address the cousins. I sat next to her.

Everyone returned a meek 'hi' in response.

'Do you think what is happening here is right?' Ananya said. Duke and his cousins looked down, avoiding eye contact. My cousins huddled next to Minti, trying to keep her calm.

Rajji mama and Kamla mami gave helpless looks to Duke's parents as all of them wanted to peek into Ananya's conference. Shipra masi walked over to the younger set.

'What are you doing?' Shipra masi said to Ananya, 'Minti's life will be ruined if they leave.'

'I think her life will be ruined if they stay. Aunty, please, give us some privacy. You make sure Duke's parents stay put,' Ananya said.

As Shipra masi left, Ananya turned to Duke, 'Yes, you. Stand up if you can.'

Duke stood up. He was six inches taller than Ananya and twice her weight. Of course, these anatomical facts didn't register with my mad girlfriend.

'What do you do, Duke?' Ananya asked.

'I am a software engineer,' he said.

'How much do you make?' Ananya said.

Duke kept quiet.

'Tell me,' Ananya said in a loud voice.

'Ten thousand a month,' he said, in a heavy Punjabi accent.

'Great, I make twenty-five thousand. Still, can you tell me what have you done to deserve a wedding like this? What have you done to deserve a car to be gifted to you?'

'I, I am the b . . . boy's side,' Duke stammered.

'So? Have you seen Minti?' Ananya said.

Duke nodded.

'You are having an arranged marriage. That is why you are getting a girl like her. If you had to woo her, can you even in your dreams have a girlfriend like her?'

Duke kept quiet as he shifted his largeness from one leg to the other.

'What?' Ananya said.

'This is too much,' Duke said.

'I am too much,' Ananya agreed and gave Duke a Bharatnatyam-style glare. She spoke again.

'Do you know what Minti's parents had to go through to do this wedding for you? That car cost two and half years of your salary, Mr Duke! These two parties have thrown him into debt. Now you want an Accent? It won't be your Accent, it will be what you managed to wrench out of a helpless father who didn't want a drama at his daughter's wedding to turn into a scandal.'

It was too many words for Duke to process at one go. He was stunned, like the rest of the cousins, more by Ananya's confidence and fluent English than what she was saying.

'Sit down,' Ananya said. Duke complied instantly. Ananya turned to everyone, 'Listen, all brothers and sisters of Duke, there isn't going to be any Accent. The elders have shown their true colours, now it is down to Duke and all of you. If he wants to take Minti with respect, he should say so. If he doesn't, then he is just a schmuck and we don't want the wedding.'

'Ananya beta. . . .' Rajji mama came to us as the youngsters' meeting had gone for too long.

'Almost done, uncle,' Ananya said. 'Five minutes, Duke. Make up your mind.'

Everyone fell silent as Ananya Swaminathan, brand manager HLL, MBA, rated best girl by popular vote at IIMA and rated best girlfriend by my own vote, forced the younger generation in Duke's family to think.

49

The cousins fell silent as seconds ticked past. Duke wanted to say something, but he noticed his parents' sour faces from far and kept quiet. He huddled with his own cousins as they exchanged whispers with each other. He stood up again and spoke to Ananya after four minutes.

'Excuse me, madam,' Duke said.

'I'm Ananya. What?'

'Can we go to the grown-ups? I want to talk to my mother.'

'About what?' Ananya said and blocked him.

'Why are you so dominating? Let me go.'

'Let's all go,' Ananya said.

All the cousins stood up from their chairs. We walked up to the grown-ups. Duke went to his mother.

'Mummy, I want to marry Minti.'

Duke's mother gave her son a shocked look.

'But they have betrayed us, beta,' Duke's father said.

Rajji mama dived towards their feet again. Ananya stopped him.

'Daddy, I have kept quiet for so long, no? Everything you have decided. Now whatever it is, don't spoil my marriage.'

'Beta, but they promised us,' Duke's mother said.

'Mummy, enough! And why this drama of keeping their jewellery? What do you think? I can't buy my own car?'

'Five minutes are over,' Ananya said, 'Should we pack up or. . . .'

'What kind of a girl are you? You are not even giving me time to convince,' Duke said to Ananya.

One of Duke's uncles stood up. 'Let's start-ji. We can't spoil our children's happy day. We are already late for the jaimala ceremony.'

'Are they OK?' Rajji mama said, looking at Duke's parents.

'Don't worry, misunderstandings happen. We don't have to spoil a lifelong relationship,' Duke's uncle said as he signalled for all the other relatives to stand up.

'Everyone, please enjoy the snacks,' Duke said. It was enough cue for his relatives to jump at the waiters. It is cruel to keep Punjabis away from their food at a wedding, especially when most of them had no stake in the car anyway.

Our side of the family hugged Duke's parents. They didn't hug back, but at least they didn't push us away. Rajji mama brought a box of mithai and fed Duke's parents a piece each in their mouths. The sugar rush improved their expression. The DJ started the music. The wedding was back on.

One girl stood back until everyone vacated their sofas and went to the stage. It was the South Indian girl who had come with me all the way from Chennai.

'What did she say to him?,' Shipra masi asked me. She took her bag back and redistributed the ornaments. I shrugged my shoulders.

'Very wise girl,' Kamla aunty gave Ananya a hug. 'Thank you, beta. You kept our izzat.'

'But tell me one thing, you earn twenty-five thousand?' Rajni aunty asked the question everyone wanted to ask.

My mother came and gave Ananya a smiling nod. Even though my mother didn't say anything, I knew it meant a lot.

'She's not that bad,' Shipra masi told my mother during jaimala.

'You've scored girl, you know you have,' I said to Ananya as we tossed flower petals on Duke and Minti.

50

'So, mom,' I said, 'as I was saying.' We were in the kitchen.

'You've said that four times. Do you actually have something to say!' my mother said. She removed boiling tea from the stove.

'Ananya leaves tomorrow,' I said.

'OK,' she said. She passed me a cup of tea.

'I called her home to meet us before she left.'

'And,' my mother said.

'We'd like to know your decision,' I said.

'It's your decision,' she said.

'OK, your opinion, which is important for me to make my decision.'

'Uff, you and your MBA terms,' my mother said.

Ananya came home in the afternoon. My mother cut a melon as we sat at the dining table.

'So mom, the unthinkable happened. Your relatives like Ananya. Now, do I have your permission to marry her?'

'You don't need my permission,' my mother said, passing me melon slices.

'Not permission, approval. Do we have your approval?' I said.

She gave a few slices of fruit to Ananya.

'Is that a yes?' I said.

'Kamla aunty and Rajji mama are quite fond of her,' my mother said.

'Do *you* like me, aunty? Tell me if you are not convinced,' Ananya said.

'Of course, I do, beta,' my mother said, her hand on Ananya's head. 'But there are other people too, your side of the family.'

'My family likes Krish a lot!'

'Yes, but what about the families liking each other? You two may be happy, but we adults have to get along with the adults from your side. You remember Sabarmati Ashram?'

'Be patient, mom. Over time, the families will get close,' I said.

Ananya brought up the topic of my father one last time before she left. 'Krish's dad won't agree?' Ananya said.

My mother gave a wry smile. 'He won't let us watch TV, forget Krish choosing his bride. It's fine, my siblings are enough. Otherwise, it will never happen,' my mother said.

Ananya nodded. My mother went to her room and returned with two gold bangles.

'No aunty,' Ananya said, even as my mother shoved it down her wrists and kissed her head.

Happiness floated like rose petals in the air and I imagined fist pumping my hands three times.

～

'So what's the next step? The wedding date?'

Ananya and I were on our long-distance call from our respective offices.

'You know your mother is right, there is a gap here,' Ananya said.

'What gap?' I said.

'My parents like you. Your mother likes me. What about them liking each other? Remember the Ahmedabad disaster?' Ananya said.

'Yeah but,' I said. 'Oh man, I thought we were done.'

'No, the two families have to unite. Trust me, it will be worth it. We should make them meet,' she said.

'Where? I'll come to Chennai with my mother?' I said.

'No, let's go to a neutral venue without relatives.'

'Good point. Let me organise something,' I ended the call.

I went back to work. I didn't have a fixed division or boss in Citibank Delhi yet. I floated between departments, pretending to be useful. I had a temporary stint in the credit cards division. I had to come up with a credit card promotion plan, something I had no interest or expertise in. I opened the existing brochure of offers for our credit card customers. We had a special deal on a package to Goa.

I picked up the phone and called Ananya again. 'Goa,' I said. 'Let's all go to Goa. Nothing like the sea, sun and sand to make the two families bond. Plus, it will be fun for us, too. What say, next month?'

'It won't be cheap,' she said.

'Isn't love the best investment?' I said and fumbled through my cards to call the travel agent.

Act 5:
Goa

51

'I am telling you now only. I don't like her mother—arrogant woman,' my mom said as we waited at the taxi stand. My mother and I landed at the Dabolim Airport in Goa two hours before Ananya and her parents did. I had tried to time the flights as close as possible.

'It's not arrogance. They are quiet people,' I said.

'Don't be under their spell,' my mother said.

'I'm not. OK, here they come, remember to smile,' I said.

Ananya's parents came face to face with my mother for the second time.

'Hello Kavita-ji,' Ananya's father said. They exchanged greetings, not warm and cuddly like Delhi airports, but not completely ice-cold either.

I had hired a Qualis. I helped the driver load Ananya's bags into the car. My mother gave me a puzzled look.

'What?' I said.

She shook her head.

I sat in front. Ananya's family took the middle seat.

'Oh, I'll sit at the back,' my mother said.

'OK,' Ananya's mother said.

I realised the faux pas. 'No, mom, I will take the backseat,' I said. My mother declined as she had already taken her place.

'Park Hyatt,' I said. The driver turned the car towards South Goa. My mother took out a plastic packet from her bag.

'Here, for you,' my mother said and passed a sari to Ananya's mother.

Ananya's mother turned around and took the packet. 'Thank you,' she said.

'It's tussar silk,' my mother said, 'I bought it from the Assam emporium.'

'Silk is very popular in the South also, we have Kanjeevaram saris,' Ananya's mother said and she kept the sari in her bag.

We didn't speak much until we reached the resort.

Hotel staff received us with a garland of flowers and a fruit-punch welcome drink. None of us had ever stayed in a five-star hotel.

'Isn't this expensive?' my mother said.

'They gave me a deal. I promised I'll get Citibank to do their annual conference here,' I said.

'Welcome, Mr Krish, we have two garden view rooms booked for you,' the receptionist said. 'And I have some good news. On one of the rooms, we are offering an upgrade to a larger, sea-view room.'

'Wow,' Ananya said, 'I've never stayed in a sea-view room.'

Of course, Ananya and I weren't staying together. I was to share a room with my mother while Ananya would be with her parents. And since they were three of them, I made the choice.

'Ananya, your family can take the larger room. Mom and I will take the other one,' I said.

The bell-boys carried the luggage to our room. 'Nice place, no?' I said to my mother as we passed a flower garden.

My mother did not respond.

'Everything OK?' I said.

My mother gave a brief nod. She kept quiet until we had reached the room.

'They are very rude people,' my mother said.

'Who? The hotel staff?' I said as I opened the curtains to see the garden view.

'Shut up, these people you want to make your in-laws. Are they in-laws? They are making their son-in-law pick up luggage?'

'Huh? When?' I asked.

'At the airport. You don't even realise you have become their servant?'

'I. . . .' I said, searching for a response, 'I wanted to help.'

'Nonsense, and why did they take the sea-view room? We are the boy's side.'

'They are more people. Besides, do you care? Isn't the garden pretty?'

'Whatever, have you noticed their biggest blunder?' she said.

'What?'

'They didn't get anything. I gave their daughter two bangles. They should have some shame.'

In Punjabi terms, Ananya's parents had committed a cognisable offence. You don't meet the boy's side empty-handed. Ever.

'And I gave her a silk sari for two thousand bucks. She didn't even appreciate it.'

'She did.'

'No, she was bragging about her South saris,' my mother said.

This is one of the huge downsides about getting married. A guy has to get involved in discussions about saris and gold.

'Mom, we have come here to get to know them. Don't pre-judge, please. And now, get ready for dinner.'

'You will take their side only. You are trapped.' She muttered, 'Stupid boy, doesn't know his own value.'

52

Few things bring out the differences between Punjabis and Tamilians than buffet meals. Tamilians see it like any other meal. They will load up on white rice first, followed by daal and curds and anything that has little black dots of mustard, coconut or curry leaves.

For Punjabis, food triggers an emotional response, like say music. And the array of dishes available in a buffet is akin to the Philharmonic orchestra. The idea is to load as many calories as possible onto one plate, as most party caterers charge based on the number of plates used. Also, like my mother explained since childhood, never take a dish that is easily prepared at home or whose ingredients are cheap. So, no yellow daal, boring gobi aloo or green salad. The focus is on chicken, dishes with dry fruits in them and exotic desserts.

'You can take more than one plate here, mom,' I said as she tossed three servings of butter chicken for me.

'Really? No extra charge?' she said.

We returned to our table. 'You are having rice?' my mother said as she saw the others' plates.

They nodded as they ate with spoons. Their fingers itched to feel the squishy texture of rice mixed with curd and daal. Ananya had made them curb their primal instincts to prevent shocking my mother.

'Chicken is too good. Did you try?' my mother said and lifted up a piece to offer them.

'We are vegetarian,' Ananya's mother said coldly even as the chicken leg hung mid-air.

'Oh,' my mother said.

'It's OK, aunty, I will try it,' Ananya said.

We ate in much silence with only our chewing making a sound.

'Amma, something something,' Ananya whispered in Tamil, egging her on to talk.

'Your husband didn't come?' Ananya's mother said.

'No, he is not well. Doctor has told him not to travel by air,' my mother said.

'There is a train to Goa from Delhi,' Ananya's father supplied. Ananya gave her father a glance, making him return to his food.

'We don't travel by train,' my mother said, lying of course. I have no idea why.

She continued, 'Actually, Punjabis are quite large-hearted people. We like to live well. When we meet people, we give them nice gifts.'

'Mom, do you want dessert? There is mango ice-cream,' I said.

She ignored me. 'Yeah, we never meet anyone empty-handed. Oh and meeting the boy's side empty-handed, unthinkable,' my mother said as I gently stamped her foot.

'OK, I've booked a car for sightseeing tomorrow. Please be in the coffee shop by seven,' I said.

'Illa sightseeing,' Ananya's mother mumbled.

'Sure, we'll be there,' Ananya said.

Ananya and I met for a walk post-dinner at Park Hyatt's private beach.

'My parents are upset,' Ananya said, 'your mother should learn to talk.'

The waves splashed the shore as many tourist couples walked hand-in-hand in front of us. I bet they weren't discussing the mood swings of their future in-laws.

'Your parents should know how to behave,' I said.

There we were, at one of the most romantic locations in India, having our first marital discord. In an Indian love marriage, by the time everyone gets on board, one wonders if there is any love left.

'How can they behave better?' she said.

'I will tell you. But you must do exactly as I say,' I said.

'If it is reasonable,' said my sensible girlfriend.

'Step one, buy my mother an expensive gift.'

'Really?'

'Yes, step two, when we go out in Goa tomorrow, always offer to pay.'

'Everywhere?'

'Yes, at restaurants, to taxis or anywhere else. And when you offer, she will say no. But insist, if needed, snatch her purse to prevent her from paying. In Punjabis, this is considered OK, even affectionate.'

Ananya's jaw went slack.

'Step three, never let me do any work when everyone's around. For example, at the breakfast table, tell your mother to bring toast for me.'

She snorted.

'That's what my mom expects. Do it,' I said.

Her face looked defiant.

'I beg you,' I said.

'Anything else?' she said.

'Yes, step four is to make love to me on the beach.'

'Nice try, pretty Punjabi boy. But sorry, nothing's happening until we cross the finish line now.'

'Ananya, c'mon' I coaxed.

'We have to fix the family situation. I'm too tense to think of anything else,' Ananya said.

'OK, if tomorrow goes well, then can we do it on the beach? We will call it Operation Beach Passion.'

'We'll see. Beach Passion,' she smiled and smacked my head. 'Let's go back, my dad is waiting for me.'

The day tour of Goa went off without any fireworks, mainly due to the presence of a friendly Goan tour guide. We went to Bom Jesus Basilica, the oldest church in Goa.

'Light a candle with someone you love,' the guide said. I had to choose between Ananya and my mother. Given the sensitivity of the trip, I went with the latter.

We also visited Dona Paula, the climax location for the movie *Ek Duje Ke Liye*.

'Famous movie shot here. North Indian boy, South Indian girl. Difficult to get along, so they die,' the guide said.

'What else could have happened?' my mother smirked. I let it pass.

Ananya's parents stayed back in Panjim for shopping.

53

We met Ananya's parents at dinner. All buffet meals at Park Hyatt were paid for as part of the package. They came to the coffee shop with three big brown bags.

'Kavita-ji, this is for you,' Ananya's father passed the bags to my mother.

'No, no, what is the need?' my mother simpered as she took the gifts.

The first bag had three saris. The second bag had four shirts for me. The third bag contained sweets, savoury snacks and Goan cashews.

I cruised the buffet counters with Ananya.

'Enough or does she want more?' Ananya said.

'It's cool. This is exactly what works,' I reassured her.

All of us sat at the table and ate in silence. I always found it scary to eat with Ananya's family, who ate their meals as if in mourning. If I found the lack of conversation awkward, my mother hated it. She shifted in her seat several times. The only sound was cutlery clanging on the plates. My mother spoke after five minutes. 'See, how times have changed. Our kids decide, and we have to meet each other.'

'Yes, initially we had a big shock. But Krish lived in Chennai for six months. Once we knew him, we were OK,' Ananya's mother said in her naturally stern voice.

'What OK? You must be jumping with joy inside. Where will you find such a qualified boy like him?' my mother said. I prayed Ananya's mother wouldn't bite at the bait. Of course, she did.

'Actually, we do get qualified boys. Tamils value education a lot. All her uncles are engineers or doctors. Ananya had many matches from the USA.'

'Yeah, but they must be all dark boys. Were there any as fair as Krish? Looks-wise you cannot match Punjabis,' my mother said, without any apparent viciousness in her voice. I almost choked on the spaghetti in my mouth.

'Mom, they changed dessert today,' I coughed, 'do you like bread pudding?'

'And my brothers are also doing well,' my mother said. 'Ask Ananya what a wedding she has attended. They gave a Santro to the groom. You may have landed my son, but it doesn't mean he has no value.'

Ananya imitated a stunned goldfish while I shook my head to deny responsibility for that statement.

'We haven't trapped anyone,' Ananya's mother said finally. 'He used to keep coming to our house. We are decent people so we couldn't say no.'

'Mom,' Ananya said.

'Why should I be quiet and get falsely accused? We haven't trapped anyone. Aren't we suffering? We all know Krish's father is against this. Our relatives will ask. Still we are accepting it,' Ananya's mother said.

'What are you accepting? You don't even deserve my boy,' my mother said, her voice nice and loud.

'Please don't shout. We are educated people,' Ananya's father said.

'Are you saying we are not educated?' my mother challenged.

'He meant "we" as in all of us, right, uncle? We are *all* educated,' I hastily put in.

'Will you continue to take their side and clap while your mother gets insulted?' my mother asked.

'No mom,' I said, wondering if I had taken sides. 'I won't.'

Ananya's family spoke to each other in Tamil. Uncle looked especially distressed as he took short, jerky breaths.

'My father is not well. We will go back to our room,' Ananya said.

I looked at him in alarm.

'Krish, we will see you later,' Ananya added.

'Mom,' I said in protest after they left.

'What? Is there bread pudding? Let's get some,' she said.

My mother and I came back to our room. She pretended nothing had happened.

'How does this remote work? I want to watch my serial,' she said.

'Mom, you could have behaved better there,' I said.

My mother didn't answer in words. She responded in nuclear weapons. Tears rolled down her cheeks.

'Oh please,' I said.

My mother didn't respond. She switched to her favourite soap where a son was throwing his old parents out of his house. She cried along with the TV parents, correlating their situation to hers. Yeah right, she was staying in Park Hyatt and ate four kinds of ice-creams and bread pudding for dessert. But, of course, all sons are villains playing into the hands of their wives.

'We can't have a conversation if you watch this stupid serial,' I said.

'This is not stupid. This is hundred percent reality,' she retorted.

I switched off the TV. My mother folded her hands. 'Please have mercy on me,' she said, 'don't subject me to this.'

The doorbell rang. I opened the door. Ananya stood there, her face equally wreathed in tears. When estrogen attacks you on all sides, there is not much you can do.

'What happened?' I said.

'Dad's chest is hurting,' Ananya said, fighting back her sobs.

'Should I call a doctor?' I said.

'No, he is fine now. But something else can help.'

'What?' I said.

'Is your mom inside? Can I talk to her?' she said.

'Sure.' I stepped back.

Ananya came in and told my mother who was sitting on the bed, 'Aunty, I think you should apologise to my parents.'

'Yes it is always my fault,' my mother mocked, looking at me for support.

'Aunty, please don't generalise. We spent four hours in Panjim today buying gifts for you. My parents did whatever Krish asked us to do.'

'What?' my mother said.

'Aunty, you have insulted them. They have not trapped anyone. They were dead against Krish to begin with. And now they have accepted him, they'd like some dignity.'

'I am not. . . .' my mother started to talk.

'OK, enough,' I said.

Both the women turned to me.

'Get your parents here,' I said, 'let's talk this straight. Everyone has hurt everyone.'

'No Krish, today my parents didn't do anything,' Ananya said.

My mother went into the bathroom.

'Ananya, try and understand,' I whispered. 'You push my mother into a corner, it will get worse. Let's make it a mutual apology.' I walked Ananya to the door.

'I don't like this,' Ananya said at the door.

'Bring everyone here, please,' I said.

I came back into the room. My mother had washed her face.

'I've called all of them here. Let's have a frank talk,' I said.

She kept quiet.

'What's up, mom? Say something,' I said. I wanted my mother to vent out before Ananya arrived with her parents.

'You saw Ananya? Have you seen any girl talk to her mother-in-law like that?' my mother demanded.

'She is a little feminist type, I admit,' I said.

'She is telling me to apologise. Can you imagine Minti talking to Duke's mother like that?'

'She is different. She is confident, independent and intelligent. But she is caring and sensitive too.'

'She is too intelligent to be a good daughter-in-law.'

I had no clue how to respond to that, but I had to calm her. 'She isn't that intelligent, mom,' I assured her. 'She did economics, but I beat her in that subject.'

'We don't have bahus in Punjabis like that, no matter how high-profile. We keep them straight,' my mother said.

'So we will too,' I said, to pacify her.

'She is out of control.'

'Mom, she is with her parents here. But I am marrying only her; once she comes to our house, we can control her. You only say, no, that South Indians are docile and scared,' I said whatever my mother needed to hear.

'I don't want my daughter-in-law to raise her voice or answer me back. She has to be under my thumb.'

'Fine, make her toe the line' I said, 'but be normal now.'

'I heard that,' Ananya said, her face red. Ananya stood there with her parents. Damn, I hadn't shut the door after Ananya left.

'Ananya? I didn't realise you were here,' I said.

'And I didn't realise what I was doing. So, I will be taught to toe the line after marriage. Well done, Krish, it's not just your mother, it is you as well,' Ananya said.

'Ananya, I. . . .' Both women stared at me with tear-ready eyes, ready to shoot their ultimate emotional laser weapon.

Ananya's father tapped his wife's shoulder, signalling departure.

'I told my parents your mother will apologise. But you guys are making bigger plans,' Ananya said and walked out of the room with her parents.

I ran out and caught up with Ananya. 'Wait, where are you going?'

'We're done,' she said, her words firm despite the wobbly voice.

'What do you mean?'

'It's over,' Ananya clarified, 'between you and me.'

'Are you breaking up with me? What? Ananya, are you crazy? I was manipulating her so she'd calm down.'

'I hate manipulations, Krish, and I hate manipulators even more,' Ananya said and broke into tears.

Ananya's father came towards us and held Ananya's hand. 'It's not about communities. It's about the kind of people we want to be with,' he said.

I stood alone in the corridor as Ananya's family walked away and the ground tilted around my feet.

Needless to say, Operation Beach Passion was not executed that night.

The Final Act:
Delhi & Chennai & Delhi & Chennai

54

I turned workaholic after Goa, spending fourteen maniacal hours a day in the office. I even brought the company laptop home to slog more. I achieved twice my work targets, I didn't socialise, I didn't see movies and I stopped going to restaurants.

'You have a great future,' Rannvijay, my new boss, told me.

When Citibank sees a great future in you, it means you have no life at present. 'Thanks, Rannvijay,' I said.

'Though you could do with a shave. What's with the new look? Growing a beard? And you look weak. . . . Take care of your health.'

I had tried to call Ananya several times after my return. Her parents would not pass her the phone if I called home. In her office, the receptionist would tell me she was in a meeting. When I did reach her, she'd make an excuse and not converse. Ananya had a cell-phone now, but she had stopped taking any calls from Delhi. One day I had a visitor in office from Citibank Mumbai. I requested him for his phone to make a call.

'Hello,' Ananya picked up the phone.

'Hi, don't hang up. It's me,' I said.

'Krish, please . . . whose phone is this?'

'A colleague from the Mumbai office. Listen, I am sorry, for the tenth time. Your receptionist will have a count of my earlier attempts.'

'Krish, this isn't about an apology.'

'Then stop sulking.'

'I am not sulking; I am doing what maximises everyone's happiness in the long term.'

I scratched my head to respond to her corporate-vision type answer. 'What about you and me?'

'For my own sake, I can't let make my parents feel small.'

'Don't you miss me?' I said.

She kept silent. I checked the phone; I had spent four minutes on the call. My colleague gave me puzzled looks as to why I had to use his phone.

'Ananya? I said, do you miss me?'

'What's the point? Say, I forgive you, what will change? Will your mother change? Will her bias towards me, towards South Indians, towards the girl's side, change?'

'She is good at heart, Ananya. Believe me she is,' I said.

'Oh really, why don't you have her apologise to my parents then?' she said.

It was my turn to stay silent.

'See,' she said.

'She is sensitive about everything right now.'

'No, she has a chip on her shoulder about being from the groom's side.'

I let out a sigh. 'Ananya, what happened to our plans to elope? Run away with me,' I said.

'And go where? To my caring, nurturing mother-in-law?' Ananya said, 'No, I want to marry where my parents are treated as equals.'

'You should have been born a boy,' I said.

'That's so sexist, I would have hung up if I didn't care for you.'

'Do you care or not? Don't you love me? Isn't our love above everything?'

'Don't ask impractical questions,' she said, her voice heavy.

'Can I do anything? Anything?' I said desperately.

'Don't call me again. Help me get over this,' she said.

'I love you,' I said.

'Bye, Krish.'

I came home and sat down in front of the TV. For dysfunctional families, television is the biggest boon. Without this electronic glue, millions of Indian families will fall apart.

The music channels showed songs of everlasting love. The couples seemed insanely happy. Perhaps, they were all from the same state, religion, caste and culture and their parents were completely in sync with each other. Otherwise, how can you fall in love in India? Some grown-ups in your house are bound to get pissed off.

My mother didn't talk about Goa or show any signs of remorse. She did feel a little guilty about my low mood; her penance consisted of cooking paneer dishes everyday.

'I've made paneer bhurji. You'll have paranthas with it?' she said.

I didn't respond. She took my lack of protest for a yes. She returned with dinner in twenty minutes. 'You want white butter?' my mother asked.

I shook my head.

'Too much work in office? There is a Canara Bank near our house. Should I talk to the manager for a job?'

'No, office is OK,' I said.

I tried to eat, but couldn't. I had not eaten anything for three days. I hid the paranthas in my laptop bag when she wasn't looking.

'Shipra masi has recommended another girl. They have a bungalow in Shalimar Bagh. Would you like to see her?' she said.

I stared at my mother.

'What?' she said.

'I'll marry her. No need to see her. Fine?' I said.

'Krish, don't say like that. When have I forced you?'

'What is the point of me seeing these girls? What am I supposed to check out in one hour? Her complexion? Figure – fat or slim? Is the marble in her home real? None of this matters when you have to spend your life with a person, so might as well save time. The parents should do the meeting. Whoever massages your ego more, say yes.'

'What has happened to you? These multinationals are sucking your blood,' my mother said.

'Can you apologise to Ananya's parents?' I said.

My mother didn't respond. She stood up from the sofa and went into the kitchen.

I followed her 'Why can't you do it?' I said.

She didn't answer me. She dabbed at dishwashing detergent with a sponge and scrubbed the utensils. She addressed an imaginary audience:

'First a useless husband, now a useless son. I had thought, after my son's marriage I will get respect. I said yes to his choice of girl, but at least behave like the girl's side. Now he wants me to fall at their feet. What is so great about this girl? Shipra is right, everyone is selfish.'

'Stop it, mom, I am not telling you to grovel. You can apologise over the phone.'

'Apologise for what? Is it wrong to expect what is due to me? Didn't I look after your grandmother until she died?'

'Didn't Ananya help set Duke's family right? Didn't you say yes then?'

'I was wrong. I hadn't met her parents then. I've never met such a dry breed of people. Look at how they eat dinner, like it is a punishment. Ananya's mother – does she ever laugh? Dark from outside, dark from inside.'

The doorbell rang. My father had come back from another of his lacklustre business ventures. I switched off the TV and opened the door. I had told him the partial truth about Goa. I had said there was an office conference there and that I was taking mom along. I had become quiet after my return and didn't even bother to fight with him anymore. He came inside and noticed the silence between my mother and me. There were several evenings these days at home when no one spoke to anyone.

'Have you decided to stop talking to your mother, too?' my father asked as he sat on the sofa and removed his shoes.

It's none of your business, would have been my usual response. But I had fought enough with the world. Another argument wouldn't have yielded anything.

'We'll be fine,' I said. I wished my mother would bring his dinner soon.

'Are you not enjoying your job?' my father said.

'The job is good. They said I've a great future,' I said. I don't know why I said the last line. Somehow, I felt the need to tell my father I was doing well.

'Why are you upset with your mother?' he said.

OK, it was enough. 'It's none of your business,' I said.

'Are you telling me my own family is not my business?' he said.

'Dad, enough. I am too tired to argue.'

My mother brought him dinner and I went back to my room. I took out Ananya's pictures. I tossed and turned in bed wondering what to do next. When you can't sleep, your mind comes up with weird schemes. I couldn't do it over the phone. I had to go in person to do it.

I woke up at four and took a shower.

'You are going to office now?' my mother said as she heard me get ready.

'I have a presentation, I'll be back late,' I said.

I took an auto to the airport. I plonked a month's salary to take my cross-country joyride.

'Same day return trip to Chennai please,' I said at the Indian Airlines counter.

55

Chennai seemed embarrassingly familiar on my second trip. I could throw in Tamil terms and negotiate with autos, I knew the main roads. I reached Ananya's office at eleven.

'Hi, I'm Krish,' I said to the receptionist.

'Oh, that Krish,' she said and called Ananya.

Ananya came out. I opened my arms to embrace her, but she shook hands.

'I came for the day,' I said, as we sat in the HLL cafeteria.

'You shouldn't have,' she said. 'What's with the unshaven look? And why do you seem so weak? Are you sick?'

'I want to meet your parents,' I said.

'There is no use. No matter how charming you are, they don't trust you anymore,' Ananya said.

'Do you trust me?'

'Irrelevant,' she said.

'I'll go to your place,' I said.

'Don't, Harish's parents are in town. They will visit my parents today.'

I took a deep breath to keep my temper in control. 'At least spend the day with me,' I said.

'I can't. I have work. Besides, it is not good for my parents' reputation.'

Blood rushed up my face. 'What reputation? What about Ahmedabad? What about when you'd lie to them to meet me in Chennai? What about Ratna Stores?' My voice was as loud as my body was tired.

She stood up. 'Please don't create a scene at my workplace.'

'Please don't play with my life.'

'I'm not doing anything! Be strong, move on,' she said. 'It's not easy for me. So please, let me be.'

She went back to her office, leaving me still sitting there burning with fatigue and fury. I hadn't shaved for ten days. Other girls in the cafeteria stayed away from me; I resembled a Kollywood villain who could rape anyone anywhere anytime. My flight didn't leave until the evening. I had half a day and no money to spend. Like a total loser, I decided to go to Citibank and visit Bala.

'Krish!' Bala said, shocked at my presence and appearance.

'Hi, how is the champion of the South?'

'I'm fine, but you look fucked,' he said.

'I am,' I said and slumped in front of him.

Bala ordered coffee for both of us. He pulled his chair forward, eager to hear the gossip from the other office.

'Is Citi Delhi screwing you? Don't tell me you want to come back.'

'Fuck off Bala, you think Citibank can get the better of me?' I said.

'Someone clearly has. Boy, your eyes. Do you have conjunctivitis?'

I shook my head. He touched my arm.

'Dude, you have high fever. Do you want to see a doc?'

'I want a drink. Can you get me a drink?' I said.

'Now? It is not even lunchtime.'

My stomach roiled and I retched. Thankfully, nothing came out and Bala's office could maintain its pre-me conditions.

'You are sick. My cousin is a doctor, I'll call him. He works in City Hospital on the next street.'

'What do girls think? We can't live without them?' I muttered. I couldn't believe I was venting out to Bala. But I needed someone, anyone.

Bala dropped me at the clinic run by his cousin, Dr Ramachandran or Dr Ram. Dr Ram had returned from the US two years ago after being a general surgeon, working on cancer research and collecting several top degrees. He told me to go to the examination bed as he collected his instruments.

'I'll see you later then,' Bala said.

'You South Indians have too much brain but too little heart,' I said to Bala as he left.

'I heard that,' Dr Ram said as he came to me. He put a cold stethoscope on my chest.

'So, this is a situation involving a girl?' Dr Ram asked.

'What girl?'

'When did you eat last?' he said.

'I don't remember,' I said.

'What's that smell?' the doc said. He sniffed his way to my laptop bag. Stale paranthas stank up the room. 'What's this?'

'Last night's dinner,' I said. 'Oh, my laptop, I hope it is OK.'

I opened my laptop and switched the power on. It worked fine.

'Can I see it?' Dr Ram said, pointing to my computer.

'Yes sure, are you looking to buy one?' I said.

He didn't respond. He spent five minutes at my computer and gave it back to me.

'What?'

'You should rest and eat food for sure. But you also need to see a psychiatrist.'

'What? Why?' I said. Sure, I am a bit of a psycho, but I didn't want to make it official.

'What's the name of this girl?' Dr Ram said.

'What girl? I don't like girls.'

'Bala said she is Tamilian. Ananya Swaminathan who stays in Mylapore, right?' he said.

'I don't like Tamilians,' I screamed. 'And don't mention her name or neighbourhood.'

'Good, because the psychiatrist I am referring you to is a Tamilian girl. Dr Iyer is upstairs. Please go now.'

'Doctor, I have to catch a flight. I am fine.'

I pushed myself off the bed. My legs felt as if the blood had drained from them. I couldn't balance. I fell on the floor.

Dr Ram helped me back up.

'What problem do I have?' I said, worried for the first time about my illness.

He handed me the specialist referral letter as he spoke again.

'There's no precise medical term. But some would refer to it as the early signs of a nervous breakdown.'

56

'So, that's it, I've told you everything,' I said.

Dr Neeta Iyer broke into laughter as I finished my story.

'This is insane. You find comedy in my tragedy?' I was miffed.

She didn't stop laughing.

'I'm paying you to treat me,' I said and checked the time. 'And I have to leave for the airport in twenty minutes.'

It dawned on me that I had spoken to her for four hours. I had no money for this extravagance.

'Sorry,' she said, 'you reminded me of my first boyfriend. He was North Indian.'

'You didn't marry him?'

'He didn't want to commit,' she shook her head.

'Oh, sorry,' I said.

'It's OK. I'm over it.'

'Of course you are, you are a therapist. You should be able to cure yourself, if nothing else.'

She walked to the window. 'Ah Krish, it doesn't work like that. A broken heart is the hardest to repair.'

I sighed. 'Do you accept Citibank credit cards?' I opened my wallet.

'It's fine, send me a cheque later,' she said. 'You should have eloped.'

'We thought we will win our parents over. Where's the joy of getting married if your parents won't smile on your wedding day?' I said.

She came to me and patted my shoulder.

'You have to leave. So, what do I do now? Do you want pills?' she said.

'You mean anti-depressants? Aren't they bad for you?'

'Yeah, but depends on how bad you feel right now. I don't want you googling for suicide recipes.'

'I won't,' I said, 'I'll probably wither away anyway. Is there another option apart from pills?'

'There's therapy, sessions like this. It takes a few months though. I can try and find a therapist for you in Delhi.'

'No, if my Punjabi family finds out, I'm done. They'll say I am mental or something.'

'You're not. But you know, there is one thing you can try yourself.'

'What?'

'When you told me your story, why did you mention that episode with Guruji?'

'At the Aurobindo Ashram?'

'Yes, it didn't really have a connection with Ananya or her parents. But you remember everything he said.'

'Yes, about forgiveness.'

'Yes, maybe it has some significance,' she said.

I kept quiet. The clock in her room told me it was time for my return journey. I took her leave.

'Airport, vegamaa,' I said as I hailed an auto.

57

I knew I had to eat, my brain knew this, but my body wouldn't hear of it. The day after returning from Chennai, I only had soup at office; at home I pretended I'd already had dinner. My mother asked me when I wanted to shave. She wanted to schedule a meeting with the new girl. I told her I had decided to keep a beard for the rest of my life. She made a face and left the room.

My father came home at ten. He looked extra tired. His normally tucked in shirt was out, and his hair wasn't neatly combed as usual. He sat in front of me.

'I've eaten dinner,' he told my mother.

'I don't know why I even cook,' my mother grumbled as she left the room.

'You came back late last night,' my father said to me. I had reached home only at midnight from the airport.

'I had to work late,' I said.

'Everything OK?' he said.

I nodded.

'I had a really bad day,' my father said. 'My pension papers are stuck in government offices. Bloody lazy buggers.'

I nodded without paying attention. My thoughts were all over the place, but none in his department. I felt immense longing and loathing for Ananya at the same time. I felt resentment towards my mother. My own problems, at least in my mind, were far bigger than some retirement files stuck in a government office.

'Now they have asked me to submit three different letters. I have to get them typed tomorrow,' my father said.

When my father had to suffer, he forgot his own vocation – of making others suffer. He hadn't shouted once since he had come home.

'Do you know a place where I can get letters typed? You have a computer, no?' my father said.

'Yes, I do,' I said.

My father continued to look at me expectantly.

'OK, I'll type them now and get a printout from office tomorrow,' I said. I anyway wanted more work to distract myself. I opened my laptop.

'Thank you,' he said, words we did not know lived inside of him.

I wrote his three applications in the next thirty minutes.

'How's your friend?' he said to me.

'Which friend?' I said.

'The girl who came from Chennai to attend the wedding,' he said.

The mention of Ananya was enough to stir up my emotions. I felt like someone had punched me in the stomach. Maybe I should take those anti-depression pills, I thought.

'I don't know. Must be fine,' I said after a minute's pause.

'You are not in touch with her?'

'Everyone has busy lives, dad,' I dismissed. 'Your letters are done. I'll get a printout tomorrow.' I shut down my computer.

'It is good that we talk sometimes,' my father said.

'Good night, dad,' I said and left for my room.

I lay in bed and that is when the depression hit me full force. Dr Iyer was right, no pill could be as bad for me as I felt right now. I lay motionless. I felt like I'd never be able to get out of bed again. I thought of every person in my life. One by one, I convinced myself how each of them hated me. If I were gone tomorrow, they'd all be happier. And considering how crappy I felt, there was no reason for me to stick around anyway. I had no one I could talk to about my situation, except at five hundred bucks an hour. I hated money, I hated Citibank, I hated my job and I hated all human beings on earth.

Calm down, Krish, this is going to pass, I told myself. This was the sensible me talking. *No baby, this time you are so fucked. This is how you will feel for the rest of your life,* the freaked-out me said. *That's nonsense. Whatever crap happens in life, one gets used to it. You aren't the first guy facing a break-up,* sensible-me said. *Yes, but nobody loves the way I do. So, nobody feels as hurt as I do,* freaked-out me said. *Yeah, right,* sensible-me said and yawned, *can we sleep? You know you need to.*

Are you crazy? How can you sleep when we can stay up all night and worry about this? the freaked-out me said.

The world's most sensible person and the biggest idiot both stay within us. The worst part is, you can't even tell who is who.

58

'Where's dad?' I asked my mother, 'he hasn't told me how many copies he wants.'

Though I sat for breakfast before going to office, I drank only a glass of milk. Solids were still indigestible. I wanted to rush to work and occupy my mind before it sank into its black-hole hell again.

'Morning walk,' my mother said.

'Why doesn't he keep a mobile?' I said as I wore my shoes to leave for office.

'Get four copies of each, worst case,' my mother said.

It wasn't a big deal. However, it didn't take a lot to piss me off these days.

'Like I have nothing better to do in office,' I said.

'All you grumpy people in the house, please leave,' my mother said and folded her hands. 'I don't know when you will forget her.'

'I don't know when you'll end your drama,' I said.

'This girl. . . .' my mother started.

'Bye,' I said hurriedly and sprinted out of the house.

I came home late at night. I had stuck to juice and milk all day.

'Again no dinner? Where are you eating these days, and look at you, so weak. And please shave,' my mother said.

'Is dad back?' I said, 'Here are his papers.'

I took out the printouts and kept them on the table. My mother shook her head and told me that he hadn't come all day.

'Please, give these to him,' I said.

I went to my room and lay down in bed. Scared of black-hole land, I kept the lights on. I read the newspaper, paying extra attention to each article to keep my mind busy. An item girl with her picture in a bikini said she wanted to be taken seriously. I found her request quite reasonable.

My father returned at midnight.

'You think this is a hotel?' I said as I opened the door. I hadn't fought with him for weeks, so it was about time anyway.

My father didn't respond.

'Here are your printouts. I didn't know how many copies you'd need.'

'Thanks,' my father said.

'Where do you go so late? Your real estate agency work can't take this long,' I said.

'I am not answerable to you,' my father said.

'And that is why we are an officially fucked-up family,' I said.

I came back to my room. I slammed the door shut as I prepared for another night with the devils in my head. I promised myself to call Dr Iyer in the morning and get a prescription for those happy drugs. Fuck the side effects, I couldn't take the mind monsters anymore.

I fell semi-asleep at three in the night. Persistent rings woke me up. I checked my watch; 5 a.m. Who the hell was calling at this hour?

I woke up groggy with a headache already in place. I reached the living room. I picked up the phone, ready to scream at the milkman or whoever else felt it was OK to call now.

'Hello,' a female voice said.

'Ananya?' I said. I knew that voice too well.

'Thanks sweetie, thank you so much,' Ananya said. Had she dialled the right number?

'What?' I said, still not fully in my senses.

'You fixed everything. Thank you so much,' she said, her voice super-excited.

'What did I do?' I blinked sleepily.

'Don't pretend! You should have at least told me.'

'Told you what?'

'That your dad is coming to Chennai,' Ananya said.

'What?' I said and woke up in an instant.

'Stop behaving like a dumbo. He spent seven hours with my parents yesterday. He assured them that I would be treated like a daughter and apologised for any past misgivings.'

'*My* dad?' I tried for clarification.

'Yeah, my parents feel so much better after meeting him. In fact, they asked me if I have a date in mind. Can you imagine?' Ananya spoke so fast, it was hard to catch her words.

'Huh, really?' I said.

'Oh, wake up properly and call me. I love you, baby. Sorry about the day before, I'd been so disturbed.'

'Me too,' I said.

'What? You too love me or you too are disturbed.'

'Both,' I said, 'but wait, my dad came to your house?'

'You seriously didn't know.'

'No,' I said.

'Wow,' she said, 'please thank him from my side.'

I went to my parents' room. They were still asleep. I don't know why, but I did a totally sappy thing. I slid right into the middle and put an arm around them both. In a minute, I was fast asleep.

I woke up five hours later, at ten. My parents were not in the room. I sprang out of bed, panicking at how late I was for office. I came outside.

'Where's dad?' I said as I saw my mother.

'In the balcony,' my mother said.

My father sat on a chair, digging up mud in one of the flower pots. He saw me but kept quiet. I wondered what I should say to him. I picked up another spade and started digging with him.

'Dad, you went to Chennai?'

'News travels fast,' he said. He didn't look up from the flower pot.

'Why? I mean, how come?'

'My son needed help,' my father said as he pulled out the weeds from the soil. His voice had been plain, yet I felt a lump in my throat.

He placed a sapling in the pot and put freshly dug mud around it. I came and sat next to him and pressed the soil with my thumb.

'How did you know?' I said.

His eyes met mine, he said, 'Because I am your father. A bad father, but I am still your father.'

He continued, 'And even though you feel I have let you down in the past, I felt I should do my bit this time. A life partner is important. Ananya is a nice girl. You shouldn't lose her.'

'Thanks, dad,' I said, fighting back tears.

'You're welcome,' he said. He gave me a hug. 'I'm not perfect. But don't deprive me of my son in my final years,' he said.

I hugged him back. Tears slipped out as I let go of any self-control. The world celebrates children and their mothers, but we need fathers too.

I closed my eyes. I remembered Guruji. I stood on top of a green mountain, watching a beautiful sunrise. As I held my father, the heavy cloak fell off, making me feel light again.

'I won't come for the wedding though,' my father said.

'Why?' I said, surprised.

'Your mother won't go without her relatives. I don't know what I will do there if they are there.'

'You won't come for your own son's wedding?' I said.

'Ananya is coming to our home only,' my father said.

I felt too much gratitude towards him at that moment to be mad at him.

'You *have* to come. I'm late for work, but I'll convince you later,' I said.

59

'Like I said, much simpler for us if you get your relatives to Chennai,' Ananya said.

'How do I get them all? I can't afford so many air tickets,' I said.

We were on our countless pre-nuptial calls.

'They won't fly down themselves?' Ananya said.

'Are you crazy? We have to take care of the baraat, until they reach you, of course.'

'Only you understand these Punjabi customs,' Ananya said.

'You'd better too,' I said.

'It's a Tamil style wedding,' Ananya said.

'What?' I said.

'Yeah, what else do you expect in Chennai? Anyway, won't your relatives like to see something different?'

'Actually, no,' I said.

'We'll see, and you can take the train to Chennai. The Rajdhani Express takes twenty-eight hours.'

'That's a long ride with relatives,' I said.

'You've waited so long for this, what's another day?' Ananya said and ended the call.

'You really won't come? I have your tickets.'

My father kept silent. My mother sat next to me at the dining table.

'Why does it have to be a choice? Why can't mom get her relatives and you come as well?' I said. *Why can't we be a normal family for once?* I thought. I guess there are no normal families in the world. Everyone is a psycho, and the average of all psychos is what we call normal.

'He feels they have insulted him in the past,' my mother said.

'And he hasn't insulted them?' I said, 'Anyway, what does it have to do with my wedding? Dad, say something.'

'You have my blessings. Don't expect my presence,' my father said.

'His drama never ends,' my mother said. 'He himself went to Chennai and said yes to the Madrasis. This wouldn't even have happened otherwise. Now when everyone in my family is waiting for the wedding, he stops them. Why? Because he can't see them happy. Most of all, he doesn't want to see me happy.' She then broke into tears.

'Is that the case, dad?'

'No, I've given you a choice,' he said.

'Which son will not want his father to come?' my mother said, 'This is not a choice. This is blackmail.'

'Whatever you want to call it. If this wedding is happening because of me, then I should get to choose the guests.'

'No dad,' I said, 'Mom has equal rights, too. Unfortunately, I belong to both of you.'

'So, you decide,' my father said.

My mother and dad looked at me. I paced up and down the room for ten minutes.

'Dad, mom's family has to come. You do what you have to do,' I said and left the room.

Rajji mama had arranged a two-man dholak band at the Hazrat Nizamuddin station. I helped locate the thirty-seven II-tier AC berths reserved for my relatives in the Rajdhani Express compartment. Two of my mother's cousin sisters had decided to join at the last minute and we had to accommodate them as well. My mother made up a wonderful story about my father's viral fever that could be malaria. Everyone knew the reality, and apart from the awkwardness of fibbing to Ananya's parents again, people were relieved, as my dad equalled to no fun.

'You can't talk half the things when your husband is here,' as Shipra masi told my mother.

I stood inside the bogie, matching everyone's ticket to their berth. Rajji mama dragged me out. 'You have to dance a little, no? This is the baraat leaving,' he said.

At four in the afternoon, hundreds of bored passengers on the platform watched the free entertainment provided by our family. The dholak men jogged along the train and argued with mama over the payment. They couldn't squeeze much out of him as the train had picked up speed.

I came inside my compartment, which the ladies had turned into a sari shop. The entire lower berths were filled with the dresses everyone planned to wear for each of the functions.

'This is beautiful,' my seventy-year-old distant aunt said as she fondled a magenta sari with real gold-work. Women never get too old for admiring saris.

My younger cousins had taken over the next compartment. The girls had their make-up kits open. They discussed the sharing of mascaras. I see why whole families get excited about a wedding; there's something in it for everyone.

I came outside to stand at the compartment door. The train whizzed past Agra, Gwalior and Jhansi over the next few hours. I still had a day to go as the train traversed through this huge country, cutting through the states I had battled for the last year. These states make up our nation. These states also divide our nation. And in some cases, these states play havoc in our love lives.

I came inside when the train reached Bhopal at dinnertime. My relatives couldn't contain their excitement that Rajdhani Express offered free meals.

'Take non-veg, the Madrasis won't give you any,' Shipra masi advised everyone.

'OK aunty, for the next three days, there are no Madrasis, only Tamilians,' I said.

Shipra masi separated the foil from her chicken. 'Yes, yes, I know. Tamil Nadu is the state. But we are going to Madras only, no? Why does the ticket say Chennai?'

'It's the same. Like Delhi and Dilli,' Kamla mami said as she slurped her chicken sweet corn soup.

'Is it true their chief minister is an ex-film heroine?' my mother's cousin said.

'Yes-ji,' another aunt said, 'these South Indian women are quite clever.'

'God has given them a brain, nothing else,' came another loose comment and I considered jumping off the train.

60

Ananya's father checked my clan into twenty rooms at the Sangeetha Residency in Mylapore. The rooms were basic, but clean and air-conditioned. 'What happened to your father? We just met him,' he asked.

'It's a viral fever that could become malaria,' I said.

'Is that possible?'

'It happens in Delhi. Anyway, what's the schedule?' I regulated the conversation.

'We have a puja tomorrow afternoon and another one in the evening. The wedding muhurtam will be in the morning day after tomorrow,' he said.

'Uncle, what about a DJ? There is no party?' I was aghast for my kith and kin.

'We have a reception party day after evening. Have your fun there,' he said and turned to my mother, 'Kavita jee, Shipra jee, can I talk to you for a second?'

My mother, Shipra masi and Ananya's father stepped away from me and other relatives. They spoke for five minutes. My mother rejoined me. Shipra masi went to the reception to collect her keys.

'What?' I said as we climbed up the steps towards our hotel rooms.

'Nothing,' my mother said.

'It's my marriage. I deserve to know.'

'They asked me if I wanted a special gift,' my mother said. Perhaps, Ananya had recounted Minti's wedding to her parents.

'And? What did you say?' I said, eyeing my mother with suspicision.

'Don't talk to me in that voice,' my mother said.

'What exactly did you say, mom?' I said, my tone worse, 'what? Did you send him to buy a car or split ACs or what?'

'That's what you think of me. Don't you?' my mother said as we reached the first floor. She paused to catch her breath.

Shipra masi's expensive sandals could be heard four seconds before she arrived to join us on the first floor.

'See this stupid sister of mine. She said no to any big gifts,' Shipra masi said to me.

'You did?' I said to my mother.

My mother looked at me.

'You will never understand how much I love you,' my mother said.

I hung my head down in shame. My mother smacked the back of my head. I deserved a slap.

Shipra masi waved her hands as she spoke.

'You and your mother, both the same – impractical. She tells him, "I sent my son to do one MBA, I am getting two MBAs in return. Ananya is the best gift,"' Shipra masi said, 'OK, she earns a lot, but Kavita, why say no if someone is ready to give. Why not grab it.'

'Because we are not that kind of people, Shipra masi,' I said and gave my mother a hug, 'she is all talk. But she can never behave like Duke's mother. Never,' I said.

I came into my hotel room where ten cousins, six aunts and four uncles sat on my bed. I sat on the floor as space was at a premium. We had twenty rooms to choose from, but my relatives would rather be cramped together than miss out on juicy gossip session.

The younger cousins battled for the TV remote. I repeated the schedule to my aunts.

'They are big bores. How can they do puja the whole day?' Kamla mami said.

'They don't even have sangeet?' my mother said.

'I think they are trying to save money,' Shipra masi said.

'What language will the pujas be in? Madrasi?' another aunt said.

'Tamil, maybe Sanskrit,' I said.

'I am not coming,' my mother said.

I glared at my mother.

'Where do we eat?' an aunt expressed everyone's concern.

'The meals are in the dining hall at the wedding venue. Let's go to bed, we have to wake up early,' I said.

We had planned to meet in the hotel lobby at seven-thirty in the morning. We only left at nine.

'What is the address?' Rajji mama said.

I took out the piece of paper Ananya's dad had given me.

'I can't read this,' Rajji mama said.

I took the paper back. It said:

Arulmigu Kapaleeswarar Karpagambal Thirumana Mandapam
16, Venkatesa Agraharam Street, Mylapore, Chennai

After three attempts at reading it, I had a headache. I counted the letters, my wedding venue had fifty alphabets in it. Delhi never gets this complicated. One of my older cousins had her wedding in Batra Banquets, another one in Bawa Hall.

We struggled for twenty minutes on the streets of Mylapore before we reached the venue. Fortunately, the locals had abbreviated the name of the place to AKKT Mandapam. From actors to political parties to wedding halls, Tamilians love to keep complicated names first and then make acronyms for the same.

'What do you mean breakfast is finished?' Shipra masi said.

'Illa, illa,' a pot-bellied, dark-complexioned, hirsute chef said and shook his hand. He wore a lungi and a chef's cap. If he wore the cap to prevent hair in the food, he needed a body sheath, given his hairy arms and chest.

'Orunimishum,' I said, 'what happened?'

'Your son speaks Tamil?' Shipra masi said to my mother.

My mother rolled her eyes.

'No, I don't. It's a common word for wait a second,' I said.

'Now he belongs to them. They'll make him do anything,' my mother lamented loudly.

'Mom, please. Let me resolve this,' I said.

'What will you resolve? They will make us cook food also,' my mother said.

'Everybody, please sit in the dining hall,' I said, then turned to the chef. 'Can't you make something?'

'Who will make tiffin then? We have to serve it at eleven,' the chef said.

I checked my watch. It was nine-thirty. My family would have medical emergencies if kept hungry for that long.

'We want something now,' I said, 'anything quick.'

'What about tiffin?' the chef said.

'We don't want tiffin. We'll only come back for lunch later.'

'Girl's side wants tiffin. They came for breakfast at 6.30,' the chef said.

Rajji mama came up to me. 'Bribe him,' he whispered.

I thought about the ethics of bribing at my own wedding to feed myself.

'Wokay, I go now, I am busy,' the chef said and mumbled to himself, 'pundai maganey, thaayoli koodhi.'

'Anna, wait,' I said.

The chef looked at me in amazement. How can a person with a heavy Delhi accent toss in a Tamil word or two?

I kept a hundred-rupee note in my hand and shook hands with him. Perplexed, he examined the currency.

'We are giving you out of happiness,' my uncle said.

'I can make upma fast,' the chef said.

'What is upma?' my uncle said.

'Salty halwa. No, not upma. Can you make dosas?' I said.

'For dosa one by one making no staff now. Then lunch also delayed,' the chef said mournfully.

We settled on idlis. There would be no sambhar. However, the chef had a drum full of coconut chutney, enough to pave roads with.

My family sat in the dining hall as servers placed banana leaves in front of them.

'We have to eat leaves?' Shipra masi said, 'What are we? Cows?'

'It's the plate,' I said, 'and there is no cutlery.'

'They have hardly any expense in weddings, how lucky,' Kamla aunty said.

Forty of us consumed at least two hundred idlis.

Ananya's father came when we had finished. 'There wasn't breakfast? I am sorry,' he said.

'It's fine,' I said, 'we came late.'

'Hello, Kavita-ji,' Ananya's father said with folded hands, as per Ananya's instructions. He took the bucket of idli from the server and served one to my mother.

'Hello,' my mother responded, a hint of pride in her voice as her siblings saw her being served by the girl's father. This is what grown-ups live for anyway, considering they have so little fun otherwise.

'How's Krish's father feeling now?' Ananya's father said next.

'He's better, he had soup last night and porridge in the morning. He is taking rest now. He sends his regards,' my mother said.

Ananya's father nodded in concern.

'What are the ceremonies today, uncle?' I asked for my relatives' benefit.

'First, we have the *Vrutham*, the wedding initiation prayers. We also have *Nischayathartham*, the formal engagement ceremony where we set the auspicious time for the wedding and give gifts to close relatives,' Ananya's father said.

My aunts only paid attention to the last four words.

We came to the main hall, the centre of action for the next two days. Every ceremony of my wedding took place in this room. In the middle of the hall, there was a fire urn, not too different from Punjabi weddings. However, in our weddings people only came around the fire after eating their dinner and dessert. Here, everyone lived around the fire. I sat down on the floor. Four priests started the mantras. Close relatives sat on the floor, while distant and arthritic ones sat on chairs in the back rows. The priests at the *Vrutham* chanted so loud, it scared some of my little cousins into crying and made it impossible to talk. My aunts behind me shifted their positions several times.

'Should we do a city tour later?' Kamla aunty said.

'What is there to see in Chennai? If you want to see Madrasis, there are enough in this room,' Shipra masi said.

I saw Ananya's relatives. I recognised a few aunts. The younger cousins had come down from abroad. They sat in traditional Tamil attire, clutching their mineral water bottles.

'Ananya didi,' Minti said as Ananya came inside. She wore a maroon Kanjeevaram sari with a mustard yellow-gold border. Her tightly braided hair made her look like a cute schoolgirl. Her face had make up, and Ananya looked prettier than any girl on any Tamil film poster ever made. Her eyes looked deep, due to the kaajal around it. For a few seconds I couldn't recognise her as my Ananya. Was this the same girl I met in the mess line fighting for sambhar?

Our eyes met briefly. She gave me a little smile, enquiring on how she looked.

I nodded, yes she looked more beautiful than she ever had.

The prayers continued for another hour. Smoke filled the room. The priests kept adding twigs and spoonfuls of ghee to the fire. Ananya and I exchanged glances and smiled several times. *Was it really happening? Was I finally getting married, with consent from everyone I shared my DNA with?*

The priest asked for my father. My mother told him he was unwell.

I thought of dad again. *Why are adults so stuck up?*

'What's your grandparents' village?' Ananya's dad asked me. The priests required it for the *Nischayathartham* ceremony.

I had no idea. I turned to my mother. She turned to my aunts. My aunts debated what answer to give them.

'Lahore,' my mother said, after their discussion.

'Lahore in Pakistan?' Ananya's father said.

He seemed worried; I was scared he'd change his mind again.

'My grandparents had come to Delhi after the Partition,' I explained to him.

He nodded.

'Uncle, when is the marriage done? Like it is irreversible and no one can object to it afterwards?'

'What do you mean?' he said.

'Nothing,' I said as the priest called me to make a donation.

I gave him a hundred-rupee note. He declined it with full fervor.

'Don't give him directly, put it in the *thamboolam*,' Ananya's father said, referring to the puja plates.

I placed the money in the plate. I decorated it with a banana, paan leaves and betel nut. I offered it again and the priest accepted it. He announced the wedding details – the non-abbreviated name of the venue, the lagnam, the star and tomorrow's date.

'Six-thirty muhurtam,' the priest said.

'In the morning?' Rajji mama said, shocked.

Ananya's relatives congratulated each other on the formal setting of the time. My relatives were aghast.

'This is a wedding or a torture? It's like catching an early morning flight,' Kamla aunty said.

Fortunately, Ananya's mother calmed the ladies by bringing in ten bags full of gifts.

'Mrs Kamla,' she announced, reading out from the first bag. Each gift had the receiver's name, relationship with me and a code word for what was inside.

'Me,' Kamla aunty said and raised her hand like a child marking attendance in class. There's something about presents that turns everyone into kids.

'We'll open them in our hotel,' Shipra masi said after the end of the prize distribution ceremony.

'And now, we will have lunch,' Ananya's father said, inviting us all to the dining hall to a meal of rice, sambhar, rasam, vegetables, curd and payasam.

'We're trapped. No paneer here,' Kamla aunty said as we moved to the paneer-less dining hall.

61

'So, what's the plan for tonight?' Rajji mama said after we came back to the hotel.

'There is dinner at the dining hall at eight,' I said.

'Please, I can't have any more rice,' Shipra masi said. The ladies had opened their Kanjeevaram sari gifts. I had told Ananya to leave the price tags on. My relatives praised Ananya a little more as they noticed each sari cost three thousand bucks.

'What's after dinner?' Rajji mama said.

'The muhurtam is six-thirty. Let's sleep early.'

'See Kavita, how your son has become a Madrasi,' Kamla aunty said and everyone laughed like she had cracked the best joke in the world.

I made a face.

'How can we sleep early? It is your wedding,' Kamla aunty pulled my cheeks.

'So, what do you want to do?' I said.

'We'll organise a party. Minti's daddy, come let's go,' Kamla aunty said and they went out.

'And you go to the beauty parlour to get a facial,' my mother said.

'Me?'

'Yes, but be careful. The beauty parlours can make you black,' Shipra masi said and my clan found another reason to guffaw like only Punjabis can.

I can't really call the party Rajji mama organised for me as a bachelor's party, especially since all my aunts were present. However, the makeshift arrangements gave it a single-guy-bash feel. Rajji mama had come back with two bottles of whisky, one bottle of vodka and a crate of beer. Kamla aunty also brought chips and juice for the ladies.

'Let the ladies also have a drink tonight,' Rajji mama proclaimed as many aunties feigned horror. My cousins had already booked the vodka bottle.

'Ice,' Rajji mama told a waiter at the hotel and gave him hundred bucks. He returned with a bucketful.

'You have a music system?' Rajji mama asked the waiter. The waiter agreed to borrow one from his friend for another hundred bucks. The choice of music was a challenge though, and we had to limit ourselves to the soundtracks of the movies *Roja* and *Gentleman*. The lyrics were Tamil but at least the tunes were familiar.

'After two drinks, you will be able to understand the Tamil words also,' Raji mama said.

The men took Room 301, my room. The women went to 302, while the teenage and young cousins were in 303. The under-thirteens stayed in 304, watching cartoon channels on cable TV. The under-fives and over-seventy-fives were cooped up in 305, the latter babysitting the former.

Rajji mama kept shuttling from 301 to 302, to gossip with the ladies and discuss stocks and real estate with the men in 301.

'It's eleven,' I reminded my relatives, 'we should sleep,'

'Oh, shut up,' Rajji mama said and hugged me happily. 'If we sleep now, we won't wake up at all. Let's keep going until morning.'

The party continued and rooms 301, 302 and 303 turned into discos. The *Indian* soundtrack was played five times. I realised if my relatives didn't sleep, we may never make it to the wedding. I went down to the lobby at half past midnight.

'Call the cops,' I told the front desk.

'What?' the manager said, 'You are the groom.'

'Yes, and I have a six-thirty muhurtam. I need to be there at five with all of them. They are in no mood to rest.'

The manager laughed. Rajji mama had bribed him well. 'Don't worry, sir, I will stop them in half an hour.'

A car stopped outside the hotel just then and a person stepped out. Even in the darkness I could tell who it was. I immediately sprinted up the stairs, my heart beating fast. Rajji mama was close-dancing with Kamla aunty in 302 to a sad song from *Roja*.

'My dad's here,' I announced.

In two minutes flat, our nightclubs shut down as if there was a police raid. Everyone went into their rooms to sleep. The corridor was stark silent as my dad climbed up to the third floor.

'Dad,' I said.

We looked at each other for a few seconds. He had decided to come, after all. I couldn't think beyond that fact. I didn't push him for a reason either. He was like me; we Indian men don't do emotions too well.

'You haven't slept? Aren't you getting married in a few hours?' he asked mildly.

I didn't respond. He walked towards 301. I stopped him. The last thing I wanted him to see was the debauchery of my maternal uncles.

'There are more rooms upstairs. This one needs repairs,' I said and took him to the next floor. I left him there to change. My mother was in 301, trying to clean it as fast as possible.

'It's fine, he is upstairs,' I said.

'What's he doing here?' my mother said, 'He's come to create trouble?'

'No,' I said, 'He's fine. He came to attend my wedding.'

'Now? He has come now?'

'It's OK, mom, you go to bed. I'll tell him you are asleep,' I said. I kissed my mother on the cheek and went up.

My father had changed into a white kurta pajama.

'Thank you, dad,' I said.

'Don't be silly,' he said. 'Where's your mother?'

'Everyone slept early. We have to wake up at four,' I said.

'Oh, I'm keeping you up. Are you sleeping here?'

I nodded and switched off the lights. I lay down next to only him, probably for the first time in twenty years.

'I love you, son,' he said, his eyes closed.

I choked up. The words meant as much to me as when Ananya had said them the first time.

'I love you too,' I said, and wondered which love story I was really chasing anyway.

62

I had to pour mugfuls of water over their faces to wake up my relatives. Rajji mama had a severe hangover. I had slept only three hours and had a splitting headache. We asked room service for triple strength coffee.

'This is inhuman, how can they get married at this time?' my mother said. She opened her suitcase to take out her new sari for the occasion.

Ananya's father had sent a bus to our hotel for the two-hundred-metre journey. I waited outside while every female in my clan blow-dried hair and applied lipstick. Panic calls started at five-fifteen.

'The priests have lit the fire. Chants have begun,' Ananya's father said.

'Two more old ladies, coming real soon,' I said and hung up the phone.

We reached the mandapam at five-thirty. Ananya's relatives had already taken the best seats. I waded through them to sit in front of the priests.

'The mother sits here,' the priest said, 'and if the father is not there then a senior male relative. . . .'

'My father is here,' I said.

Ananya's parents sprang up from their seats. 'Welcome,' Ananya's father said, 'How is your fever?'

'What fever?' my father said as he took his place.

The priests continued their fervent chants. Rajji mama passed on Saridon strips as everyone with a hangover took a pill. Ananya's uncles passed copies of *The Hindu* to each other as they continued to gather knowledge through the wedding.

'Come, Krish,' Ananya's father said after five minutes of prayers.

'What?'

'You have to change. I am supposed to help you,' he said matter-of-factly.

I had worn a new rust-coloured silk kurta pajama my mother had bought for me. 'This doesn't work?' I said.

Ananya giggled. Ananya's father shook his head and stood up. I followed him to the room next to the main hall. He ominously bolted the door. 'Take off your clothes,' he said.

'What?' I said as he fingered my kurta's hem to help me take it off.

'I will do it myself,' I said hastily. I removed my kurta.

'Pajama also,' he said, reminding me of my college ragging days.

'Is this necessary?' I snapped, wondering if my strip-tease would make the mantras more effective.

He didn't respond. His hands were about to reach my pajama cord when I decided to get rid of my modesty myself. I had worn a white underwear with Mickey Mouses prancing all over it.

'Why are you wearing . . . this?"

I had brought a pack of six Disney-themed underwear. Considering I was going to get married and Ananya liked cartoon characters, I had thought she'd find it cute. Of course, I couldn't give this reason to my future father-in-law.

'How was I to know it will be on display?' I said.

Ananya's dad had a worried expression.

'Why, what's wrong?' I said.

'You have to wear this veshti,' Ananya's dad said and gave me a translucent cream-coloured lungi. It resembled the bathing dress worn by Mandakini in *Ram Teri Ganga Maili*.

'I have to wear this? How?' I held it up. The early morning rays came right through it.

'Come, I'll show you,' Ananya's dad said, and horror of horrors, tucked half his hand into my underwear. I wondered if a groom can sue his father-in-law for molestation.

'Please, let me try first,' I said. Of course, out of nervousness I couldn't focus. The veshti kept slipping and I stood there in my Mickey Mouse underwear, almost in tears.

'Allow me, it will take only a minute,' Ananya's father said gently, like a doctor convincing a kid for an injection.

I closed my eyes. *This is the absolute last, last humiliation I will go through to get the love of my life*, I thought. A few hours more and this will be over. Uncle's hand came too close for comfort as he tried to ensure a snug fit. Some say this ceremony is designed to ensure that the groom has his equipment in place. Well, he surely did a good job finding out.

'Are we done?' I said as uncle adjusted the final pleats.

I saw myself in the mirror. My first topless meeting with the world was about to take place. Little Mickey Mouses were grinning through my translucent veshti. OK, it is only for a little while more, I told myself.

'See, now all your wedding pictures will have Mickey Mouse,' uncle said, confirming that my humiliation would continue for the rest of my life.

'Do you want to change your underwear? You can wear mine. Should we exchange?' he asked.

I looked at him, wondering if he actually said what he just said. 'Let's go. I have to get married.'

We came outside and my cousins burst into laughter when they saw me.

'Mickey Mouse,' my five-year-old cousin screamed, ensuring that all guests would now freely spot it.

Ananya sat in a gorgeous nine-yard dark red silk sari. She wore diamond and gold necklaces. She looked like an accessible goddess.

'What's with the underwear?' she whispered to me.

'I bought it for you . . . I mean us,' I said.

'Excuse me?' she said as the priest scolded us for talking and asked us to focus on the prayers. Someone tied a scarf over my eyes so I couldn't see anything for ten minutes as prayers continued. It could be the punishment for talking to the bride during the wedding, but no one explained why. Prayers continued even after the scarf was removed.

'OK, now you go for Kashi Yatra,' the priest said after an hour. He gave me an umbrella and a copy of the Gita.

'What's that?' I said.

Ananya's father gave me the details. I had to stand up and announce I wasn't interested in the wedding and was going to Kashi, or Varanasi, to become a sadhu. I didn't know why they gave me an umbrella, but I had to open it and place it over my head as I walked out. Ananya's father would come after me and convince me that I should marry his daughter instead.

I decided to do an extra good job with this ceremony, especially as I had messed up with the veshti. I stood up, gave Ananya's parents a disgusted look and sprinted out of the hall. Ananya's father followed me but I walked way faster than him. I came to the main road outside the hall. I walked on to the street. An auto saw me and came near me.

'Where, where?' he said, his engine still sputtering in first gear.

'Kashi,' I said.

'Kashi where?' he said.

'Varanasi, in U.P.,' I said.

'Central Station? Seventy rupees, sir,' he said.

I turned over and saw Ananya's dad twenty metres behind me. Well, you only get married once, so I decided to do the best Kasi Yatra ceremony ever.

I sat inside the auto. The auto sped off.

'Hey,' Ananya's dad screamed at full volume.

'Who's that?' the auto driver said.

'Nothing,' I said, 'stop.'

I came out of the auto. Ananya's father came running to me.

'What are you doing?' he said, panting after the jog.

'Going to Kashi,' I said and smiled, 'you didn't tell me when to stop.'

He grabbed my arm tight. 'Come inside,' he said, dragging me towards the mandapam.

'Hey, aren't you supposed to convince me?' I said.

We had some more Tamil ceremonies. We had *Maalai Maatral*, which involved an exchange of garlands like the Punjabi jaimala. However, Ananya's relatives lifted her high, making it difficult for me to reach her head. My own relatives took it as a personal challenge and lifted me even higher. Rajji mama took a while to realise that it was only a game and almost got into a fight with one of Ananya's uncles. After that, we had *Oonjal* where Ananya and I sat on a swing as her relatives fed us small pieces of banana soaked in milk. Finally, we came back to sit around the fire. Ananya sat on her father's lap for the final *kanyadaan*.

'Yes,' I whispered to myself, 'it's almost over.'

Ananya and I held a coconut dipped in turmeric. Ananya's mother poured water over it. Ananya couldn't hold back her tears, sitting in her father's lap. I tied a gold necklace with a flat rectangular pendant around her neck, called the taali, in the *Mangalyadharanam*.

The priests told us to stand up for the *Saptapathi*, or the seven sacred steps. Ananya's sari and my veshti were connected in a knot and held hands. I had felt her touch after months.

'Are you OK?' I said as she sniffed.

'You are not a girl, you won't understand,' Ananya said, and thus began a lifetime of 'you won't understand' statements married men have to endure everyday.

I placed my feet under Ananya's feet and helped her take seven steps around the fire. I slipped silver rings onto her toes.

Everyone clapped as I came back up.

'What?' I said.

'It's over, now go around the room and take blessings from everyone,' the head priest said.

I looked at Mr Swami and his wife. They were no longer Ananya's parents. They were my in-laws. I had done it. The two states had become one.

'Do namaskaram,' the priest instructed us. Ananya and I lay fully flat on the ground in front of every elder relative to bless us. It is the only wedding ritual in the world that involves a workout.

'My blessings are always with you,' my father said as he stopped us from lying down fully in front of him.

'God bless you,' Shipra masi said as I lay down in front of her, 'But I'm sleepy. Let's go back to the hotel.'

63

'He has a speech?' I said. Ananya and I sat on regal chairs at the venue of our reception. At least this function felt familiar to my relatives as they saw food stalls in the open garden. We were at the Madras Boat Club. Coloured lights twined around the trees; the lakeside venue was a welcome change from the unpronounceable smoke-filled mandapam.

'Yeah, he wanted to do a powerpoint, but I stopped him. He even came to the hotel to show the speech to you.'

'When?' I said, 'I was there only.'

'Sleeping all day,' Ananya said. 'He only heard snores.'

'You didn't sleep?' I said.

'No way, we have so many out of town guests. I haven't slept for the last two days.'

'So, how do you manage to look so beautiful?' I said.

She blushed. It matched her clothes. She wore a pink lehnga with heavy gold and silver embroidery for the evening, a surprise for my relatives and a bit of a shock for her own aunts. However, it was too late and Ananya was already married – to me. Screw you, Pure Harish, I thought, though I cursed myself for thinking of him at all.

'Congratulations,' some random person came to the stage to meet us and we smiled for pictures for the hundredth time.

Dinner did have North Indian choices, but the flavours were a bit off.

'They've made gobi aaloo with coconut oil,' Minti complained.

'We are all going back tomorrow,' I said. 'You'll have your paranthas soon. Now don't make a face and eat ice-cream.'

'When are we cutting the cake?' one of my younger cousins said, pointing to the eggless cake kept in the middle of the garden. Next to the cake, there was a dais with chairs around it.

A waiter rang a hand-bell, announcing the speech and cake-cutting ceremony. Relatives came around and sat on the chairs. The Tamilians and Punjabis looked at each other. People had not come to attend my wedding, they had come to a live human museum of the other community.

'But when will the DJ start?' my cousin said.

'Patience,' I said.

Ananya and I stood next to the cake. Ananya took the mike to speak first. 'Thank you everyone for coming here. I am so grateful to all of you that you decided to share our happiness. Yes, ours is quite a different wedding, and it has taken us a while to get here, making it all the more special. I'd like my amazing father to share a few words with you.'

Ananya clapped and the rest of the crowd applauded as well.

My father and mother sat together with a smile on their face. At least for tonight, they'd decided to get along.

'Hello, everyone,' Ananya's dad said. 'I'd like someone from the boy's side later to say a few words as well.'

He looked at my father. My father folded his hands to say no.

'I'll talk,' Rajji mama said and raised his hand. He had obviously found the Boat Club bar.

'Welcome everyone,' Ananya's father started, 'I never liked giving speeches. However, in the last year, helped by my son-in-law, I've gained the confidence to talk in public.'

Everyone turned to look at me. OK, making office presentations is one thing, confessionals in front of your community quite another. I hoped he knew what he was doing.

'I know the number one topic all of you have discussed in this party—why is Swami marrying his daughter to a North Indian fellow? I know it, as we would have done the same.'

Sniggers ran through the crowd.

'In fact, when Ananya first told us about Krish, we were quite upset. As all Tamilians know, we are so proud of our own culture. We also thought our daughter is one in a million, she will get the best of boys in our own community. Why must she go for a Punjabi boy?'

Everyone who wore a Kanjeevaram sari in the crowd nodded. The Punjabis kept a straight face.

'We did our best to discourage her. We didn't treat Krish well even though he moved to Chennai for us. We even showed her Tamil boys. But you know kids of today, they do what they want to do.'

This time all gave understanding nods.

'So why do parents object to this?' he said and adjusted his glasses. 'It is not only about another community. It is the fact your daughter has found a boy for herself. We as parents feel disobeyed, left out and disappointed. We bring our children up from babies to adults, how can they ignore us like this? All our frustration comes out in anger. How much we hate love marriages, isn't it?'

Ananya's aunts smiled.

'But we forget that this has happened because your child had love to give to someone in this world. Is that such a bad thing? Where did the child learn to love? From us, after all, the person they loved first is you.'

Ananya clasped my arm and clenched it tight. The crowd listened with full attention.

'Actually, the choice is simple. When your child decides to love a new person, you can either see it as a chance to hate some people – the person they choose and their families. Which is what we did for a while. However, you can also see it as a chance to love some more people. And since when did loving more people become a bad thing?'

He paused to have a glass of water and continued. 'Yes, the Tamilian in me is a little disappointed. But the Indian in me is quite happy. And more than anything, the human being in me is happy. After all, we've decided to use this opportunity to create more loved ones for ourselves.'

When he kept the mike down, Ananya hugged him hard. The crowd burst into applause. Ananya and I cut the cake through the resounding claps. We fed each other and our respective in-laws a piece. The cameraman gathered both sets of parents for a picture.

'Ananya, see, both our parents. They are smiling,' I said.

Rajji mama stood up and came to the mike for his speech.

'Stop Minti's daddy, he has had six pegs,' Kamla aunty said.

Rajji mama took the mike and raised his hand. 'Ladies and gentleman,' he said.

I went up to him.

'Rajji mama, enough. You are too cool to make boring speeches,' I whispered in his ear.

'Really? We should answer them, no?' he said.

'It's not a competition,' I said.

He said into the mike, 'Ladies and gentlemen of Tamil Nadu, thank you very much. Now we invite you to some Punjabi-style dancing with the DJ at the backside.'

My cousins flew off their chairs and surged towards the dance floor.

The song collection was a mixture of Tamil and Hindi film music. They had one Punjabi music CD, which Rajji mama had instructed to play in a loop. My family dominated the dance floor, but Ananya urged her aunts and uncles to join in as well. I guess they were my family too now.

Rajji mama avoided a bad fall while trying a particularly difficult bhangra-break dance fusion step to impress my new relatives. My cousins pushed me and Ananya together for a close dance. I held Ananya to me as we moved on the dance floor.

'Ananya,' I whispered in her ear.

'What?' she said softly.

'I love you and your father and your mother and your brother and your relatives,' I said.

'I love you and your clan, too,' she said.

We kissed as Tamils and Punjabis danced around us.

'So, the self-imposed exile is over now? You said we'll only do it when we cross the finish line,' I said.

'Is that all you men think about?' she said.

'Only for the sake of uniting the nation,' I said.

Epilogue

A couple of years later

'Do I have to be here?' I asked Ananya who lay in the delivery room. A curtain spread mid-way across the bed separated her lower and upper body. The doctors had given her a half-body anesthetic, which enabled her to stay awake during the C-section. A team of specialists hid behind the curtain cutting up her stomach.

'He has a knife,' I said, peeping at the doctors. My head felt dizzy.

'Don't freak me out. Talk about something else,' she said. 'How's the book going?'

'Well, the fifth publisher rejected it yesterday,' I said and stood up again to take a peek. 'At least I can go to the sixth one now . . . wow, there is blood.'

'Sit down if you can't handle the sight, and stop being so scared. I can't feel a thing because of this epidural,' she said. The doctor had recommended a caesarian without general anesthesia.

'If only you could see,' I said, 'wow, I see a leg. It's like Aliens 3.'

'Shut up,' she said.

'Hey, it's a boy,' I said.

'Does he look like me?'

'I don't know. I haven't seen the face yet. I've only seen the you-know-what.'

The doctor took out the whole baby.

'Thank you, doctor, thank you so much,' I said emotionally and moved to shake his hand.

'Wait,' the doctor said through his masked face.

'What?' Ananya said.

'I don't know,' I said. 'Oh wait, there's another leg. Wow, there's another boy.'

'Twins?' she said in disbelief, looking ready to faint.

'Yes,' the doctor said, 'Congratulations.'

The nurse cleaned up the two babies and gave them to me.

'Be careful,' she said as I took one in each arm.

'You are from two different states, right? So, what will be their state?' the nurse said and chuckled.

'They'll be from a state called India,' I said.